MURDER
ON 34th STREET

MURDER
ON 34th STREET

EDWARD I. KOCH

and Wendy Corsi Staub

Concept created by Herbert Resnicow

KENSINGTON BOOKS
http://www.kensingtonbooks.com

KENSINGTON BOOKS are published by

Kensington Publishing Corp.
850 Third Avenue
New York, NY 10022

Kensington and the K logo Reg. U.S. Pat. & TM Off.

Library of Congress Card Catalog Number: 97-071433
ISBN 1-57566-232-9

First Kensington Hardcover Printing: November, 1997
10 9 8 7 6 5 4 3 2 1

Printed in the United States of America

The authors wish to acknowledge
retired police officer
B. J. Haskins
for providing helpful information on police procedure.

ONE

Chestnuts roasting in the open air . . . lavishly decorated department store windows . . . bell-ringing Santas on bustling street corners . . .

Nowhere in the world are the holidays more festive than they are right here in New York City.

And don't tell me I'm biased. I may be mayor of the Big Apple, but if you ask anyone, anywhere, which city they'd most like to visit in December, I'd be willing to bet it's my own hometown.

And this year promised to be as merry as any other—until the glorious season was interrupted by a shocking murder. . . .

I'm not foolish enough to think that you catch a cold simply by being exposed to cold weather, no matter what my grandmother used to say.

But when I woke the morning after Thanksgiving to find my nose streaming and my head hot and pounding, I couldn't help but wonder if it had anything to do with my participation in yesterday's parade.

Don't get me wrong. I didn't regret marching for hours behind the Rockettes, waving at throngs of adorable children that lined the route. But I had been feeling run-down ever since getting over the stomach virus I'd caught during my post–Election Day visit to Washington.

And I had realized, when I saw the weather Thanksgiving morning, that it wouldn't do me any good to be out in driving rain with temperatures hovering around freezing. I had already done that once this week, at a funeral for a police officer who had been killed by a sniper in Brooklyn.

Anyone who knows me can vouch for the fact that I'd be as likely to back out of marching in New York City's annual Thanksgiving Day Parade as I would be to pack my bags and retire in Sandusky.

So, there I was on Thursday, smiling and waving all the way from the Upper West Side to Herald Square.

And here I was on Friday morning, telling my driver to pull over in midtown, en route to City Hall, so that I could hop out of the car and dash into Duane Reade to pick up some of my favorite honey and lemon lozenges.

Though it was just past nine, and a light snow had been falling since dawn, I noticed that the sidewalk was crowded with business people, tourists, and early bird shoppers.

My bodyguard, Ambrose Kaloyeropoulos, insisted on coming along, of course. When you're mayor of New York City, there are very few places where you're allowed to venture unescorted—and none of them are out in public.

I found the lozenges in a hurry, and Ambrose and I made our way to the line at the front of the store.

"Hey, Ed," someone said, coming up behind me. "How's it going?"

I looked around. Most of the time when someone says, *"Hey, Ed,"* it's a total stranger. That, too, comes with the territory when you're mayor of New York.

This time, however, I actually recognized the speaker. It was the middle-aged niece of my longtime secretary, Rosemary Larkin, who had retired over a year ago.

"Louellen," I said, transferring the bag of throat drops into my left hand and shaking her hand with my right. "It's good to see you. What has your aunt been up to?"

"She's spending the winter down in Miami Beach again," Louellen informed me, adjusting her thick bifocals on her long nose. "Right about now, Aunt Ro's probably lying in the sun, drinking freshly squeezed orange juice, reading the *Times,* and chuckling about the weather we've been getting here."

"She always did hate the cold and snow." Personally, I'm not overly fond of either, but I have no intention of spending my retirement years anyplace other than right here in New York. Not that I'm opposed to winter vacations in warmer climates.

In fact, I was looking forward to my upcoming trip to Barbados, which I had been planning for months now.

Louellen was nodding her dyed blond head. "But as much as Aunt Rosemary loves the weather in Florida, she's pretty homesick. You know how she loves New York."

"Who doesn't?"

She smiled and nodded.

I covered my mouth as a cough slipped out.

"Are you coming down with something, Ed?"

"Just a little cold."

"What are you taking for it?"

"Nothing yet," I said, holding up the cellophane bag of lozenges. "But I'm going to pop one of these in just as soon as I pay for them."

"Nah," she said with a brusque shake of her head that was sharply reminiscent of her aunt. "You don't want those. They're candy."

"They're not candy," I protested. "They always work just fine."

"Think what you want," Louellen said with a shrug. "What you need is the old Larkin family remedy. Didn't Aunt Ro ever tell you about it?"

"Not that I can recall."

"What you need is a pan of hot salt water, whiskey, honey, and some oil of peppermint—do you keep oil of peppermint in the kitchen at Gracie Mansion? Why am I asking? You must," she said, as if no kitchen would be complete without the stuff.

"I'd have to check with my chef," I told her, knowing Lucien wouldn't take to my concocting a potion of hot salt water, whiskey, and honey, oil of peppermint or no oil of peppermint.

He had very definite ideas about what one did and did not do in a kitchen, as he had let me know on more than one occasion.

I knew better than to wander in and start whipping up a snack or anything else when he was on duty.

"So anyway, Ed, as I was saying, you put it all together, and you sip it. I'm telling you, you'll be good as new by tonight," Louellen promised.

"Sounds interesting," I said politely, aware that Ambrose was shifting his weight from one foot to the other and trying not to look amused.

I glanced at the head of the line, where the cashier was calling, "Void! Void! I need a manager."

"And if by chance *that* remedy doesn't work," Louellen started to say, "you need to find a rushing brook and stick your head—"

"Where are you headed this morning?" I asked her, to change the subject.

"Shopping. I wanted to buy some film for my camera." She motioned at the black nylon pouch dangling around her neck.

"Your camera?"

"I promised my grandson up in Albany that I'd take pictures of the roller coaster. It's supposed to be the largest in the Northeast."

I blinked. Had I missed something, or had she just told me she was going shopping?

"What roller coaster, Louellen?"

"The one at Highview Meadows."

"Oh."

That roller coaster.

"And I wanted to see the reindeer at the petting zoo. It's the biggest petting zoo in the Northeast."

"I see. So that's why you're going on this little expedition?"

"Of course that's not *why*. The main reason is that I have a lot of Christmas shopping to do."

"Why are you going all the way to New Jersey to shop, Louellen? Don't you live right over on Thirty-third, just off Fifth?"

She nodded, looking vaguely uncomfortable. "I *will* do some shopping here in the city, of course, Ed. But I couldn't help wondering about that gigantic new mall. It's the biggest enclosed mall in—"

"Yeah, I know, I know," I cut in. "In the Northeast."

"No," she said a little smugly. "In the world."

"It can't be."

"Oh, it is."

"Well, what's so wonderful about a huge suburban mall, when you can shop for anything you want right here on Fifth Avenue? Or Madison?" I couldn't help asking.

"It's *cold* on Fifth Avenue. And Madison. In the mall, I don't even have to wear a coat."

I couldn't argue with that. But . . .

"And anyway," she continued, pulling out a compact and checking her pink lipstick in the mirror, "it's so easy to get to Highview Meadows now that they're running that shuttle service from the corner."

"What corner?"

"That corner," she said, snapping her compact closed and pointing just outside the store.

Sure enough, there, on the opposite corner of East Thirty-fourth Street, was a cluster of people—mostly eager-looking women and teenage girls, none of them seeming to mind the fact that they were forced to wait in subzero temperatures as snowflakes drifted relentlessly from the gray sky.

I had noticed the crowd earlier as I stepped out of my car, and had assumed they were waiting to see the famed windows of Ramsey's Department Store.

But now I realized that the store was a few yards away from the throng. Even more intriguing, there was no one standing between the velvet ropes that traditionally funneled shoppers and tourists past Ramsey's windows.

Strange.

This year's display was supposed to be more spectacular than ever, with animated scenes depicting American Christmases through the ages. My good friend Sybil Baker had told me all about it. She was all jazzed about the fact that her pal Muriel, one of Ramsey's window designers, had borrowed her enormous vintage radio for the Depression-era scene.

"How much are they charging for this shuttle service?" I asked Louellen, rubbing my chin and staring at the traitorous crowd.

"It's free. And I heard that the drivers are going to be handing out vouchers for free sleigh rides at the winter carnival they've set up behind the mall."

"Is that so?"

"And someone even said they're serving free hot chocolate in the international food court."

"The *international* food court? What nationality came up with hot chocolate?" I asked wryly.

"I don't know . . . maybe the Swiss?"

I sighed and looked again at the register, really starting to get impatient. I had a ten o'clock meeting with my deputy mayor and a press conference right after that.

Luckily, the store manager had fixed the void in question and the cashier had taken the next customer in line, who was standing in front of me. Thank goodness I was almost out of there.

"You're still going to buy those things?" Louellen asked, motioning at the bag in my hand.

"You better believe it. You're still going all the way to Jersey to go shopping?"

She grinned. "You better believe it."

"Mr. Mayor, what do you think of Highview Meadows?"

The question came at the tail end of the press conference, from a twenty-something reporter whose trendy faux fur jacket and matching headband suggested she knew a thing or two about shopping.

"What do *you* think of Highview Meadows?" I shot right back at her.

"Me?" She looked a little taken aback. "To be perfectly honest, I think it's an amazing place. I can see why everyone in New York is so hot to do their Christmas shopping there instead of in Manhattan, which brings me back to my original point—"

"Highview Meadows has nothing to offer that we don't have right here in New York's many fine shopping districts. In fact, anything we offer here in New York is bigger and better—the best bargains money can buy. Does that answer whatever question you were about to ask?"

"But Highview Meadows has a skating rink and—"

"Did something happen to Rockefeller Center while I wasn't looking? Or to the Wollman Rink? Or to—"

"What about the petting zoo at the mall in Jersey?" someone called out.

I cleared my aching throat before firing back, "Have you been to the Children's Zoo in Central Park since it's been renovated? The place is incredible."

"They're offering free sleigh rides."

"And hot chocolate," another reporter, a pretty, young brunette, put in.

I guffawed as loudly as the rest of the crowd did at that.

"You need to go all the way to Jersey for free hot chocolate?" I asked the woman, who was now blushing furiously. "Honey, didn't anyone ever tell you that you weren't going to make any money in journalism?"

"But, Mr. Mayor," someone else objected, "there's no clothing tax in New Jersey. That alone has been luring shoppers out of New York until now. How can Manhattan stores compete with the added attraction of the hugest indoor mall in the world?"

"How," I retorted, "can New Jersey compete with the tree at Rockefeller Center, and Radio City Music Hall, and carriage rides in Central Park? How can one measly mall compete with the excitement of the holidays here in New York? Malls are a dime a dozen across the country, but there's only one Big Apple."

"Mr. Mayor," another reporter began, but I held up a hand and shook my head.

"I'm finished," I announced. "I've got a lousy cold and a full schedule, and the last thing I want to do is feed some ridiculous rumors about how this sprawling suburban Grinch is stealing Christmas from the Big Apple."

Perfect, I thought as I sailed from the podium and out of the press room.

Too late, I realized I'd made an enormous mistake.

Why, oh, why, had I trumpeted to every major media source in Greater New York that I had a cold?

That meant it was only a matter of time before . . .

* * *

My mother called five minutes after I arrived at Gracie Mansion Friday evening, having canceled my evening engagement because I felt so rotten. I often spend weekends at my apartment in the Village, but I was having the whole thing painted over the next few weeks.

"How are you feeling, Eddie?"

"I'm fine, Ma." Thanks to my stuffy nose, I couldn't keep it from coming out *I'b fide, Ba.*

"You don't sound fine. They said on the six o'clock news that you were very sick."

"Oh, for the love of . . ."

"I'm coming right over," Joyce Koch informed me. "With some homemade chicken soup."

When it comes to medical breakthroughs, my mother rates her homemade chicken soup right up there with the Salk vaccine. For some reason, she actually thinks I like the stuff and insists on making it for me in sickness *and* in health.

"Ma," I said patiently, "I don't need chicken soup. Especially at this hour." It was well past nine o'clock.

"Have you eaten dinner yet?"

"I was just about to."

"What were you going to have?"

I hesitated. Lucien was off tonight, since I was supposed to be dining at the new Le Cirque with friends.

"You need chicken soup," my mother repeated when I paused too long.

"All I need is to stay home tonight and rest. I'll be—"

"You need chicken soup," she said for the third time. "You also need a Glugol Muggle."

In case you were wondering, a Glugol Muggle is a wonderful concoction handed down from generation to generation on my mother's side of the family.

To make it, you squeeze the juice of a grapefruit, an orange, and a lemon into a saucepan. Add one tablespoon of honey and then one or two jiggers of your favorite liquor. I prefer scotch. Bring the ingredients to a boil and drink it immediately.

My mother did have a point.

I probably did need a Glugol Muggle. Maybe even two Glugol Muggles.

Still . . .

"You don't have to come out in the snow just to—"

"I should let my son suffer alone? No," my mother said firmly. "I'm coming. I'll be in a cab, so tell the security at the gate that your mother's on her way and not to monkey around when I get there."

I started to protest, then realized it would be useless. She probably already had the matzo balls waiting in a Tupperware container by the apartment door.

"Where's Pop?" I asked instead, reaching for a Kleenex and blowing my nose. "Tell him to drive you. It's safer than a cab in this weather."

"Lately, I don't know," she said, and I could picture her shaking her head sadly. She's been convinced my father's eyesight has been failing for years, and drags him off to an optometrist every chance she gets.

"What's wrong?" I asked absently.

"He's driving me crazy. Every time we get into the car, it's an argument. Just yesterday we were heading out to Commack to visit your cousin Sylvia, and he got into one of those EZ-Pass lanes."

Uh-oh, I thought. I knew he hadn't applied for an EZ-Pass electronic toll tag for his car, even though I had tried to explain to him that it is an incredibly efficient means of toll paying and would, in just a year, save him hours of waiting in traffic.

Pop simply couldn't grasp the notion of paying into an account and placing an electronic tag on his car so that the toll would automatically be deducted every time it passed through a toll booth. He doesn't even like to use tokens at New York's many bridges and tunnels.

To him, the only dependable means of paying tolls is the old-fashioned way, involving cash and human beings.

"So anyway," my mother went on, "I said, 'Lou, get out of the lane, you're in the wrong lane,' and he kept saying, 'What? What are you talking about?' He wouldn't budge, Eddie. Kept telling me to look how short the line was, and why would he want to get into a longer line?"

I shook my head, picturing the scene all too clearly.

"Then we got up to the booth, and he stopped and was looking for the toll collector. I said, 'Lou, that's not how it works,' and he said, 'What are you talking about?' again. And so I said to him—"

"Ma," I cut in, "I hate to interrupt, but all I asked was where is Pop tonight?"

"He's not here."

"Where is he?"

"It's Friday."

"So? It's Friday."

"So? Your father's out playing pinochle, Eddie, remember? He's been playing pinochle every Friday night for months."

"Good for him. What about you?"

"What about me?"

"Don't you have a folk dancing class to go to tonight, or something?"

"I gave that up. The girls at the center"—that would be the neighborhood senior citizens' center, around which Mom's social life revolves these days—"decided folk dancing was too strenuous after Hattie Baumgartner had an episode during one of the classes."

"What kind of episode?"

"Oh, it was nothing. That one, she's always huffing and puffing like her heart is going to give out on her any minute. She just likes the attention. So we're starting a watercolor class, but not until April."

"Why not?" I said absently, flipping through a stack of personal mail on my desk.

I stopped to open my latest statement from Ramsey's Department Store. I had recently returned the sweater I'd bought for Pop on his last birthday—he said the argyle pattern was too "busy"—and wanted to make sure the credit appeared on my account.

"Because most of us go to Florida at this time of year, Eddie. We won't start until everyone's back."

"Mmm-hmm." The Ramsey's envelope contained an announcement that the store's world-famous Santa's Winter Wonderland would be opening the Friday after Thanksgiving—which meant today.

"That reminds me, Eddie, Aunt Honey asked me if I could get her menorah back from you, so if you can—"

"What?" I looked up from the billing statement I had just unfolded. There are times when you really have to pay attention when you're talking to my mother. "Why would I have Aunt Honey's menorah?"

"Pat"—that would be my sister—"told her you borrowed it the last time you visited her in Scarsdale."

That would be this past summer.

"Why," I asked my mother, "would I borrow a menorah in July? Why would I borrow a menorah at all? I happen to have a lovely menorah of my very own that I brought back from my trip to Israel several years ago, thank you very much."

"I'm just telling you what Pat said, Eddie. Why don't you call Aunt Honey and—"

"Ma, I don't have *time* to call Aunt Honey. I don't even have time to call *you.*"

"Such a son. How did I end up with a son who can't make time for his own mother?"

Exasperated, I said, "Ma, I'm a terrific son. I always make time for—"

"I know. Can't you take a joke?" She heaved an exaggerated sigh. "I'm leaving now, Eddie. The soup is piping hot. Make sure you have a bowl and spoon waiting. And a mug for the Glugol Muggle."

I don't know how the woman does it.

Twenty minutes after hanging up the telephone, I was presented with a mug of steaming Glugol Muggle, a bowl of homemade soup, freshly squeezed orange juice, a dazzling array of over-the-counter cold remedies, and a pair of fuzzy slippers.

"I don't wear slippers," I reminded her, eyeing them dubiously.

"That's why you have a cold," Ma informed me, shoving one on my foot. "How does it fit? Too big? Too tight?"

"Where did you find slippers on the spur of the moment?"

"They were going to be one of your Hanukkah presents. I unwrapped them." She squeezed my toes through the end of the slipper and pronounced them a perfect fit. "Now eat your soup."

"But—"

"Eat."

I ate.

And as I ate, I watched the Fox ten o'clock news, rolling my eyes when they aired footage of this morning's press conference, including the discussion of Highview Meadows.

They followed that up with an interview taped earlier this evening with Barnaby Tischler, general manager of Ramsey's Department Store. Barnaby's an old friend of mine, and I wasn't pleased to see him looking drawn and worried as he spoke to the reporter about whether the new mall in New Jersey was hurting his business, which, incidentally, was already rumored to be in trouble.

"We at Ramsey's are as dedicated as we always have been to providing every shopper with personal attention and quality merchandise at competitive prices," Barnaby said—woodenly, if you ask me. And he seemed to be on edge as he adjusted his glasses on the end of his long, narrow nose.

"Do you call thirty dollars for a lipstick a bargain price?" my mother wanted to know, waving her hand at the television screen. "Melissa told Pat she paid thirty dollars for a lipstick at Ramsey's."

Melissa would be Pat's grown daughter, who lives with her husband and child on the Upper West Side.

"I'm sure," Barnaby went on, running a nervous hand through his thinning salt-and-pepper hair, "that New Yorkers are able to recognize the benefits of staying here in town to do their shopping. . . ."

"What are you putting in your lipstick that you think you can charge thirty dollars for it?" Mom demanded of the televised Barnaby Tischler. "Is it made of gold?"

"Shh," I said, trying to hear what he was saying.

" . . . and we are an old-fashioned department store that believes in old-fashioned service. Every member of our staff is committed to showing consumers that they have every reason to shop locally this holiday season. And, kids, don't forget that the one and only Santa Claus is waiting here at Ramsey's to visit with you during our first-ever extended hours in our famous fifth floor Winter Wonderland!"

I had to smile at that. The Ramsey's Santa is as integral to the fabric of this great city as I am.

The publicity surrounding the Ramsey's Santa was inspired way back in the thirties, when a skeptical little boy visited the department store, sat on his lap, and demanded proof that he was the "real" Santa.

Legend has it that Santa glanced up at the child's mother, who had been in a wheelchair after a bout with polio. In that moment when their gazes locked, she suddenly felt a tingling sensation in her legs. Moments later she was standing and taking tentative steps for the first time in a year.

A handful of people witnessed what happened that day. One of them was a newspaper reporter waiting in line to see Santa with his toddler, and he wrote the story as a Christmas Eve feature. It was picked up by wire services everywhere, and sales at Ramsey's skyrocketed.

Nobody seemed bothered by the fact that no one had thought to get the names of the child or his mother so that the story could be verified. And a subsequent revelation that the reporter happened to be a distant cousin of Cornelius Ramsey, the store's founder, did nothing to diminish the magical aura that would surround the Ramsey's Santa for decades. The giant store on Thirty-fourth Street has been a cornerstone of the Manhattan retail scene ever since.

Until now, that is. As I mentioned, the word is that Ramsey's has been in trouble for some time now.

Apparently, I wasn't the only one who'd heard that particular rumor.

". . . and I would like to ask you, Mr. Tischler," the television reporter was saying, "is it true that Ramsey's sales have plummeted drastically over the past year, while sales at Weatherly Brothers, your Thirty-fourth Street neighbor, have improved tremendously?"

"I can't speak for Weatherly Brothers," Barnaby said stiffly, "but I wouldn't say our sales have 'plummeted drastically.' Ramsey's, like many other retailers, has simply been feeling the effects of a rather cautious economic climate."

"Well, I'll take Ramsey's over Weatherly Brothers any day," said Mom, always one to put her two cents in. "I'll never forget the time I bought that expensive dress from them for Pat's wedding—do you remember that, Eddie?—and the sequins started dropping off while I was doing the hora. Remember? Shiny turquoise sequins were rolling all over the dance floor."

"How could I forget? One dropped into Uncle Reuben's cognac."

"Oh, that one and his liquor. He couldn't put his drink down for a few minutes to dance at his niece's wedding? But, you know, he almost choked on that sequin. He could have died and ruined Pat's wedding, all because of that crazy dress."

"Well, I don't know about *that* . . ."

Mom ignored me, on a roll. "When I took it back to Weatherly Brothers and showed the department manager what happened, he said I must have been dancing too hard. I said, 'Who do you think I am? Ginger Rogers?' Dancing too hard . . . Did you ever hear of such a thing?"

"No," I told her honestly, "I never did."

"You know, Eddie," she went on, bouncing off the subject in her usual way, "it's a shame that everyone's leaving New York to do their holiday shopping across the river. I finished mine in June—you know how I like to get things done ahead of time—but if I hadn't, you can bet I wouldn't be on that shuttle to Jersey like the other girls at the center."

So even the "girls" at the center were making the trip to Highview Meadows? That was remarkable, considering that some of them complain about having to cross an avenue to catch a bus.

I know this because several of my mother's friends lobbied me last year to set up bus stops directly opposite each other on both the east and west sides of Lexington Avenue in front of their building. They informed me that the buses traveling downtown could then stop on alternate sides.

"But that would mean you would have to wait twice as long for a bus to stop," I pointed out patiently.

"Well," came the reply, "that would be easy to fix if you just use your brain. All you have to do is put twice as many buses on the route."

There's no arguing with the girls at the center, so I wisely kept my mouth shut. And these days, whenever I run into one of them while I'm visiting my parents, I assure her that I'm still working on the bus problem.

"What are you going to do about this problem, Eddie?" Mom asked, and it took me a moment to realize she was talking about the Jersey shopping center.

"I don't know," I told her, rubbing my chin thoughtfully. "Short of blowing the whole place up, I'm not sure what I can do."

"Eddie!"

"I'm kidding, Ma."

"I knew that," she said defensively, patting me on the arm. "You'll come up with something, Eddie. That's why you're the mayor."

"But you're the mayor, Ed," Barnaby Tischler protested on Monday night in his office, leaning forward in his chair and placing his oversized palms facedown on his desk. "There has to be *something* you can do. That's why I called you here to meet with me."

I shrugged and took a handkerchief out of my suit pocket, blowing my nose. I was on the tail end of what had turned out to be a nasty cold, and would have liked nothing better, after a long Monday at the office and a charity banquet on Staten Island, than to have gone back to Gracie Mansion to collapse.

But Barnaby had phoned this morning and practically begged me for this private late-night meeting in his office, tucked into the cavernous depths of the old store's top floor.

It was a large and drafty office reminiscent of some downtown loft space, with tall windows overlooking Thirty-fourth Street. It contained your standard business furniture as well as a stationary bike and a treadmill. Odd, I thought, considering that Barnaby Tishler is a tall, gaunt Abe Lincoln of a guy who looks as though he's never exercised a single moment in his fifty-odd years.

I told him, "I can't *force* people to stay in town to buy their holiday gifts, Barnaby. This Jersey thing is a problem we've been wrestling with for decades, all year round. We've always lost shoppers who want to go across the state border to Jersey and Connecticut and beat the clothing tax."

"Believe me, I know that. But this is different, Ed. That mall has shuttle stops all over Manhattan, and a lot of them are right in front of our big department stores. They're snatching customers right out from under our noses. People who were headed into my store have been changing their minds at the last minute when they see the shuttles, and they're going to Jersey instead. Can't you do something?"

"I wish I could. But nobody has been breaking any laws, Barnaby. Can't *you* do something?"

"Believe me, I'm trying. I'm doing everything I can do. I'm advertising like crazy, offering coupons and other incentives. I'm even extending our hours. We're going to be open twenty-four hours around the clock on every weekend from now until Christmas to accommodate people who can't find time to shop because of work schedules."

"That's a great idea."

"It's not going to be enough, Ed. Ramsey's is as much a part of Manhattan as Bloomingdale's and Macy's, but I don't know how much longer we're going to stay open. If things don't pick up this season, I'm going to have to file Chapter Eleven."

"I'm sorry to hear that. It would be a terrible shame."

"Yes, it would. And that's not all."

Something in his tone caused me to lean forward in my worn visitor's chair. "What's going on, Barnaby?"

He glanced at the closed office door as though expecting to see the silhouette of an eavesdropper against the frosted glass window. There was no one there.

Still, his voice was nearly a whisper as he said, "Someone has been making bomb threats."

"I heard about the one that happened during your Columbus Day sale," I said, remembering that they had evacuated the store, brought in the police department's special bomb squad, and found nothing.

"There was one during our Election Day sale too."

I had been traveling the following day, I remembered—I was

in Washington the rest of that week. I hadn't heard about it, or any others.

"Was that all?"

He shook his head. "There was one on Saturday too. That one I managed to keep out of the papers, but, Ed, this can't go on. People are going to be *afraid* to shop at Ramsey's."

"Who do you suspect of making the threats."

"Simon Weatherly," he said promptly. "Who else could it be?"

I was vaguely acquainted with the young manager of Weatherly Brothers, a descendant of the store's wealthy founding family. Simon had recently taken over the business from his ailing uncle, Mortimer. I had heard several longtime employees had quit soon afterward. Apparently, Simon's people-management skills left much to be desired.

Which wasn't surprising. On the few occasions when our paths had crossed, he had struck me as a spoiled, imperious character.

Still, that didn't mean he was behind the bomb threats to Ramsey's, and I pointed that out to Barnaby, who shook his head.

"It's him," he said. "He's determined to put me out of business. He wants to buy our building and move Weatherly Brothers in. Our store is far bigger, and it's located on the corner."

"But, Barnaby, do you actually think he would stoop so low as to phone in bomb threats?"

"I don't think there's any limit as to how low Simon Weatherly would stoop to eliminate the competition, Ed."

"Do you have any proof that he's behind this?"

"Not a shred. But my gut instinct—"

He was cut off in mid-sentence by a sudden commotion from somewhere outside the office.

"What the heck is that?" I asked. "It sounds like dogs barking."

"It *is* dogs barking." Barnaby shoved his chair back and strode to the door, throwing it open. "It's part of our store security system. We release several Dobermans into the store after closing, to make sure no would-be thief is hiding on the premises."

"Dobermans?" I frowned. "Isn't that sort of . . . outdated, when it comes to security?"

"Oh, we implement quite a few modern security measures as well, Ed. But we have found in this area, as in many others, that you can't beat certain old-fashioned techniques. And, as you know, we pride ourselves on being an old-fashioned kind of store." Barnaby peered out into the hall, where the barking sound coming from one of the floors below seemed to be growing more frantic.

I glimpsed my bodyguard for the evening, Mohammed Johnson, who was stationed just outside Barnaby's office. He appeared more cagey and alert than ever, his thick brows narrowed over his dark eyes as he gazed down the hall in the direction of the barking. Either he isn't crazy about dogs, or he sensed that something wasn't quite right.

"Hmmm," Barnaby said, looking troubled.

"What is it?"

"The dogs sound more frenzied than they usually do. They might have found something."

"You mean someone?"

"It could be nothing." Barnaby turned away from the door. "A couple of years back, they sniffed out a terrified computer repairman who was here after hours, fixing a glitch in the system in our payroll department."

"Interesting," I commented, unable to help feeling vaguely unsettled.

Maybe it was just the prospect of being hounded by those dogs myself as I headed out of the store later. I could see the headlines tomorrow: "MAYOR ATTACKED BY PACK OF ANGRY DOGS."

Or maybe, in retrospect, the sense of trepidation that stole over me was due to some sixth sense that told me something was about to happen.

Something huge and horrible.

"As I was saying," Barnaby continued, returning to his desk and speaking loudly over the racket the Dobermans were making, "I don't have evidence that specifically points to Simon Weatherly, and he's denying any involvement."

"How do you know that?"

"Because I called him here for a meeting to confront him with the situation. You know, man-to-man."

"When was this?"

"Just this evening. He stormed out of here an hour ago. He

was furious when I asked him if he knew anything about the bomb threats. As I said, he denied everything."

"Well then, maybe he's not responsible."

"Of course he is. Who else would—"

The ringing of the telephone on his desk caused yet another interruption.

"Excuse me, Ed," he said, picking it up. "Tischler here . . . what? What happened? Why don't you just tell me—" He broke off and listened briefly, then said, sounding resigned, "All right, I'll be down there in a second."

He hung up the phone, already on his feet, reaching for the suit coat he had draped over the back of his chair. "That was my security chief. Something's going on downstairs."

"Did the dogs find someone hiding in the store?"

"I have no idea. It's probably nothing." He paused, and I knew he was thinking of Simon Weatherly and the bomb threats. "I *hope* it's nothing. I'll be back in a few minutes."

Oh, no, you don't, I thought, jumping up and following him to the door. "I'm coming with you."

No way was I going to sit there like a potential late-night snack for that bunch of Dobermans on the loose, even with Mohammed stationed nearby.

Barnaby, perhaps reading my mind, didn't argue. He led the way back down the dimly lit hallway lined with offices, past the elevators to a door marked EXIT, saying, "Let's take the stairs. It's only one floor below, and these old elevators take too long."

Mohammed and I followed him down the dank stairwell to the fifth floor, and through another door, where we found ourselves in another hallway. The place was a maze, I thought as we made several turns, approaching the sound of dogs and voices.

Whatever was going on had the dogs in a frenzy, I decided, and said as much to Barnaby.

"I hope it's just another computer repairman," he told me, looking distracted as we pushed through a set of double doors.

"Something tells me it isn't, Barnaby," I said, reading the sign over the door. "Unless you keep computers in the employees' locker rooms."

"I just hope it isn't anything disastrous," Barnaby returned, moments before we rounded a corner, opened another door, marked RESTRICTED, and saw a cluster of security guards and barking, jumping black Dobermans several yards down a long hall. They were gathered around an open door. Several of the guards held the dogs' leashes, and appeared to be struggling to quiet them.

It wasn't clear at first what had them in such an uproar.

But as we approached, I realized that the open door led to a storage closet, and whatever it was must be lying on the floor just inside.

"Mr. Tischler, I'm afraid—" The security guard who had glanced up and started to speak stopped short when he saw me. "Good evening, Mr. Mayor."

I nodded politely, and Barnaby stepped forward.

"What is it, Collins?" he asked. "What's going on?"

"You'd better take a look," he said, stepping aside and motioning at whatever lay waiting inside the closet.

I was right behind Barnaby, peering over his shoulder.

The expletive that spilled from his lips was echoed by one of my own.

There, on the floor, lying in a pool of blood, was a crumpled figure clad in a familiar crimson velour suit with white fleece trim.

Someone had murdered the Ramsey's Santa Claus.

TWO

"Drink this, Barnaby," I said firmly, placing a glass of cold water, fetched from a nearby cooler by Mohammed, in his badly trembling hands.

He obeyed blindly, seated stiffly on a bench beside a row of employee lockers.

Down the hall, a team of detectives from the New York Police Department was examining the body and the grisly scene.

"I can't believe this could happen," Barnaby said, handing the glass back to me and burying his head in his hands. "What could anyone have done to deserve such a death?"

I thought back to the gala event just before Thanksgiving, when this year's Ramsey's Santa had made his first public appearance. His true identity, in keeping with tradition, had been withheld as part of the store's Santa gimmick.

"What was his name?" I asked Barnaby.

"The Santa?" He sounded hesitant. "I have no idea which one it was."

I frowned. "I thought you use only one."

That, too, was a part of the Ramsey's legend.

Unlike other big department stores, which have an entire staff of Santas, many on duty simultaneously in carefully contrived, mazelike settings, Ramsey's boasts of an old-fashioned single-Santa policy in keeping with their old-fashioned tradition of service.

Each year the store's search for the perfect Santa begins in the summer months, amid considerable publicity. There are always hundreds of applicants, some from as far away as California and Florida. Everyone, it seems, is eager for the chance to carry on the Ramsey's legend.

Now Barnaby looked distinctly cagey as he informed me, "Until this year, we *have* used only one Santa. But I'm afraid that just wasn't working out for us anymore, Ed. We had to go to a multi-Santa situation like the other stores. It was the only way we could compete."

"What do you mean?"

"When you have only one Santa, you're limited to relatively short shifts. After all, the guy has to take breaks. He has to go home eventually. And when he's not there, the kids can't see him. They're unhappy. They leave the store. And that means, obviously, that their parents leave with them. When the parents leave, they obviously stop spending—"

"Obviously," I cut in. "But that means you're lying to the public, Barnaby. You deliberately created a media circus around the Santa-selection process this year, just as you have in the past."

"But I never—"

"Let me finish. You led the public to believe that there's only one lucky candidate—make that *unlucky*," I amended, glancing at the activity around the body down the hall, "who gets to be the Ramsey's Santa."

"I know."

"That's all you have to say?"

He bristled. "What do you want me to say? This is progress, Ed. We can't keep doing *everything* the old-fashioned way. We're losing money here. And anyway, very few people know about the new setup. We've had very tight security behind the Winter Wonderland enterprise, and only those directly involved have access to the area. That spot where the body was found was in the restricted area. No one not involved with the Santa setup is allowed past the door opening to that hallway—it leads down to the Wonderland display."

"It doesn't seem possible that you can keep such an enormous secret, Barnaby."

"Everyone—the security people, our few employees who have knowledge of the situation, and, of course, all the elves and Santas—has been required to sign statements that he or she will reveal to no one—including the press, of course—that there is more than one Ramsey's Santa."

"I see."

I have to admit, the whole idea of such clandestine action revolving around a mere Santa Claus display seemed vaguely ridiculous to me.

Yet, a man connected with the operation had just been murdered.

The behind-the-scenes details concerning the Winter Wonderland had taken on serious implications.

Footsteps approaching from down a nearby hall caused both of us to look up.

A police detective was walking quickly toward us. He was a tall, handsome, dark-haired Latino who appeared to be in his early forties, if that.

"Mr. Mayor, Mr. Tischler, I'm Detective Lazaro," he said, his black eyes somber. "I'm with the homicide squad. We've secured the crime scene. The police forensic unit has arrived, and so have pathologists from the medical examiner's office. We need your cooperation with the investigation, as witnesses."

"Of course," I responded promptly.

Barnaby protested, "We didn't witness anything. We were in my office—"

"We're going to need to ask both of you a few questions," the detective interrupted.

"Certainly," I said, standing.

I had become familiar with the specifics of crime-scene investigations, having recently been present at homicide scenes both at City Hall and at the Regal Theater over on West Forty-sixth Street. Of course, I went on to solve both those cases, as you may have heard.

"Mr. Tischler, we'll speak with you first—that is, if you don't mind, Mr. Mayor."

"Not at all."

I watched as he led the badly rattled Barnaby down a hall to a small office that had been turned into a makeshift interrogation room.

As soon as they were out of sight, I made my way—preceded by a wary Mohammed, of course—back toward the closet where the body had been found. The area had been cordoned off by the police. Before trying to get closer to the body, I took note of the surroundings.

Rows of employee lockers ran along either side of the closet, with benches scattered about the large room. There were several vending machines along one wall, and one of those coolers that held a large, upside-down blue plastic bottle of spring water.

In addition to the closet, there were doorways leading to men's and women's rest rooms, and another that was marked PRIVATE. AUTHORIZED PERSONNEL ONLY.

I noticed a display of framed photos running the entire length of the wall opposite the lockers and stepped over to investigate. Each frame bore a brass plate containing the year in which the photo was taken, and they dated back to the early nineteen twenties.

They appeared to be group shots of the store employees taken at the annual Ramsey's Christmas party. I spent a few minutes idly glancing over them.

Then I moved back toward the closet, noting that the Dobermans were nowhere to be seen, and most of the store's security force had dispersed. Uniformed officers stood by as police photographers snapped pictures of the scene and detectives bustled around, dusting for fingerprints and examining the body.

"I'm afraid we're going to have to ask you to step back, Mr. Mayor."

I turned and nodded at a chubby young cop who had spotted me hovering on the fringes. He had an open snack-sized bag of Fritos in his hand and was munching as he spoke.

"I just wanted to see what was going on over here," I told him, incredulous that anyone could think to buy a snack from the vending machines in the midst of this horror.

"Just a routine homicide investigation." His eyes shifted from mine, and I glanced in the direction they had taken.

He appeared to be ogling a uniformed female police officer.

She was trim and attractive, with a long blond braid poking from beneath her cap.

She looked vaguely familiar. I figured I must have seen her at the policeman's funeral last week, which had been mobbed with not just uniformed officers, but hundreds of friends and family members. New York City cops are the finest citizens around.

Well, most of them, I thought, glancing back at the detective, whose lecherous eyes were trained on the attractive female cop across the room.

"Have you identified the victim yet?" I asked him.

He reluctantly returned his attention to me, popped another chip into his mouth, and rubbed his balding head, looking hesitant.

"As you know, Officer . . ."

"Holt," he supplied when I paused for his name. "Doug Holt."

"Officer Holt, I'm the mayor of this city, and a potential witness to the crime," I pointed out. "What reason could you possibly have for withholding information about the victim's identity? I'll find out soon enough."

"I guess everyone will." He shrugged, finished crunching the chip, and swallowed. Then he revealed, "According to the wallet they found in his pocket, his name is Angelo Calvino. He's seventy-two. Lives down in Little Italy."

"Any motive?"

He lowered his voice and rattled his cellophane bag as he reached inside for another handful of chips. "If you ask me, it was probably a mob hit."

"And you're basing this information on . . . ?"

"You saw him. Shot in the back of the head, execution style. And as I said, he lives down in Little Italy."

"A lot of people live down in Little Italy," I said brusquely. "The vast majority of them are not involved with the mob."

"Some are."

"If I were you, Officer Holt, I would resist the urge to jump to conclusions. I would also wipe my mouth," I said, noticing the pronounced film of orange seasoning the chips had left around his lips.

I turned and walked away, sidling closer to the body. The Fritoeating officer was either too humiliated to stop me, or had returned his attention to the pretty female cop nearby.

In any case, I managed to position myself close enough to take in some specific details of the murder scene.

Lest you conclude that I'm some kind of ghoul, allow me to point out that I was driven closer not by mere morbid curiosity, but by a genuine desire to help with the investigation.

Given my past successes in cracking high-profile murder cases, I had been forced to acknowledge, privately and publicly, that I happen to be gifted with extraordinary powers of instinct and reasoning. As any professional detective will attest, both those traits are crucial to the process of crime solving.

With politics firmly and fondly standing as my primary vocation, I had no intention of pursuing a career with the NYPD.

By the same token, I shoulder an enormous responsibility to the citizens of this city, and I had no intention of allowing the dangerous and despicable murderer of one of their most beloved icons to roam free, not to mention destroy the world-renowned ambience of New York at Christmastime.

And so I did what any mayor would do under the circumstances. I vowed to do whatever I could to help New York's Finest solve this case. That meant taking advantage of both my proximity to the crime scene and my God-given talents.

The man on the floor was lying on his stomach, his limbs twisted in a grotesque position. He wore a familiar red velour suit with white trim, a matching cap, and black boots. From beneath the hat and his prone face, I could see tufts of white from his hair and whiskers.

They were spattered with scarlet splotches.

And the upper portion of the suit was so soaked with blood from the gaping head wound that it was difficult to tell where the velour left off and the fuzzy white trim began. But as I edged closer, I saw that the blood was a darker shade of red—that indicated it was beginning to dry.

My sharp ears heard a familiar voice announce from somewhere in the vicinity of the body, "Warm to the touch. No evidence of rigor mortis."

I didn't have to position myself any closer to know who was

speaking. Even if I hadn't instantly recognized the figure crouched by the corpse, I would have realized the distinctly gravelly voice belonged to Darius Jones, a friend of mine who happens to be a forensic pathologist. He had obviously been sent by the medical examiner's office to investigate.

"My preliminary conclusion is that death most likely occurred within the past three hours," Jones announced, straightening and addressing his assistant and one of the detectives standing by. "However, that is, as you understand, a tentative conclusion. Go ahead and bag the hands."

I strained to hear what else they were saying, but couldn't quite make it out.

Then somebody called the detective away, and I seized the opportunity to zero in on Darius.

"Mr. Mayor!" he exclaimed, his large mocha-colored eyes glad, as always, to see me, yet understandably puzzled. "What are you doing here?"

"I just happened to be meeting with Barnaby Tischler in his office upstairs when the body was discovered."

He let out a low whistle. "Talk about a coincidence. For a minute there I thought maybe the homicide squad had made you an official detective."

I chuckled and shook my head.

"They should. If it weren't for you, they would have two unsolved cases on their hands."

"I'm sure they would eventually have solved both the Kreig murder and the Matthews case. But I like to do what I can," I acknowledged. "For the good of the city."

"Well, it looks to me like you've got your hands full with this case." He glanced over at the body, which was still being photographed. "When it hits the papers that the Ramsey's Santa has been murdered . . ." He trailed off, shaking his head. "Think of all the children who will be devastated."

"I am thinking of them. That's why I'm going to work with the detectives, if I can, to find out who did this. Is there anything you can tell me about the condition of the body?"

He looked around as if to ensure that no one was eavesdropping, then said in a low voice, "I'm not supposed to give out information to anyone other than the authorities."

"The mayor *is* an authority, Darius."

"True . . ." Still, he hesitated.

I was about to bribe him with the promise of that green peppercorn pâté he adores, when he finally shrugged and started talking.

"The victim was killed within the last three hours. Single gunshot wound to the head, fired at close range. No sign of a struggle."

"Where was he killed?"

"It doesn't look like the body has been moved. I would guess that he was shoved from behind into the closet and immediately killed right where he fell."

"Did they find the weapon?"

"Not yet. The investigators are searching the vicinity though."

"Anything else you can tell me?"

"At this point? No. The autopsy will—"

"There you are, Mr. Mayor."

I turned to see Detective Lazaro standing behind us. He didn't appear pleased to find me chatting with a pathologist.

"If you'll come with me, please," he said crisply. "We're ready to question you."

"Absolutely," I agreed amiably, and, trailed by Mohammed, followed him down the hall.

"Would you please state your name and address for the record?"

I blinked. "Edward I. Koch. Gracie Mansion. New York, New York."

The detective smiled faintly and made a note on the pad in his hand. "Just following procedure, Mr. Mayor."

"Of course."

"What was your purpose for being on the premises this evening?"

"I was meeting with Barnaby Tischler. He's an old acquaintance of mine."

"Acquaintance or friend?"

"Friend," I amended.

"That's what he said. What was the purpose of the meeting?"

"He asked me to discuss the problem Ramsey's Department

Store is having with the new Highview Meadows mall over in Jersey."

"The problem being . . . ?"

"Ramsey's is losing business to them. They're running shuttles for shoppers from the corner of Thirty-fourth Street right outside his store. He wanted to know what I could do about that."

"And what can you do?"

"Nothing," I told him bluntly. "They're not breaking any laws."

"Did he mention any other problems the store is facing?"

"Besides financial ones?"

The detective nodded.

"He did say that there have been several bomb threats in the past few months."

"Did he mention suspecting anyone in particular?"

"Yes, he did."

"And that would be . . . ?"

"Simon Weatherly."

"What did he say about Weatherly specifically?"

I recounted my conversation with Barnaby to the best of my ability, then asked whether the detective thought the bomb threats were linked to the murder.

"If you don't mind, Mr. Mayor, I'm asking the questions here," he said politely. "Did you notice anything unusual at any time during your visit to Mr. Tischler?"

"Aside from the Dobermans suddenly going wild downstairs— I'm assuming that occurred at the point when they discovered the body in the closet—no, I didn't."

"How did Mr. Tischler react to the disturbance?"

"He seemed mildly concerned. He went to the door and listened."

"Did he comment as to what might have caused the dogs to bark?"

"He said it was probably nothing. He mentioned that the dogs had found a computer repairman on the premises late one night. That was all he said about it, until the telephone call came from security."

"How did he react to the call?"

"He seemed concerned, but he wasn't aware until we got down here that someone had been murdered."

"How do you know that?"

"How do I—Because he didn't say anyone had been murdered. And he was visibly shaken when we saw the body. Barnaby isn't a suspect in this case, is he, Detective?"

"As I said earlier, Mr. Mayor, I'm the one who's asking the questions here." He sounded considerably less polite than he had before. "Is there any additional information you can add to aid in our investigation?"

"I'm afraid there isn't at this point. I didn't see or hear anything unusual, as I said."

"I would appreciate, Mr. Mayor, if you would keep all the details of this case to yourself."

"Of course I will. You didn't think I'd go blabbing inside information to the press, now, did you?"

He offered a tight smile. "No, I didn't. And I apologize for taking up so much of your valuable time, Mr. Mayor. I realize you are a busy man."

"Never too busy to lend a hand when it comes to something like this, Detective. In fact, I fully intend to assist the police department with this investigation, as I have in the past."

He pursed his lips. "That won't be necessary, Mr. Mayor. The homicide squad is quite capable—"

"I didn't say it wasn't capable, Detective. Only that I intend to provide whatever insight I can into this murder."

"As I said, if there is any additional information you can provide—"

"And as I said, I have nothing to add at this point. When I do have information, I will be glad to share it with you."

He hesitated, then threw up his hands in a helpless gesture. "You go ahead and do whatever it is that you feel is necessary, Mr. Mayor."

"I always do," I said with a curt nod.

When we emerged from the makeshift interview room, Detective Lazaro told Mohammed that he would find a police officer to escort us downstairs to my car.

"That isn't necessary," I said. "We know the way."

"It *is* necessary. This is a crime scene. Officer Varinski?" The detective beckoned to a nearby cop.

It turned out to be the attractive blonde I had seen earlier.

"Yes?" She smiled pleasantly, but it didn't reach her pale blue eyes. She looked distinctly rattled. I wondered if she was new on the force. Maybe this was her first murder.

Then again, maybe not.

Maybe some cops never get used to the sight and smell of blood and gore. I know I wouldn't.

"Would you mind escorting the mayor and his bodyguard to the main entrance on Thirty-fourth Street?" the detective asked her.

"Not at all."

Mohammed radioed into his walkie-talkie for my driver to bring the car around, then told the female cop he remembered her from when he worked in the same precinct a few years back.

"Katrina, isn't it?" he asked her.

She smiled faintly and nodded.

"I'm Mohammed Johnson."

"You kind of look familiar," she said in a hesitant way that told me she didn't recall him.

"I do?"

"But I can't quite remember . . ."

"That's not surprising," Mohammed said. "I worked in the precinct for only a few months, and you were busy planning your wedding at the time. I remember some of the guys teasing you about having a stash of those bridal magazines in your locker."

"Yeah, well, they still like to tease me," she said a little grimly.

I didn't doubt that a young, exceptionally attractive female police officer inspired some measure of attention from her fellow officers, and not all of it pleasant.

"Thank you again for your help, Mr. Mayor," Lazaro said, shaking my hand.

"No problem. I'll be in touch," I told him before following the female officer down the hall.

She turned left where I expected her to turn right, and right where I thought we should turn left.

"This place really is a maze," I commented as we stepped into a narrow stairwell marked EMPLOYEES ONLY.

"It does seem like one, doesn't it," the officer agreed, holding the banister with one hand and fiddling with the tip of her braid with the other as we descended several flights to the first floor.

I found myself scanning the shadows, perhaps half expecting to see a blood-covered killer lurking there.

For some reason, I suddenly became aware of the unsettling notion that danger was hovering nearby. My heart started pounding and my hands clenched into nervous fists.

Feeling ridiculous, I told myself the killer had to be long gone. If he had concealed himself anywhere in the store, that pack of panting Dobermans would undoubtedly have sniffed him out long before now.

And anyway, I was perfectly safe, in the company of not only my own armed bodyguard, but an armed police officer. I decided my mind must be playing tricks on me.

Still, I was relieved when we emerged into the dimly lit cosmetics department. The officer swiftly led the way to the main entrance, where two more uniformed cops were stationed, along with a Ramsey's security guard, who quickly unlocked one set of doors for us.

I saw him blatantly looking the blond officer up and down the way the detective upstairs had done, but he stopped when he saw that I had noticed what he was doing.

I turned to her and thanked her for the escort.

"Are you all right?" I asked her, noticing that she still seemed vaguely upset.

"I'm fine," she assured me with a faint smile. "It's just upsetting to work on cases like this."

I noticed one of the uniformed cops nudging the other, a burly oaf who nodded and muttered, "That's why female officers should be assigned to desk jobs. They can't hack the rough stuff."

That sexist comment deserved a retort.

Before I could open my mouth to offer one, the woman, Officer Varinski, turned to him.

But instead of blasting the chauvinist, she merely said, "Maybe you're right, Jake. I can't speak for all women, but when it comes to violence, I can't help feeling like a real wimp. It bothers me to see someone gunned down in cold blood like that poor man upstairs."

With that, she turned, nodded politely at me, and went back into the store.

I shook my head, bemused. Most of the female cops I've met would have jumped down a guy's throat for even hinting that they're weaker—physically or emotionally—than male officers. But this one had somehow managed to put him into his place without even raising her voice.

Mohammed and I were halfway down the icy sidewalk, heading toward the familiar black sedan parked at the curb, when a photographer jumped out at me, causing me to gasp and jump.

"Mr. Mayor," a reporter I hadn't noticed before called out. "Is it true that someone has been murdered inside Ramsey's?"

"No comment," I said gruffly, still blinking from the camera's flash, and pushed my way past the nosy media hound to the car.

Only when I was safely in the backseat and my driver was pulling away from the curb, turning the corner and heading uptown, did I allow myself to heave a big sigh of relief.

It's not often that I manage to spook myself like that.

Then again, it's not often that I'm thrust into the middle of a murder scene.

"Are you all right, Mr. Mayor?" Mohammed asked, looking concerned.

"I'm fine, thanks, Mohammed." I turned to look out the window at the twinkling white Christmas lights that sparkled in the trees dotting the island in the middle of Park Avenue.

So festive, I thought, noticing that a light snow was falling. On a nearby sidewalk, a uniformed doorman was standing on a ladder to hang an enormous boxwood wreath over the door of an apartment building.

With another sigh, I vowed once again to do everything I could to catch the murderer and protect New York's reputation as the merriest city in the world.

_____ THREE

By Wednesday, my cold was entirely gone, thanks to daily doses of Glugol Muggle.

I certainly hadn't been able to grab any extra rest. In fact, Tuesday had been more hectic than usual, thanks to a number of issues.

One was the weather. Temperatures in the metropolitan region had plunged drastically. The high on Tuesday was ten degrees, with a windchill factor of minus twenty. That was positively balmy compared to the forecast for Wednesday.

After consulting my corporation counsel's office, I announced at a Tuesday afternoon press conference that as long as the weather remained dangerously cold, the homeless would be removed from the city streets—involuntarily if necessary—and brought to shelters.

This decision was, predictably, met with a media uproar. The last time I issued such a decree because of perilous weather conditions, we had homeless people threatening physical harm to the social workers trying to drag them into shelter-bound vans and thus, save their lives.

The city's lawyers declared Tuesday, as they had in the past, that we were well within the law to forcibly remove anyone who willingly exposed himself to the elements, meaning they were oblivious—due to drugs, alcohol, or mental illness—to the life-threatening cold.

I informed the press that I would stick to my guns on this issue once again.

Also on Tuesday, in the midst of budget meetings and public relations ceremonies, I met with Rockefeller Center officials regarding next Monday's tree-lighting ceremony. I had agreed to emcee the event, which would be nationally televised live during prime time.

And then there was the Ramsey's murder.

Because it had happened late Monday evening, the Tuesday morning papers had gone to press too late to report the crime. But by Tuesday evening there wasn't a person in New York— probably in the entire country—who hadn't heard that the famed Ramsey's Santa had been gunned down in the store.

Along with that information, the press revealed that witnesses at the crime scene included none other than yours truly.

As a result, I arrived at City Hall early Wednesday morning to find a familiar barrage of reporters and cameras waiting for me.

"It's this homeless thing," Lou Sabatino, one of my bodyguards, commented as he eyed the throng.

"No, it isn't," I told him. "It's the Ramsey's murder."

"You think?"

"Didn't you see the ten o'clock news last night? They're claiming I was summoned to the scene of the crime *after* the body was discovered."

"Because . . . ?"

"The homicide squad needed my help with the investigation."

"That might be true," Lou conceded, adding hastily, "the part about their needing your help, I mean. You've got a knack for crime solving, Mr. Mayor."

"I'm not denying that. But our homicide squad is not a bunch of helpless, bumbling idiots, as the media would like to portray them. I just happened to have been in the store Monday night when that body was found. And I'm going to make sure the press understands that loud and clear."

He grinned. "I'm sure you will."

I buttoned the top button of my charcoal cashmere overcoat,

put on my fleece-lined leather gloves, and tucked my gray wool scarf around my neck.

"Ready, Mr. Mayor?" Lou asked, settling a knit cap on his head.

"Ready."

"You're all nuts!" I proclaimed the instant I stepped from my car amid an urgent chorus of *Mr. Mayor*s and a blinding array of flashing flashbulbs and television lights.

I blasted them, "It's forty below zero with the windchill this morning. Nothing I have to say could be worth freezing your buns off."

"Mr. Mayor, who killed Angelo Calvino?"

"Who do I look like, the Amazing Kreskin?" I shot back, my breath frosty in the frigid morning air.

"What were you doing at the scene of the murder?"

"What was the motive?"

"Is it true that you've joined the homicide squad as a detective?

The final question made me roll my eyes and snort, "Ridiculous! Of course I haven't joined the homicide squad. I already have a job, remember? I happen to be mayor of this wonderful city," I retorted, adding, "And as mayor, I have a responsibility to its citizens. I will personally and professionally do everything I can to ensure that the police catch the vicious killer responsible for this heinous crime."

"How do you explain your presence at the scene of yet another high-profile local murder?"

"Coincidence," I barked. "What other explanation did you have in mind? And now, if you'll excuse me, I'm going inside to thaw out. I would advise you all to do the same."

Ignoring the protests and questions flung at my back by the reporters, I allowed my team of bodyguards to hustle me inside City Hall, which was bustling with activity even at this early hour.

I paused at my secretary, Maria Perez's, desk in the outer office.

"Good morning, Mr. Mayor," she said with a businesslike smile. "How are you feeling today?"

"Better, thanks. Any messages?"

"Only from the press. They keep calling about the murder. I keep referring them to your press secretary."

"Good. He'll keep telling them 'no comment.' He's getting very good at that."

I didn't have any appointments scheduled until my nine o'clock meeting with Bob Denisovich, my commissioner for Housing Preservation and Development, and MacDonald J. Lawrence, a Manhattan real estate tycoon who wanted to raze a historic midtown cathedral to build an eighty-story steel and glass condominium.

Once I was seated at my desk—which, incidentally, had once belonged to the great Fiorello La Guardia himself—with a steaming mug of Martinson's coffee, I turned my attention to this morning's papers.

Predictably, the first headline I picked up screamed, "SANTA SLAYING STUMPS SLEUTHS."

I scanned the article and learned that the police had no potential suspects at this time, nor had they established a motive.

Barnaby Tischler had released a statement saying, "On behalf of Ramsey's Department Store, I would like to offer my condolences to the Calvino family. We are all deeply saddened by this tragedy and will cooperate with the police to ensure that the killer is found."

The store, which had been closed all day Tuesday, would reopen this morning. Tischler was quoted in the paper as saying that he would employ heightened security measures to ensure the safety of both Ramsey's employees and customers. Furthermore, "a new Ramsey's Santa" would be on hand to greet children in the Winter Wonderland.

I snorted at that. The papers hadn't revealed the store's deep, dark secret—that there had been more than one Santa all along. I had to wonder whether that was because of Barnaby's efforts to cover it up, or because it was one of the incidentals about the case that the police didn't want revealed to the press.

In case you didn't know, detectives always withhold key information when they're investigating a murder case. That way, they can ensure that there are certain facts that only the killer would know. That's one technique they use to corner bad guys.

I continued to read about the Ramsey's case, plowing through extensive coverage in all the local newspapers, where it was front-page news, and a couple of out-of-town papers, where it was reserved for less prominent placement.

A sidebar about the victim in Manhattan's number one tabloid, *The Daily Register,* showed a photo of a smiling elderly man with a full head of white hair. Angelo Calvino, a seventy-two-year-old widower and a retired cabdriver, had no known enemies according to his distraught only child, an adult daughter, Amy, who had flown in late Tuesday from her home in Phoenix.

She told reporters that her father had lived a simple life since her mother had died back in 1989. He had lived alone in a modest apartment two doors down Mulberry Street from Benito One, which is one of my favorite restaurants in Little Italy.

As it happened, I would be dining there tomorrow evening with my good friend Sybil Baker, who is the veteran gossip columnist for *The Daily Register.* We had made the date over this past week-end, when she called and told me she had a hankering for Benito's gnocchi with tomato sauce. Her husband, Claude, who works for the U.N. and is constantly globe-trotting, hates Italian food, particularly gnocchi, so whenever he leaves town, Sybil—who adores Italian food, particularly gnocchi—makes it a point to call me to dine with her on Mulberry Street.

I made a mental note to stop by Calvino's apartment while I was in the neighborhood tomorrow, to see what I could find out. The police would already have searched the place and interrogated the neighbors, but you never know.

I might just be able to pick up on some interesting clue that they had missed.

Wednesday afternoon, in lieu of a time-consuming lunch at one of the neighborhood restaurants, I gobbled down some low-fat saltines and a bowl of Campbell's cream of mushroom soup I'd prepared myself in the kitchenette adjoining my office. As I ate, I went over a report from one of the city's financial advisers—grim news, as usual.

In the back of my mind, of course, was the Ramsey's murder. However, I was doing my best not to let it distract me from my work. I had enough to worry about at the moment, with the usual budget woes. I had managed to make a five-minute phone call this morning to Detective Lazaro, to see if there was anything he could tell me about the case that hadn't already been in the papers.

There wasn't.

Why was I surprised?

There are certain members of the homicide squad who bristle at the thought of outsiders intruding on their turf. In fact, I was reminded of a conversation I had had not long ago with Charley Deacon, a detective friend of mine who has risen through the ranks of the New York Police Department.

He told me that the crime-solving business is as competitive as any other. Every detective wants to be the one to solve the case, making true teamwork, especially in high-profile cases, a bit of an anomaly.

Which would explain why Detective Lazaro wasn't the most effusive conversationalist I had ever encountered.

I did manage to confirm what I already knew—that no weapon had been recovered, that no suspicious prints had been found at the scene, and there was no sign of a struggle. The time of death had been established as having occurred between nine-thirty and ten-thirty P.M. Since the store had closed at ten, and Calvino would have left his post in the Wonderland shortly afterward, he had probably been killed between ten-ten and ten-thirty.

Lazaro was clearly eager to cut our conversation short, and I finally allowed him to wriggle off the line after deciding I wasn't going to learn anything new from him.

I was about to return to the speech I was writing for a charity benefit I would be attending that evening, when my secretary buzzed me on my intercom.

That was unusual, because I had instructed her not to disturb me until one-thirty, and it was only a quarter past the hour. Maria is nothing if not efficient.

"What is it, Maria?" I asked, concerned, as I picked up the receiver.

"I'm so very sorry to disturb you, Mr. Mayor, but there's an important call for you. I told him you weren't available, but he insisted—"

"Who is the caller?"

"Barnaby Tischler."

"Go ahead and put him through."

I leaned back in my chair, and a moment later a familiar voice was saying, "Ed, thanks for taking the call."

"No problem," I said, and found that the connection sounded somewhat distant and tinny. I frowned. "Do you have me on speakerphone, Barnaby?"

"Yes," he said, seeming oddly out of breath. He went on. "I'm in my office, on my treadmill, trying to burn off some of this nervous energy."

"Well, what's going on?"

"Nothing. That's the problem."

"What do you mean?"

"The cops are dillydallying around with this thing, Ed. They have no idea who killed Calvino, no motive, nothing."

"Do they have any theories at all?"

"If they do, they're not telling me. I keep asking if they've questioned Simon Weatherly, and all they say is that they're checking into every lead. There *are* no other leads, Ed."

"How do you know?"

"Who else would want to gun down a wonderful person like Angelo Calvino? Everybody he knew loved the guy, and the motive couldn't have been robbery. He wasn't well off by any means. His wallet was still in his pocket, with fifteen dollars and a couple of subway tokens, and he was still wearing his Timex. Anyway, who would think to mug an old guy in a Santa suit?"

"No, robbery wouldn't be the motive," I agreed. "Listen, Barnaby, how many people have you told about the Winter Wonderland scam you're running this year?"

There was an abrupt telltale click that meant the speakerphone had been disconnected, and then Barnaby's voice, sounding suddenly intimate in my ear, was asking nervously, "What do you mean?"

"How many people know that you hired multiple Santas this year?"

"I went over this with you before." He paused to huff and puff a little, apparently still winded from the treadmill. Then he informed me, "The only people who know about the situation are the few employees and security personnel who are directly involved with the display, and as I said before, they're required to sign a statement that they will not reveal the situation to anyone. Oh, and, of course, the Santas themselves know."

"How many are there?"

"I'd rather not say."

"Barnaby . . ."

"I had a total of eight, but two quit, so now there are six," he said reluctantly, then added, "I mean, five . . . because of Calvino's . . . you know."

"Who else knows about this?"

"Nobody. Oh, well, except for my wife—not that Wanda has anything to do with this mess. And then there's *you*. You know about it. You haven't said anything to anyone, have you?"

"No. Do the police know?"

"Of course the police know. They deliberately haven't told the press, and not just because it would ruin my reputation."

Hmm. Just as I had suspected. This was obviously part of the information that was being withheld in an effort to nail the killer.

"Anyway," Barnaby went on, sounding glum, "I've had a handful of employees—and, as I said, two Santas—quit on me since yesterday morning."

"Why?"

"Why do you think? They're terrified. And so are my customers, Ed. What few actual customers there are."

"The store is empty, huh?"

"Actually, it's been more crowded than it normally is on a Wednesday morning, but most of the people who showed up today are curiosity seekers and reporters. They're all sniffing around for the gory details. No one seems to be buying anything."

"That's a shame."

"I've had a security consultant in my office all morning, working on an upgrade for our system. Because of the bomb threats *and* the murder, he strongly suggested placing metal detectors at every entrance to the store."

"Isn't that a bit expensive? And extreme?"

"It would be a hell of a lot more extreme to be forced to shut down my store because people don't feel safe shopping here, Ed."

He had a point. "What are you going to do?"

"What *can* I do? I'm going to put in the detectors. They'll be in place by the end of the week. And I'm beefing up my security staff."

"Do you think the murder was connected to the bomb threats?"

There was a pause. Then Barnaby said, "I would bet my life on it, Ed. Simon Weatherly—"

"You don't even know he was behind the bomb threats," I reminded him.

"I know. He wants me out of business. He wants my building. And he's a low-down SOB. I'm positive he would stop at nothing to get what he wants. Not even murder."

"I wouldn't go around saying that to too many people, Barnaby. You don't have proof."

"Yet. That's where I really need your help, Ed. You have to look into this for me. If I go snooping around Weatherly Brothers, everyone will clam up. But you . . . you're the mayor. And you're charming."

"I do have a way of winning people's confidence," I admitted with a modest shrug. Who could argue with that? You don't get repeatedly elected mayor of New York if people don't like and trust you.

I went on. "Actually, I already had plans to see what I could uncover with this case, Barnaby."

"So I heard. The press has you joining the police department as a homicide detective. You haven't, have you?"

"What do *you* think?"

"I think it's a shame they don't give you more credit for the two cases you've already solved. With your amazing brain, Ed, you could be catching murderers full-time."

Where had I heard that before? "Listen, my amazing brain is already occupied with the many challenging problems that come with running this city, Barnaby. But I promise you that I'll do everything I can to find out who killed your Santa."

"Thanks, Ed."

"I called the detective in charge of the case earlier today, to see if there was anything new he could tell me."

"And . . . ?"

"They're working on it, Barnaby. And so am I. The preliminary

autopsy report showed that Calvino died of a single gunshot wound
to the head—"

"What kind of gun?"

"Nine-millimeter pistol," I said, "and there were no signs of
a struggle. Someone came up and ambushed him from behind,
and there had to be a silencer on the gun, because there were
other employees in the vicinity, and they heard nothing."

"I just know it was Simon. He's a sneaky son of—"

"Barnaby, I know Weatherly's not exactly your closest pal, but
there are other possibilities here."

"Such as?"

"Like I said, I'm working on it."

"I really appreciate your help, Ed."

I could hear the despair in his voice. I wanted to reassure him,
to tell him not to worry, that I was positive everything would be
okay.

As everyone knows, politicians who never lie are few and far
between these days. However, I happen to be one of them.

And so, all I said to poor Barnaby was good-bye.

"Uncle Eddie!"

Only one person in the world calls me that.

I turned around and, sure enough, there, sweeping across the
crowded grand ballroom of the Marriott Marquis hotel, was my
sister Pat's daughter—my lovely niece, Melissa. She was radiant
in a floor-length midnight-blue-velvet gown, her long, dark curls
swept on top of her head to show off not just her lovely features,
but the dazzling diamonds and sapphires at her ears and throat.
She looked more like a glamorous young fashion model than the
thirty-five-year-old married mother of a toddler.

"I knew you would be here somewhere, Missy," I said after
excusing myself from the police commissioner and his wife, with
whom I had been chatting. I kissed my niece on the cheek.
"Where's Remy?"

"Making the rounds with his mother. Where else?"

Melissa's husband, Dr. Remy Beltran, is the son of the late
Raoul Beltran, who, of course, is widely renowned as one of the
wealthiest philanthropists in New York. Sadly, Raoul had died of

a heart attack just this past summer while yachting in the West Indies.

His wife, Melissa's mother-in-law, Michelle, had replaced him as chairperson of tonight's gala fund-raiser for the children's literacy fund, and it was she who had recently talked me into cohosting the festivities.

I really didn't mind, although it had taken some shuffling to fit the gala into my jammed schedule. Thanks to the holidays and my upcoming vacation to Barbados, which would keep me away from my duties for a week later this month, the days of December were even more hectic than usual.

Melissa told me, "I thought you would appreciate knowing that when we saw you on television yesterday during that press conference, your grand-niece started shouting, 'Hi, Uncle Eddie, it's me! Hello! Uncle Eddie?' She couldn't figure out why you weren't talking back to her."

I chuckled, thinking fondly of the precocious, towheaded tot who can be a docile miniature lady one moment and a holy terror the next.

The last time Melissa had brought her to visit me at Gracie Mansion, Schuyler had somehow managed to unlock a cabinet filled with eighteenth-century collectibles. She proceeded to construct a wobbly tower of stacked bone china teacups. Luckily, my housekeeper happened to stumble onto the scene in the nick of time.

"What else has Schuyler been up to lately?" I asked my niece.

Melissa made a weary face and sighed. "We're giving potty training another try this week. Don't ask for details."

"Believe me, I won't," I promised readily, and plucked a stuffed mushroom from a tray held by a passing waiter.

"And she has decided she wants that hideous giggling Henrietta Hyena puppet that's sold out of every toy department in the country. We're on a waiting list at F.A.O. Schwarz, but there's no guarantee they'll get a new shipment before January. I'm telling you, Uncle Ed, my life has been so hectic lately, I don't know if I'm coming or going."

She was certainly her mother's daughter. Pat always was—and

still is—an expert at making a huge fiasco out of the slightest setback.

"I'm a mental and physical wreck," Melissa informed me.

"Well, you're looking lovely, as always, Missy."

She brightened. "Thanks—that's sweet of you. You're very dashing in that tuxedo yourself, Uncle Ed," she said, smiling. "Will you be going to the Hanukkah celebration at my mother's this weekend?"

"Absolutely," I said, making a mental note to buy the last few gifts I needed before Saturday. "You know I wouldn't miss Pat's potato latkes with homemade applesauce and sour cream."

"I know. It's because of you that Mommy's having the get-together now instead of during the actual holiday later in the month, since you'll be away on vacation then."

"She's thoughtful that way, your mother," I said.

I swallowed the last morsel of my stuffed mushroom and made a mental note to cut back on my food intake for the rest of the week to compensate for all the rich, traditional Jewish holiday foods my sister would be serving.

"Schuyler is very excited about Hanukkah this year," Melissa confided in the endearing fashion of a mother who is head over heels with her precious child and can't resist regaling others with tales from the nursery. "I helped her make a menorah out of beads and clay. And she's just—"

"You're not going to let her light it, are you?" I cut in, horrified by the sudden mental image of my pint-sized niece brandishing flaming candles.

"Of course not! Anyway, as I was saying, Schuyler's thrilled about Christmas too. She keeps wondering how Santa Claus is going to get out of the fireplace when he comes down the chimney. I've told her a thousand times that we'll move the fire screen on Christmas Eve so he won't be trapped. And, of course, we've promised not to light a fire on that particular night."

"No, you wouldn't want poor Santa to drop into a pile of smoldering wood," I agreed.

I thought about how nice it was that my niece and her husband had managed to work out their religious differences so that their child was so well adjusted. Schuyler is being raised in the Jewish faith, but Melissa and her husband celebrate Christian holidays and traditions too. When Melissa married Remy, who is Catholic, a few years back, my sister and her husband had their reservations. But Remy has proven to be such a wonderful husband and father that they eventually accepted the interfaith union.

"Speaking of Santa," Melissa went on, her expression sobering, "what a terrible shock that murder was!"

"Terrible," I agreed cautiously, knowing precisely which murder she meant. But the ballroom was crowded, and I wasn't particularly eager to be overheard discussing the case.

"Were you really called to the scene as an official homicide investigator, Uncle Ed?"

"Missy, how many times have I told you not to believe everything you read?"

"I know, but . . . remember last summer when *The Daily Register* reported that you were rushed to the hospital with chest pains while you were vacationing in Venice? That turned out to be absolutely true."

"It was true," I admitted, "but all I had was an acute case of indigestion from eating one too many sausage ravioli."

More like *ten* too many, I admitted to myself.

"Well," Melissa said, "my point is, the papers aren't always wrong. And after you solved those last two murders, I honestly wouldn't be surprised if the police department appointed you an honorary detective. Who do you think is responsible for the killing?"

"Miniature quiche?" A waiter popped up, brandishing a silver tray loaded with tantalizing hors d'oeuvres.

"Yes, thank you." Melissa helped herself and glanced at me. "Do you want one, Uncle Ed?"

"Do I *want* one? Yes. Will I have one? Not on your life. I'm under doctor's standing orders to watch the cholesterol and fat. And that quiche is loaded with both."

"Ah, *that* must be why it's so delicious," said Melissa, who had fortunately inherited my sister's bone structure *and* metabolism. She nibbled her tiny pastry and prompted me, "Anyway, as you were saying, about the murder, Uncle Ed . . . ?"

But the waiter seemed to be hovering, and I sensed that his ears were awaiting my reply.

I cleared my throat pointedly and gave him a withering look that promptly caused him to skitter away with his miniature quiches.

Then I turned back to Melissa and said, "I have no idea who killed Angelo Calvino. As far as I know, the police haven't found any viable suspects yet either."

"Well, I'm just sick about the whole thing. Remy had planned to take Schuyler to see the Ramsey's Santa next week, but now we just don't feel that it's safe to set foot in that store. I think that he's going to take her over to see the Santa at Weatherly Brothers, or maybe Macy's, instead."

I thought of my earlier conversation with Barnaby Tischler, of his beefed-up security and his expensive metal detectors.

"I'm not so sure Ramsey's isn't safe," I told Melissa tentatively.

"Someone was murdered there, Uncle Ed. I can't afford to take chances with my little girl's life."

Who could argue with a statement like that?

"No," I agreed, "you certainly can't do that."

"Still, it's a shame . . ."

"What's a shame?"

We glanced up, and I saw that my tall, handsome nephew-in-law had joined us.

"How have you been, Uncle Ed?" he asked, greeting me with a handshake and a clap on the back.

"All things considered, not bad, Remy."

"What were the two of you talking about just now? What's a shame?" he repeated.

"I was telling Uncle Ed how you had planned to take Schuyler to see the Ramsey's Santa next week," Melissa told her husband.

"Oh, that." Regret filled his voice. "My father took me to the store to see Santa every year, even after I was too old to believe. In fact, I pretended to believe in Santa long after I knew the truth just so that we could keep up those visits. It was such a special day for the two of us—first, we would see the Ramsey's Santa, and then we would walk down the block to the Empire State Building and take the elevator to the one hundred and second floor to look out over the city."

I smiled, thinking back to my own fond father-and-son memories. When I was a very young child and we still lived in the Bronx, Pop and I would take the subway to Manhattan together every once in a while, to the Merkin Deli, where we would each get a pastrami on rye and a celery tonic. I cherished those rare moments when I had my father all to myself.

"Dad was a busy man," Remy was saying, a faraway look in his eyes. "There were so many days when he was too busy to see me at all. But those annual December visits to Santa and the Empire State Building were our tradition." He sighed and shook his head. "And now that Dad is gone, and I have a child of my own, I was looking forward to carrying on the tradition. Schuyler has never been to the top of the Empire State Building, and she has never met the Ramsey's Santa."

"Weatherly Brothers and Macy's are both right down the street from the Empire State Building too, Remy," Melissa pointed out gently. "You can still go up there."

"Weatherly Brothers doesn't even have a toy department. It just wouldn't be the same."

No, I thought sadly. It wouldn't be the same.

I thought about the countless other children and parents who had been robbed of something precious and meaningful this Christmas, and I found my hands clenching into fists just thinking about the abominable murder.

I personally intended to see that whoever had killed the Ramsey's Santa was going to pay dearly.

_____ FOUR

    I had several reasons for walking over to Little Italy on Thursday evening despite the frigid temperatures that still gripped the city.

For one thing, Mulberry Street is practically a stone's throw from City Hall, so it wouldn't make sense to take a car.

For another, my doctor has been hounding me to exercise more, and it's not easy for a mayor to make time for the gym as often as he would like.

Besides, it always makes me happy to be out on the streets of my city, where I can experience the sights and sounds and smells that are so uniquely New York.

The final reason: I do some of my best thinking while I'm walking. And on this particular evening I had a lot to think about.

According to today's papers, there had been no new developments in the "Santa slaughter," as the case had been dubbed by the press. No leads, no potential suspects, nothing to report about the investigation itself.

What *was* mentioned was something that I already knew—that very few shoppers had visited Ramsey's Department Store since the murder.

Barnaby Tischler was quoted as saying his store was perfectly safe; that he had beefed up his security staff and was taking additional "precautionary measures." He added that his special extended weekend shopping hours would continue through the holiday season as planned, with the store being open around the clock on Fridays and Saturdays from now until Christmas.

Meanwhile, Simon Weatherly was quoted as saying that his store was increasing its inventory "to accommodate the overflow of regular Ramsey's customers, who will be warmly welcomed and assisted by the polished, professional sales associates here at Weatherly Brothers."

In addition, his store would hold a bonus preholiday sale extravaganza this coming weekend, with ten percent off every item of clothing in the store. This was in direct response to the competition from Highview Meadows, where there is no sales tax on clothing.

Simon glibly asked New Yorkers, "Why go all the way across the river to Jersey to save eight percent when you can stay close to home and save ten?" which, anyone would admit, made an awful lot of sense.

On top of that, there would be "a free toy for every kiddie who visits the world-renowned Weatherly Brothers Santa."

I should point out that until last night there was nothing particularly world-renowned about the Weatherly Brothers Santa. That changed when one of those newsmagazine television crews interviewed several members of Simon's staff as part of a live update on the Ramsey's murder. One of the Weatherly Brothers Santas told the reporter that you couldn't pay him enough to take the Santa throne vacated by Angelo Calvino's murder.

"That store has always given me bad vibes," the would-be jolly old elf announced with a shudder as Simon Weatherly nodded solemnly in the background.

As I walked briskly up Broadway through lower Manhattan, surreptitiously flanked, as always, by two bodyguards with another pair trailing behind, I wondered if Weatherly really was behind the whole thing, as Barnaby had suggested.

There was no doubt that the rivalry between the neighboring Ramsey's and Weatherly Brothers department stores was even more notorious than that of Macy's and the now-defunct Gimbel's.

And there was no question that if Ramsey's went out of business, Weatherly Brothers would benefit, not only with increased sales, but, as Barnaby had pointed out, by taking over the more desirable location on Thirty-fourth Street.

Ramsey's occupies a stately limestone corner building reminiscent of a grand, graceful era in urban architecture. The imposing structure is six stories tall with vast display windows at street level, shaded by Ramsey's signature red and gray striped awnings. The interior, with its polished plank floors, high ceilings, ornate columns, and sweeping stairways, still exhibits many of the original fixtures from the store's Gay Nineties heyday. Narrow wooden escalators and caged elevators reminiscent of the turn of the century are still in service. The entire place gives off an undeniable old-world charm.

In contrast, the boxy three-story building that houses Weatherly Brothers is located in the middle of the block, roughly one-third the size of Ramsey's, and displaying, in my opinion, far less architectural allure. I have seldom ventured into the store, but I distinctly recall lots of cold marble and dimly lit nooks. The store, both inside and out, displays an aura of forced elegance reflected not just in the snooty sales staff, but in Mortimer Weatherly himself.

I have long been acquainted with the old man, whose father and uncle founded Weatherly Brothers in 1902. He is a Machiavellian businessman, impossible to like, yet reportedly scrupulous.

His nephew Simon, on the other hand, is a sallow, glowering character who never quite seems to make eye contact with anyone. Before Mortimer retired not long ago, there was talk that he intended to sell the business rather than allow Simon to take over. Apparently, the old man didn't think much of his only heir. But when the time came, Weatherly Brothers stayed in the family, with Simon taking over and Mortimer retiring to his chateau in Europe, ostensibly to put as much distance as possible between himself and his beloved department store, now in Simon's inept hands.

Surprisingly, despite reportedly disgruntled employees, the younger Weatherly had managed to keep the place afloat, with its sales currently surpassing those of its longtime competitor, Ramsey's. Now Simon clearly intended to move in for the kill by shrewdly capitalizing on his rival store's blizzard of bad press.

Rumor also had it that he was planning to expand his business

to include other departments, such as housewares and home elec-
tronics. Unlike Ramsey's and Macy's and Bloomingdale's, Weatherly Brothers had always dealt strictly in apparel, accessories, and
cosmetics.

In the current location there simply wasn't room to add other
types of merchandise. So there would be another benefit to taking
over the larger Ramsey's building.

But was Simon Weatherly actually behind the dastardly murder?
I must admit, he was my prime—and, yes, only—suspect.

Still, I didn't have nearly enough information about the case.

I couldn't overlook one of the oldest mottos of crime solving:
to know the victim is to know the criminal.

And that was precisely what I had in mind as I strode toward
Angelo Calvino's apartment that chilly Thursday evening.

I have spent many happy hours in the midst of the several-
block stretch of Mulberry Street that makes up the heart of Little
Italy. As one who enjoys dining and socializing, I can't help being
drawn to the casual, homey atmosphere that pervades even the
most upscale restaurants in the neighborhood. I always enjoy stroll-
ing past the small ethnic groceries and pastry shops, shoulder to
shoulder with some of the most colorful characters and tourists
the city has to offer.

I have been known to spend hours meandering along Mulberry,
especially during the renowned Italian festivals and feast days,
when I'm bound to see countless familiar faces in the crowds. But
tonight my pace was vigorous, and it was everything my guards
could do to keep up with me.

"If I didn't know better, I'd think you were in training for the
next New York marathon, Mr. Mayor," Ambrose commented,
huffing frost breaths alongside me as we scurried across Grand
Street.

"The marathon *is* a grand local tradition," I admitted, stepping
carefully onto the opposite curb, careful not to slip on the icy
concrete. "And you know how I feel about participating in New
York traditions. I'll have to give it some thought. Of course, you
would have to train with me, Ambrose. Can't run all that way
alone, now, can I?"

He grunted, and I grinned.

Then I spotted the address on a four-story redbrick building nearby. This was it.

I stopped and surveyed the building, with Ambrose and my second bodyguard, Lou, taking grateful breaths beside me.

On the ground level was an Asian grocery, testimony to Chinatown's current tendency to spill across its original border, Canal Street, and into Little Italy.

To the right of the door leading to the grocery was one that apparently led to the apartments above. I walked over and gave it a try.

Locked, of course.

Though this has always been one of the safest neighborhoods in Manhattan, there are very few buildings that allow access to people off the street.

I would have to be buzzed in—a feat that might be difficult for someone other than the mayor.

I surveyed the row of bells, the residents' names written neatly alongside them in fading black ink on yellowed rectangles of paper.

3B—A. Calvino.

On the off chance that the late Mr. Calvino's daughter might be there, I pressed the button for his apartment and waited.

There was no reply.

I decided to start with his neighbor, a B. Tucci in apartment 3A.

After ringing the bell, I expected either silence or the static of a voice over the intercom, asking who was there.

Instead, the door buzzed loudly.

Startled, I shoved it open and quickly entered the dimly lit vestibule, with Ambrose, Lou, and the others right on my heels. The place smelled of Lysol and spaghetti sauce, and I could hear the evening news coming from a television set in one of the first-floor apartments as we walked toward the narrow staircase at the back of the short hallway.

On the third floor I saw that the door to apartment 3A was ajar, and hesitated on the rubber mat before tapping and calling, "Hello?"

"Come in, Donnie, before you let my heat out," came a female voice in reply as water ran and pots clattered in the background.

I glanced at my guards, who gave a group shrug.

"I'll go first," Lou said with characteristic caution, as though an opportunistic assassin might be lying in wait on the off chance that the mayor might drop by this afternoon.

I followed him into the minuscule sitting room, where countless white crocheted doilies were draped atop threadbare furniture and battered dark wooden tables. There was an old-fashioned portable television set and a stereo that when brand new, in a bygone era, would have been termed a hi-fi. On the walls were dozens of framed family photos and an enormous crucifix.

The place was sweltering, with the telltale hiss and scent of steam heat coming from the radiator in one corner.

"Must be a hundred degrees in here," Ambrose muttered, wiping his brow. "At least."

"Feels like my mother's place," Lou said, and I nodded.

My own parents, who spend part of every winter in Florida, aren't comfortable unless the thermostat is set on ninety. Whenever I visit them at this time of year, I find myself wishing I had worn shorts and a tank top.

"I'm in the kitchen," called the voice.

"*I'll* go first," I told Lou, stepping in front of him. I figured that I, as the recognizable mayor, would provide a more welcome sight than a hulking stranger would to the unknown woman who had clearly been expecting someone named Donnie.

"Hello?" I called, poking my head around the corner of what had to be the kitchen, judging by the delectable aroma that wafted to my nostrils.

A good-sized elderly woman, standing at the sink, turned and caught sight of me. Her jaw dropped and her eyebrows rose from behind her wire-rimmed glasses to disappear beneath the swoop of salt-and-pepper hair across her forehead.

She closed her mouth again a moment later, without having said a word.

"I'm sorry to barge in on you like this, ma'am," I said graciously. "As you may know, I'm Ed Koch, and these"—I gestured at the burly gang hovering in the doorway behind me—"are my bodyguards."

She only nodded, still looking stunned.

In the sink behind her, water continued to pour from the faucet.

I gestured at it and said helpfully, "Do you want to turn that off?"

She did.

Then she found her voice, wiped her hands on her aqua-print housedress, and said, "I was expecting Donnie."

"Donnie . . . ?" I prompted.

"My son. He always comes for dinner on Thursday nights. He bowls right near here, so . . ." She trailed off, shrugging.

"I won't keep you, then," I said politely. "I only wanted to talk to you if you had a few minutes to spare, Ms. . . ."

"Mrs. It's Tucci. Betty Tucci."

"It's a pleasure to meet you."

"I can't believe the mayor of New York is standing in my kitchen" was the somewhat breathless reply.

Luckily, I'm used to this sort of reaction—not that I drop by strangers' homes on a daily basis.

"Do you have a few minutes, then?" I knew that the best tactic was to put her at ease.

"Do I have a few minutes for you? I have all the time you need, Mr. Mayor. Sit," she invited, gesturing at the red Formica and stainless-steel table in a cramped corner by the lone window, which was steamed over from whatever delicious concoction was bubbling in the cast iron pot on the old white stove.

"Do you want some coffee?" she asked, bustling over to the counter as the boys and I found room around the table.

"I don't want to trouble you," I said, though I wouldn't have minded a cup.

"It's no trouble. I've got some made here in the percolator, fresh," she said, taking several white and orange flowered Corelle cups from the row of hooks along the underside of the upper cupboard. She set them on the table, along with a matching sugar bowl and creamer.

"Hungry?" she asked, returning to the counter, and it was then that I noticed the dozens of cookies cooling on baking racks. "I've

just started the Christmas baking. I only had time to make two
different kinds so far. I have to watch my stories in the afternoons,
until four o'clock," she confided. "It's like an addiction. You like
soaps, Mr. Mayor?"

"I can't say that I've had a chance to watch daytime television
in quite a while, Mrs. Tucci."

"You really should," she informed me. "You learn a lot about
people that way. Anyway, help yourself to some cookies."

"That's all right," I said, although I wouldn't have minded
sampling a biscotti or two. "I don't want to—"

"Here. Don't be shy. Eat," she interrupted me, placing a plate
of freshly baked cookies in the center of the table.

"I know why you're here," she went on, pouring coffee all
around. Her hand was shaking and she sloshed some onto the
table. "Sorry, nerves. It's not every day that the mayor drops by
for coffee."

I smiled faintly, then said, "You know why I'm here?"

"To talk about poor Angelo. Why else? I heard you were in
charge of the case—"

"I'm *not* in charge of the case," I corrected her—not that it
seemed to make any difference to her.

"What do you want to know?" she asked, dumping a teaspoon-
ful of sugar into her own coffee and shoving the plate of cookies
toward me. "Eat," she commanded again.

I obeyed, biting into a round, dark cookie covered in white
icing. It was delicious, chocolaty and spicy, with a moist, dense
texture and dotted with plump raisins.

"You like that?" she wanted to know.

I nodded. "I've never tasted anything like it before. What is
it?"

"Italian chocolate clove cookies," she told me. "My mother's
recipe."

"You're kidding. My mother makes those too," said Lou, who
was munching on an almond-studded biscotti.

"Does she soak the raisins first?"

"I'm not sure."

"You have to soak the raisins first," said Mrs. Tucci in an I-
mean-business tone. "Otherwise it's no good."

"I'll tell Ma," Lou promised.

"And you have to use melted Crisco, not butter or margarine, no matter what anyone says. That's the secret. Some people use—"

"Uh, Mrs. Tucci?" I cut in politely. "Getting back to Mr. Calvino . . ."

"Oh, yes," she said, sobering. "What did you want to know?"

"Were you acquainted with him?"

"Acquainted?" She made a snorting noise and gestured with her hands to show me that *acquainted* was an understatement. "We've lived next door to each other for the past twenty-five years. You can't help but become a part of someone's life when you're neighbors for that long. I was very friendly with him and his wife, Mary, who passed away back in the late eighties, right after their daughter left for college. Poor man went from having a family to having no one. Well . . . in a manner of speaking."

I glanced up sharply. Something in her cagey expression told me I was about to uncover important information—but that it wouldn't be easy.

"What do you mean by that, Mrs. Tucci?"

"Nothing," she said quickly—too quickly. She closed her mouth and gazed at her coffee, her mouth drawn into a firm line.

"Was Mr. Calvino . . . involved with someone?"

"I wouldn't know about that," she said briskly with a shake of her gray head.

"If you wouldn't know, who would? You said yourself that you couldn't help being a part of his life. You must have known what was going on with him."

She shrugged and sipped her coffee.

"More cookies?" she asked my still-munching bodyguards, who gladly helped themselves from the plate she pushed in their direction.

"Mrs. Tucci," I said, frustrated, "I really wish you would tell me what you know about Mr. Calvino's love life."

"His love life?" She flashed an indignant glance in my direction, but I could see in her eyes that I was on the right track. "Who said Angelo had a love life?"

"You did."

"I did?" She blinked. "I didn't say that."

I cleared my throat. "Mrs. Tucci, I really need to discuss this with you. I promise that whatever you say will not leave this room. My lips are sealed, and so are theirs."

I gestured at my bodyguards, whose lips, incidentally, were hardly sealed as they gorged themselves on Mrs. Tucci's home-made cookies.

"Maybe you and I could talk in private," I suggested, and pointedly instructed my security detail to leave us alone in the kitchen.

They adjourned to the living room reluctantly. I couldn't tell whether it was the plate of baked goods or me that they didn't want to let out of sight. Considering that I had to be as safe in Mrs. Tucci's cozy, steamy kitchen as I was in my own bed, I had a feeling it wasn't their dear mayor that they didn't want to leave behind.

In any case, as soon as they left the room I turned back to Mrs. Tucci and said in that no-nonsense, point-blank manner that has gotten me everywhere in politics and law, "Tell it to me now, Mrs. Tucci. All of it. Don't leave any details out."

She faltered.

"I'm the mayor," I said when she continued to hesitate—as though my political status were relevant to the conversation.

My ploy worked as effectively as Glugol Muggle on a nasty cold.

"You didn't hear this from me," she began.

I nodded.

She went on in a whisper, with a wary glance at the wall as though it had sprouted a microphone. "He was seeing someone."

"He was entitled," I pointed out, "wasn't he? After all, he was widowed."

"Well, *she* wasn't."

I got the picture.

Mrs. Tucci's mouth was pursed in distinct disapproval.

"Who was she?" I asked, keeping my voice low and confidential lest she suddenly decide to clam up.

She looked around furtively, as though to be sure we were,

indeed, alone in the room. Then she said, so softly that I could barely hear her, "Dinah Leary."

"Leary?"

"Shh. Yes."

I rubbed my chin. If I wasn't mistaken, *Leary* was one of the names I recalled reading on the row of buzzers downstairs.

"She lives in the building," I said, just to be sure.

She nodded. "She's always been a floozy, that one. And Gil is blind. He goes whistling off to work every day like he doesn't have a care in the world. Meanwhile, she's sneaking upstairs to Angelo's place every chance she gets. I can hear the two of them in there, giggling and laughing . . . the walls are like cardboard in this place," she added, lowering her voice further still as if to prove the point.

"How long was this going on?"

"At least a year. Maybe longer. You should have seen Angelo while they were seeing each other. He kept his hair slicked back, wore cologne, trimmed that beard of his all the time. Even got the gap between his front teeth fixed. Do you know Mary was after him to do that for years?" She shook her head as though it were a shame that the poor late Mary hadn't been as successful as her husband's mistress had in convincing him to see a dentist.

"You said *while* they were seeing each other," I pointed out. "They had stopped?"

She hesitated. "They broke it off about a month ago. I remember because it was on Halloween, which is my Donnie's birthday, and I was right here in the kitchen, frosting the chocolate almond torte I make him every year when it happened."

"When what happened?"

"The argument," she whispered. "They had a terrible argument. He was crying, Angelo. Begging her not to leave. She said he was pathetic. Said she didn't care about him anymore, that she wanted to devote herself to Gil."

"That's her husband?"

Mrs. Tucci nodded. "He's an alcoholic. Has a nasty temper when he's drunk, but when he's sober he's as calm as you please. He was diagnosed with liver problems not long ago. I know that's why Dinah suddenly dumped Angelo. She felt guilty. Finally," she tacked on in a disapproving tone.

"What about Angelo, when they were arguing? He was begging her not to dump him?"

She nodded. "He started to sound desperate. Said he was going to tell Gil about them, demand that Gil release her from their sham of a marriage."

"His words?"

"Mine."

Apparently, she really did watch a lot of daytime television.

"What did *he* say?" I asked her.

"About her marriage? That he knew it was a joke. He said, 'What, did you forget all the times you came crying to me about how Gil doesn't understand you?' He wanted to know what she was trying to prove. And she said she wasn't trying to prove nothing—her words," she added. "That's how she talks. I don't know what a nice man like Angelo saw in that woman."

"Did he ever discuss her with you?"

"Oh, no! Of course not. He didn't know I knew. Or, if he did, he wasn't the type to say anything about it. Angelo was a private man. A good man, really."

"Who killed him, Mrs. Tucci?" I asked abruptly.

She looked alarmed. "Why would I know? You don't think I had something to—"

"I'm just asking for your opinion," I said, laying a hand on her arm to calm her down. "Do you have any idea who would have wanted him dead?"

"No . . . I have no idea," she said, avoiding my gaze.

"Are you sure?"

"Positive," she murmured. "Unless . . ."

"Unless?" I prodded.

"Gil had an awful temper when he was drinking. But I'm not saying he killed Angelo," she added hastily. "Anyway, he had stopped drinking. Had to, because of his liver. The doctor said the booze was killing him. When I ran into him the other day in the hallway, he told me his only bad habit was watching the New York Jets. I said, 'But, Gil, that's not a bad habit.' He said, 'Have you seen the Jets play lately?' " She smiled.

"What about Dinah?"

"She didn't drink, as far as I know," Mrs. Tucci said, adding distastefully, "but she smoked like a fiend. Always smelled like an ashtray."

"I mean, what about Dinah's temper?" I asked patiently. "Did she ever fly off the handle?"

"Who knows?" She threw up her hands. "If you're asking whether I think Dinah killed him, I would have to say that I would find that nearly impossible to believe, Mr. Mayor. If she did it, why wouldn't she do it right here in his apartment? Why would she go all the way down to the store, where he was working, and risk being seen?"

"That's a very good question," I told her.

"Thank you." She smiled faintly. "I used to watch *Murder, She Wrote* all the time. It was too bad they had to go and take it off the air. I loved the way Angela Lansbury went around solving all those terrible crimes. She had such a good head for clues, that one. And so do you, Mr. Mayor. Are you going to be able to solve this case?"

"I certainly hope so, Mrs. Tucci. Have you discussed any of this with the police?"

"Oh, no," she said quickly. "When they came around, I answered all of their questions honestly, but I didn't tell them about his affair with Dinah."

"Why not?"

"Because they didn't ask me. And I know Dinah and Gil had nothing to do with Angelo's death. And anyway, I'm not the type of person who goes around spreading nasty gossip," she informed me primly. "I told you, this is just between you and me. And you said your lips are sealed."

"If you don't mind my asking," I said with a sigh, "why would you tell me and not the police?"

"Why?" She looked incredulous, as though it were the most pointless question she had ever heard. "Because you're the mayor."

When I got to Benito One a few doors up Mulberry Street, Sybil was already there. She wasn't hard to spot. The place is tiny, with only a handful of tables on either side of the shallow room. Besides, Sybil was wearing an enormous white faux-fur hat.

"Bad hair day?" I asked, slipping into the chair opposite her after shedding my coat.

"What, this?" She gestured to the towering hat. "My head is still frozen. I walked over from the office"—the office being relatively nearby, in SoHo—"and do you *know* how cold it is out there?"

"Come on, it's not so bad." I picked up a menu and glanced at it.

"Well then, why did you order all the homeless into shelters the past few nights?"

"Okay, so it's bad," I agreed. "I guess I've just had my mind on other things, so I haven't noticed the weather."

"Other things . . . like the murder?"

"That too," I said as though I weren't entirely preoccupied with the Calvino case at the moment.

After leaving Mrs. Tucci's apartment, I had tried Calvino's apartment again, hoping to catch his daughter there, even though Mrs. Tucci had told me she was staying uptown with friends. There was no reply. I would try and get in touch with her before she went back to Phoenix, which, according to Mrs. Tucci, wouldn't be right away. She had to settle her father's affairs and take care of giving away or selling his belongings—preferably before the end of the month, Mrs. Tucci had said, so that the apartment could be rented for January first.

Before leaving the building, I had also walked downstairs and knocked on the Learys' door. They weren't home, but I had every intention of returning. Mrs. Tucci might not believe her neighbors were capable of murder, but I had readily labeled Dinah and Gil as Suspects Number Two and Three, and I was most eager to speak with them.

"What have you found out about the case?" Sybil asked, blowing on her manicured hands to warm them.

"Not a whole lot," I hedged, looking back at the menu and scanning the vast list of pasta entrees.

Sybil is one of my dearest friends, but she *is* a gossip columnist. And when you're mayor, you never say anything in front of the press that you wouldn't trumpet over a megaphone for the whole city to hear.

"This whole thing is such a shame. You know, I used to work at Ramsey's," she said unexpectedly.

I looked up in surprise. "You did? When was that?"

"Back when I was fresh out of college and no newspaper would give a female reporter an entry-level position. I spent six months when I was twenty-one years old selling ladies' hosiery, back in the good old days when nylons were a novelty and garter belts were a given."

"Sounds interesting."

"It wasn't. Although I did make some good friends. And I got to go to a rip-roaring company Christmas party at the Waldorf-Astoria."

I thought back to the framed photos I had seen in the locker room at Ramsey's, group shots taken yearly at the employee Christmas party. I smiled faintly, thinking about how surprised I would have been to spot a youthful Sybil among the faces.

"As much as I hated being a department store saleswoman though, Ed—and as often as I got lost trying to find my way around in that drafty old maze—I would hate to see the store taken over by Weatherly Brothers," Sybil said, shaking her head. "There's something about Ramsey's that's—I don't know . . . a part of New York."

"I feel the same way."

"Then do something about it."

I raised an eyebrow at her. "Such as?"

"Find the killer. Who are the suspects?"

Before I could answer, the waiter appeared with the carafe of Merlot Sybil had ordered, as well as a generous basketful of crusty Italian bread and butter, and a plate of Benito's incredible carrots, cut diagonally in thin slices and then marinated with just the right amount of seasoning.

"Mr. Mayor," he greeted me warmly, pumping my hand with both of his clasped around it. "How are you doing?"

"You tell me," I said jovially. "How'm I doing?"

He grinned and said in his thick Italian accent, "You know you're always doing fine by me. What can I get for you tonight, eh?"

Sybil, of course, had long ago decided on the gnocchi with a delicious pale tomato sauce. Meanwhile, I selected the roasted eggplant tossed with peppers, garlic, and oil over penne. I am a fanatic for garlic.

Our waiter disappeared, and our conversation meandered to providing updates on mutual acquaintances—something Sybil, gossip queen that she is, always enjoys immensely. It seemed that since we last spoke, several days before Thanksgiving, there had been, in our admittedly vast combined social circle, more splits and spats than they pack into an entire episode of *Melrose Place* (Sybil's favorite television program, not mine).

"We're going to have one hell of a case of indigestion after eating all of this," Sybil observed when our entrees arrived after we had devoured the bread, carrots, and two tossed green salads in a light vinaigrette. "I know I'll be up all night with heart-burn . . . but it'll be worth it."

"I'm not going to eat all of mine," I informed her. "Only half. I'm watching my weight."

Sybil rolled her eyes. "You're always watching it, Ed. Live a little."

"According to my doctor, if I want to live at all, I have to have willpower, Sybil."

As it turned out, my willpower seemed to have skipped town for the time being, and I ate almost the entire plateful of pasta.

But I probably would have been up almost all night anyway, and not just because of indigestion.

As I lay in bed later at Gracie Mansion, I kept going over the Calvino murder in my mind.

I couldn't help feeling like there was something I should be remembering. But for the life of me, I couldn't put my finger on it. . . .

_____ FIVE

Friday morning I arrived at City Hall to find Erik Dolk from the corporation counsel's office waiting to see me.

I like to think of myself as an optimist, but being greeted by a grim-faced lawyer before you've had your first cup of coffee doesn't bode well for the day.

I asked him to have a seat in my office, then excused myself for a few moments to go into the small kitchenette, where I started a pot of Martinson's. No matter how pressing Dolk's business was, I couldn't—after a long, virtually sleepless night—face it without my morning beverage in hand.

I've been a java drinker all my life, and I don't care what anybody says, you can't beat my coffee. I've perfected the technique over the years, and it beats the stuff you find in those pretentious cafés that have been popping up all over town. While I'll admit to enjoying the occasional cappuccino, I usually don't go in for all those fancy, foamy drinks with ridiculous pseudo-Italian names.

I had wisely purchased, for my office, one of those automatic drip coffeemakers that allows you to pour a cup while it's still brewing. As a result, I was back in my office with my steaming mug in no time.

"Are you sure you wouldn't like some?" I asked Erik, who, judging by the weary shadows in his fair-skinned face, probably could have used a jolt of caffeine.

"I can't," he said again, and added, "The doctor took me off coffee, cigarettes, and liquor because of my ulcer."

I'll admit, being a city lawyer is a stressful job. So is being mayor. But I have, for the most part, always managed to handle the pressure without a major impact on my health, aside from the stroke I suffered a few years back.

"You look like you could use a vacation, Erik," I commented, looking at his strained expression.

"I'm going to Hawaii over the holidays."

"Good for you. I'm heading for Barbados in about ten days myself. We'll both be refreshed for the new year." I leaned back in my low-slung black leather armchair. "So tell me, what crisis is looming on the horizon before I depart for my well-deserved tropical vacation, Erik?"

"Did you happen to read about Tommi Tremaine in the paper yesterday?"

"Tommi Tremaine?" I frowned and rubbed my chin. "Doesn't ring a bell. Who is he?"

"Who is *she*," Erik corrected me.

"Who is she," I echoed dutifully.

"Tommi Tremaine is one of the homeless people who was forcibly removed from a sidewalk on Queens Boulevard on Tuesday night and brought to a shelter."

I sipped my Martinson's. "And . . . ?"

"Not only wasn't she very happy about being dragged away from the cardboard refrigerator box she calls home, but she was robbed that night in the shelter. There was a small blurb about it in the paper yesterday—I guess she marched over to *The Daily Register* on Wednesday afternoon and told a reporter what had happened."

"What, exactly, did happen?"

"Two other women pulled a knife on her, roughed her up, and stole all of her money."

"How much money?"

"Three dollars and twenty-seven cents, but that's not the point. The point is, if she had never been in that shelter against her will Tuesday night, she wouldn't have been threatened, robbed, and bruised."

"If she hadn't been in that shelter Tuesday night, she would have been a human Popsicle by Wednesday morning."

"That's beside the point."

"How can a matter of life or death be beside the point?" I demanded, annoyed with Erik's sudden apparent fascination with points.

And anyway, I had a feeling I knew what was coming.

"The point—at least *Tommi Tremaine's* point—is that she is holding the city responsible for her being robbed. She's brought a lawsuit against us, Ed."

"A woman who should be thanking us for saving her life is suing us?" I asked incredulously, and expanded, "A woman who has lost the only money she had in the world—the amount being three dollars and change—has, what? Hired a lawyer to bring a lawsuit against the City of New York?"

"That about sums it up," he said, nodding.

I rubbed my forehead, feeling a headache coming on.

And that was *before* my mother called to inform me that Aunt Honey was still insisting that I had her menorah.

Friday evening was one of those rare occasions when I didn't have an official or social obligation. What I did have was enough paperwork to keep me at the office until nearly midnight.

Which ruined not only my intention of dashing over to Little Italy to question Dinah and Gil Leary, but also my plan to finish my Hanukkah shopping by stopping by the gift shop at the Metropolitan Museum of Art on my way back to Gracie Mansion.

I do most of my gift buying there; you can't go wrong giving jewelry, scarves, ties, and suspenders that are both elegant and based on ancient designs—particularly when the prices are far better than you would find on comparable merchandise in a designer boutique.

However, the gift shop had long since closed by the time I slipped into my wool overcoat and, flanked by my security detail, made my way to the exit. I saw that it was snowing outside and paused inside the door to slip on my gloves and wrap my scarf more snugly around my neck.

"Good idea to bundle up, Mr. Mayor," commented Avery, the

amiable security guard waiting to unlock the door to let us out. "It's a nasty night to be out."

"A warm bed does sound inviting right about now," I agreed, wondering what I was going to do now that I had missed the boat with the shopping. I would have to get up early tomorrow morning and dash out to finish buying the few last-minute gifts I still needed. . . .

Wait a minute.

How could I have forgotten, until right this very moment, about Ramsey's?

Barnaby had mentioned that they would be open around the clock this weekend. I probably would have remembered that sooner if I had been able to spend any time at all thinking about the Santa murder case today, but I had been incredibly busy with my mayoral duties all day.

"I have a last-minute change of plans," I said, turning to Lou Sabatino.

"For tonight? You don't want to go straight home after all?" he asked just as Avery opened the door.

A whoosh of icy air and snowflakes swirled in around us, snatching my breath away and making me reconsider. That warm bed, a good book, and a mug of hot cocoa sounded better and better.

On the other hand, why not take advantage of Ramsey's extended hours? It would certainly be a show of good faith to my friend Barnaby.

Besides, I wouldn't have much time for shopping in the morning anyway. Pat was expecting everyone at her house by noon, and Scarsdale isn't exactly around the corner from Gracie Mansion. My sister has always insisted on starting her affairs at an ungodly early hour.

"Where do you need to go, Mr. Mayor?" Ambrose wanted to know, his teeth chattering slightly as we started down the icy pavement toward the waiting sedan.

"To Ramsey's Department Store," I said firmly, determined not to be waylaid by the cold or my exhaustion.

"Has there been another . . . emergency there?" Lou wanted to know.

"No! I just want to do some holiday shopping."

My guards glanced at each other.

"In this weather?" Ambrose wanted to know, brushing white crystallized clumps from his dark hair.

"At this hour?" Mohammed put in.

"Preferably," I said. "Unless you fellows would like to delay the proposed shopping expedition another hour or two while we stand around in the aforementioned weather, discussing the pros and cons."

They shook their heads promptly.

"You're the boss," Mohammed said as I slid into the backseat of the blessedly warm car.

As we pulled up in front of the store, I spotted a familiar figure walking along Thirty-fourth Street toward where we were parked.

It was the pretty blond police officer who had escorted me to my car the night of the murder. She had caught sight of me, too, as I stepped out of the long, shiny black car.

It wasn't hard. The street in front of Ramsey's was all but deserted, which didn't bode well for Barnaby's extended-weekend-hours gimmick.

"Hello, Mr. Mayor," she called.

I greeted her with a wave and asked, as she drew nearer, "What are you doing here? There's no trouble at the store, is there?"

"Not that I know of. This is actually my regular beat, and I'm on duty."

"Not a nice night for foot patrol."

She shrugged. "Part of the job. How's the murder investigation going?"

"You're asking me?"

Another shrug. "You would know more than I would. The homicide squad doesn't exactly give us patrol officers daily updates."

"I know what you mean."

"You're kidding. You're the mayor!"

"Right. Not a detective on the NYPD—despite reported evidence to the contrary."

"So you aren't really working on the case?"

I shrugged.

"Then why are you here?" she asked, gesturing at the store building behind her.

"I had some last-minute shopping," I explained as casually as I had to my bodyguards.

She looked at me as though I were crazy. "Now?"

"What could be more fitting for the mayor of the city that never sleeps?"

The police officer smiled faintly.

I shivered and started toward the store. "Have a pleasant evening, Officer . . ."

"Varinski," she filled in when I paused. "You too, Mr. Mayor."

The first thing I encountered upon entering the store was a metal detector similar to those used in airports.

Three security guards manned the machine, allowing my own guards, who were, of course, armed, to step around it. They would have let me go around it as well, but I insisted on walking through. I like to be treated like one of the regular folks when I'm out and about in New York, even in the wee hours of the morning.

Once we had passed security, I led the way through the cosmetics department to ladies' accessories. My guards trundled along, looking about as thrilled as they would be to accompany their wives on an all-day mall spree.

I found a glass-topped display case filled with leather gloves, and was browsing through them when an elderly saleswoman appeared. She had a pile of white curls on her head and wore a pair of glasses on a chain around her neck.

"May I help—oh!"

"Hello," I said pleasantly.

She held the glasses up to her eyes and, peering through them, announced, "Mr. Mayor, it's you!"

"Is it?" I asked, looking myself over and nodding. "You're right. It's me, all right."

She laughed longer and harder than most people would have, then told me she was my biggest fan, which explained her excessive mirth.

"I've been admiring you for, oh, almost as long as I've been working at Ramsey's," she informed me.

I doubted that, but asked politely, "How long have you been working here?"

"Almost thirty years now. I'll be getting the three-decade silver clock at this year's employee Christmas party."

"Congratulations."

"Thank you. You know, Ed, the best thing I ever did was decide to get a job when all my little birdies flew out of the nest." She smiled a twinkly smile at me and added, "They're not really birds, you know. I'm talking about my children. I have six."

"That's nice."

"Oh, it's wonderful. But I was so lonely after they all moved out, and"—she lowered her voice to a confidential whisper—"my husband and I parted right after the last was born. Anyway, I've made so many friends here at Ramsey's over the years. It's a second home to me. Just as you always say, Mr. Mayor, you have to be a friend to make a friend."

To tell the truth—and I always do—I didn't recall ever having said that. Still, it's good advice, so I didn't argue.

"Anyway," she chattered on, "I have always made it a point to try and get to know every new employee who works on my floor, and as many others as possible. I try to make everyone feel more comfortable. You know how hard it is to be the new kid on the block. That's just a saying, of course," she added with an inexplicable giggle.

I nodded and opened my mouth to say something polite, like *Well, it's been nice talking to you . . .*

But she had more to tell me. "You wouldn't believe how many people have come and gone here over the years, Ed. But I never forget a face. Names, yes. Faces, never. Sometimes people come in here shopping and I recognize them instantly, no matter how many years have passed. I'll go, 'Didn't you used to work here back in seventy-nine?' and they'll look surprised and say, 'Why, yes, I did!' Although not everyone says those exact words, but you get the point."

As she rattled on, I thought of Sybil. Women's hosiery was on the first floor. I was about to inquire whether the woman remembered her. But then I realized that no matter what lies Sybil tells publicly about her age, she had been well into her thirties by the time this particular saleswoman started working at Ramsey's.

I zeroed in on what she was saying again, my attention recaptured by the word *murder*.

"You know, Ed, one of the girls who has been here as long as I have got all rattled by that murder upstairs. She quit first thing the next morning. But I would never do that. Not just because I want my silver clock—although it will look nice on the wall over my sofa. But you know, I owe Mr. Tischler my whole career, and I wouldn't leave him in the lurch. That's why I volunteered for the overnight shift. No one else wanted it. Everyone's afraid."

"You aren't?"

"Oh, my, no." She leaned closer to me. "When you get to be our age, Ed, you can either worry constantly about dropping dead, or you can live your life with gusto."

Our age? She had to have at least fifteen years on me. Still, I liked her spirit, so I merely smiled.

"If this place ever closed down," she went on, her own expression growing serious for the first time, "I don't know what I would do. Why, I'd be lost. A person doesn't start a brand-new career at our age, Ed. You have to make sure that Ramsey's stays open."

"For your sake, I will do everything within my power to see that it does."

I resumed browsing through the gloves, with the woman hovering at my elbow.

"Anything in particular you're looking for, Ed?"

Okay, I might have liked her spirit, but I detest pushy salespeople.

I shook my head and said, "Just inspiration."

That brought on another giddy gale of laughter.

"You know, you really *are* funnier in person," she said cryptically, and added, "If you think of anything I can do for you . . . I'm Dotty."

I blinked, then realized she was pointing to a plastic name tag pinned to her cheerful red sweater.

Still, if ever a name suited a person . . .

Under Dotty's watchful gaze I worked my way through the

echoing, nearly empty first floor of the store, finding several gifts I needed and a few more that I didn't but bought anyway because it doesn't hurt to be extra generous with the people you care about.

When I was ready, Dotty rang up my purchases and informed me, with regret, that the gift-wrapping department upstairs had closed at nine.

"You know, Ed, Mr. Tischler wanted every department to be open all night, but there simply wasn't enough staff willing to stay here after dark," Dotty said, shaking her white head.

I looked around, not seeing another living soul besides my bodyguards, who were buttoning their coats, putting on gloves, and generally looking eager to get the heck out of there.

Judging by the utter lack of customers, it wouldn't matter how few Ramsey's employees were on hand to man the various departments.

". . . and Hizzoner himself was on hand last night to demonstrate to the people of New York that there's no need to stay away from Ramsey's despite the grisly murder that took place there earlier this week . . ."

I glanced up at the television set from the stationary bike I was diligently riding in a corner of my Gracie Mansion bedroom—in anticipation, of course, of the potato latkes with sour cream that I would be eating at Pat's that afternoon.

". . . Mayor Koch reportedly appeared at the store shortly after midnight, accompanied by several bodyguards. He proceeded to browse for nearly an hour and left with several packages—an assortment of gifts, according to one Ramsey's sales associate, which she declined to describe, saying she wouldn't want to give away any of his surprises for his loved ones."

I snorted at that and kept pedaling. I couldn't help remembering how, as an anniversary present a few years back, I had bought my parents tickets to a hot new Broadway premiere. The press found out about it and set off speculation that I had pulled strings to get the impossibly unavailable orchestra seats.

I hadn't. I had simply risen at four-thirty A.M. the day tickets went on sale, and I had gone to stand in line at the theater with the rest of the law-abiding, honest citizens.

But that's beside the point. By the time the truth came out, the entire city—including my parents—knew about the gift right down to the performance night I had selected and exact seats I had obtained.

"Asked over the telephone from his home to comment this morning on his longtime friend's show of good faith in his troubled business, Barnaby Tischler told reporters that 'Ed Koch has always had both excellent taste and common sense, which is why he has always shopped at Ramsey's, and will continue to do so. I hope New Yorkers will follow his lead and visit us during this holiday shopping season.' "

I lifted my left hand from the handlebars and glanced at my watch. It wasn't even nine o'clock yet.

Apparently, Dotty and the local press had been busy in the hours since I had left the store. I knew she must have tipped them off. The only other souls I had seen were the security guards and that female police officer I had met on the street, and none of them would have thought to alert the press of my presence at the store.

You had to hand it to Dotty. The woman was doing everything she could to help her beloved Ramsey's stay afloat.

I sighed and got off the bike, wiping my face on a hand towel and heading for the shower.

As much as I was looking forward to the holiday gathering at my sister's house, I was torn.

Despite spending a late night at City Hall, an enormous volume of official paperwork still awaited my perusal—as was always the case, in my position.

Then there was the Tommi Tremaine lawsuit. The news had hit the late editions of yesterday's newspapers. I had given a press conference late in the day, firmly reiterating my position on removing the homeless from the streets in dangerously inclement weather. Still, the whole thing promised to be a relentless, high-profile legal and political headache.

And then there was the murder.

I had every confidence that the NYPD's fine homicide squad was going full speed in its investigation of the case. But I had promised Barnaby that I would lend a hand, and I never break my promises.

Tomorrow was Sunday, and I had two official engagements in the morning—the first, a breakfast with several orthodox rabbis in Brooklyn, and the second, a statue dedication at Battery Park.

I decided that on the way back uptown afterward, where I would tackle the piles of paperwork waiting in my study at the mansion, I would make two stops.

I needed to check on the progress of the paint job at my apartment in the Village. I had hired an outrageously expensive painting contractor recommended by Sybil, who had promised that I would be thrilled with his work. Still, I like to be on top of things, especially when they're costing me twice as much as I had initially intended to pay.

My final order of business: I needed to talk to the Learys—Angelo Calvino's lover and her husband. I figured there was a good chance of finding them—or at least the husband—home on a Sunday afternoon, given that Mrs. Tucci had mentioned he was a diehard football fan. The Jets were playing New England up at Foxboro later that day.

For Barnaby's sake, I also had to speak to Simon Weatherly, though I had read that the police had already questioned him extensively and he had an airtight alibi for the night of the murder. I wondered if I would find him in his store on a Sunday afternoon. It wouldn't hurt to check. If he wasn't there, I didn't know when I would have a chance to track him down for questioning.

I had a hectic schedule at the office on Monday, following a nine-thirty A.M. run-through at Rockefeller Center for the following night's tree-lighting ceremony. I was to be master of ceremonies before a live national audience. It was my chance to show the world that New York was as festive as ever this season.

I couldn't know that before tomorrow night was over, Ramsey's Department Store—and, indeed, the city itself—would see its holiday ordeal take a cataclysmic twist.

SIX

The weather on Sunday afternoon had become more suited to March or April than December. The temperatures had risen sharply into the mid-fifties, transforming the piles of gray snow along the city streets into vast puddles of dirty slush on the sidewalks and in the gutters. A chilly, steady rain had been falling all day, driven by a dank breeze off the East River.

After inspecting the paint job at my apartment—which was, so far, coming along just fine—I took my car over to Little Italy. While I have been known, especially on weekends, to walk or even take the subways around town, this was not one of those occasions. Not only was the weather downright nasty, but time was of the essence.

While the breakfast with the rabbis—a delicious spread catered by one of my favorite kosher delis—had gone according to schedule, the statue dedication had been interminable, thanks to several long-winded speakers—myself not included. I have always believed in keeping things to the point, particularly when I'm forcing a captive audience to stand in an icy downpour.

The rain showed no sign of letting up when I reached Mulberry Street just before three o'clock. Accompanied by my bodyguards, I hopped out of the car and dashed for the now-familiar building where Angelo Calvino had lived. I scanned the row of names, found the Learys' apartment, 2D, and pushed the buzzer.

I waited.

When several moments had passed, I concluded no one was at home and was about to turn and leave.

Then there was a loud click, faint static, and a male voice booming over the intercom.

"Yeah?"

"Mr. Leary?"

"Yeah? Who's that?"

"Ed Koch, Mr. Leary."

"*Who?*"

"Ed Koch."

Pause.

Then, incredulously, "Ed Koch? You mean the mayor?"

"That's what I mean."

"Get out of here."

It took a moment for me to realize that the comment was not to be taken literally. He was simply expressing his disbelief that the mayor would drop by for a visit, and why wouldn't he?

"It's me, Mr. Leary," I insisted. "Really. May I come up? I'd like to talk to you."

"Now?" His tone clearly stated that this wasn't a good time. Remembering what Mrs. Tucci had told me about him, I had a feeling I knew why.

I exchanged a glance with my bodyguards.

"If it's possible," I told Gil Leary politely, "now would be very convenient for me."

Another pause.

Then a faint, "I guess so."

There was a long buzz, and I shoved the door open, stepping out of the weather at last. After wiping our shoes carefully on the worn mat in the vestibule, my bodyguards and I clomped up one flight to the second floor.

I would have known, even if I hadn't been there before and even if I weren't glancing at the letters and numbers on the neighbors' doors as we passed, that apartment 2D would be down at the end of the hall. There was no mistaking the sound of a televised football game blasting from behind the closed door.

I knocked, waited, heard Gil Leary call, "Just a second."

I figured he must be tidying up a bit, judging by how long it took for him to get to the door. That, or perhaps combing his hair, putting on a clean shirt.

Or, if he were guilty of murder and had any inkling of why I was there, disposing of telltale evidence.

"Sorry," the rotund, middle-aged man said, looking a little sheepish as he finally opened the door. I saw that there weren't enough gray strands on his head for combing, and his white tank-style T-shirt was covered in orangy-red tomato sauce splatters across his ample stomach. "I just wanted to see that play. They have a first down. You a Jets fan, Mayor?"

"I don't have much time to follow football."

That was certainly the truth.

What I neglected to mention was that even if I did have spare time, I wouldn't necessarily spend it watching sports. I could think of hundreds of more interesting ways to pass an afternoon.

"Come on in and watch with me anyhow. I guarantee I'll make a fan out of you," he said, hurriedly opening the door wide. "We can talk during the commercials. Anyway, there's only a few minutes left in the half. Score's seven–nothing, New England."

Before I could get a word in, he turned to address my bodyguards. "You fellahs like the Jets?"

They mumbled appropriate answers as we all stepped over the threshold into an apartment that for a few moments seemed to give off a welcoming, toasty warmth after the cold rain outside. But it didn't take long for me to realize that the place was as uncomfortably overheated as Mrs. Tucci's apartment had been— which explained Gil Leary's sleeveless T-shirt.

I saw that a living room window was open a crack—probably as much as the driving rain allowed—but even that did little to dispel the steam heat blasting from the radiator. That's just how it is in some of these older buildings.

"Come on, sit down," he invited, escorting us to the faded brown brocade couch against a wall. There wasn't room for all of us there, but he didn't offer to let someone sit in the only other seat in the room—a worn, rust-colored recliner by the open window.

That seat, with its threadbare headrest and lumpy padding, clearly belonged to the master of the house, who plunked himself comfortably into the cushions that seemed to have molded, over the years, to the contours of his body. He raised the footrest with an abrupt practiced crank of a lever near the floor and reached for a remote control with one hand and an open can of Planters peanuts with the other.

"Oh, hell. Look. Would you look at this? Okay, here we go. We're moving in to score. This is it. This is what we need," he muttered, so intently focused on the television screen that I didn't dare interrupt.

Still standing, I glanced instead around the room, noting that a pair of pink, fuzzy slippers peeked out from beneath the couch and a copy of *Better Homes & Gardens* lay on the coffee table. His wife clearly hadn't left him, but she didn't seem to be in the apartment at the moment. I had the feeling Gil Leary was alone.

After noting that the only photos on the wall were of the two of them, I concluded they must be childless. From what I could see in the most recent framed photos, Dinah Leary was an attractive, busty redhead who liked to display her considerable physical . . . *assets*. Her wardrobe seemed to be made up of clingy and low-cut outfits, from her wedding gown to the snug black dress she wore in a formal portrait with her husband that, judging by Gil's hairline, hadn't been taken too long ago.

I turned my attention back to the man in the recliner, who seemed oblivious to my presence.

He leaned forward in anticipation of the big score, then slammed his hand down on the armrest and groaned, "No! No! Aw, interception. Damn it!"

The game was replaced by an image of a rushing mountain stream that turned out to be the opening of a beer commercial, and Gil Leary turned to me. "Er, sorry about my language, Mr. Mayor. I get kinda caught up in things when I'm watching the Jets. Now, what can I do for you?"

I cleared my throat. "I'd like to talk to you about—"

"Can I get you a beer? Anyone?" he interrupted congenially, starting to get out of his seat.

I shook my head and my guards, perched awkwardly on the sofa, declined as well.

"Good," Leary said, "because I just remembered. We don't have any beer. The wife stopped buying it."

"Why is that?" I asked casually.

"This damn liver of mine," he told me, rubbing his stomach through the stained T-shirt, wincing slightly, as though it were tender to the touch. "It's been acting up. So the doctor told me to cut out the drinking—not that I've ever been much of a drinker, you know."

"No?" I asked, noting that he had the telltale ruddy complexion, flabby stomach, and haggard look of a man who has seen many a hangover.

"Nah," Leary said with a wave of the hand. "Listen, my drinking is nothing compared to the wife's smoking. I says to her, 'Dinah, I'll give up the booze if you'll give up the butts.' She didn't want to do it. Says the doctor hadn't given her orders the way he'd given me orders. I says to her, 'Who're you trying to kid here? Any doctor'll tell you to quit. Just go ahead and ask.' She says, 'I'm not asking.' So I tell her, 'Fine. Don't quit for the doctor. Quit for me.'"

He paused here to nod solemnly, then added, "And you know what? She quit. Cold turkey."

"She must really love you. When was this?" I asked, trying to keep my tone conversational rather than adopt the manner of a detective taking copious mental notes.

"Been almost two weeks now. She almost had a setback last week after what happened to our neighbor, Angelo."

"Oh?" I kept my voice neutral.

"Yeah. I caught her looking in the empty coffee canister in the kitchen in the middle of the night, trying to find the pack of Salems she had stashed there after she quit, for an emergency. Thing is, Mayor, I know my wife inside and out. She can't keep any secrets from me," he said pointedly.

"No?" Somehow I knew he wasn't just talking about the cigarettes.

"Nope. I got rid of those Salems the day she quit. When she figured it out she was steaming mad. But I let her yell. I knew she was more upset about Angelo than she was at me."

"Why is that?"

He shifted his weight in the chair and glanced uncomfortably at my bodyguards, whose gazes were focused on the television screen, where a car commercial was drawing to a close. Luckily, they're very good at fading into the background.

"Is that why you're here?" Leary turned his gaze back in my direction and answered my question with one of his own.

"What do you mean?" I returned.

"Are you here because of Angelo? I mean," he continued on a nervous laugh, "why else would you be here? You and I aren't exactly old prep school buddies, are we?"

"I didn't go to prep school."

"Oh, yeah? Me neither."

I smiled faintly.

"I read in the paper that you were looking into the murder," Leary told me. "Listen, I wish you luck. Just like I told those cops who was here the other day, asking questions."

"About what?"

"You know, about Angelo. He was our neighbor, after all. They wanted to know the usual stuff—"

"The usual stuff?"

"I watch a lot of detective shows. They wanted to know what Angelo was like, if we had noticed anything suspicious . . ."

"And?"

"I told them I hadn't noticed anything."

"What about your wife?"

"They talked to me and Dinah separately. But I guarantee you that she said the same thing."

The game had resumed on television, but he didn't seem to have noticed.

"Dinah was pretty broken up about what happened to Angelo." Leary's surprisingly bright blue eyes were focused on mine, and I knew he knew that I knew about his wife and Calvino. What surprised me was that *he* knew.

"Because she was in love with him?" I asked quietly.

"No!" He shook his head vehemently.

"Mr. Leary, I know about what was going on with Dinah and Angelo. You don't have to hide—"

"I'm not hiding anything," he cut in. "I know all about them too. Who doesn't? Like I told you, Dinah's never been good at keeping secrets, and not only from me. Of course, she doesn't know that I was on to her all along. Because the thing is, Mayor, he wasn't the first."

"He wasn't?"

"No. And you asked me if she was upset about what happened because she was in love with him. No, she wasn't in love with him. She loves me."

Looking into his weary blue eyes, I knew he believed that. And you know what? I actually believed, too, that she did love her husband. Still . . .

"If she loves you," I said carefully, "why would she get involved with another man? Other men," I amended, remembering what he had said.

"Because she needed the attention. Always did. Dinah had a lot of fellows buzzing around her before I came along. She loved the way they fussed over her. When we got married, I figured I could make up for all of it. Well—not just me."

"What do you mean?"

"I figured that between me and the bunch of kids we were going to have, Dinah wouldn't have a chance to be lonely. She'd have all the attention and affection she needed. But—"

Looking into his sad, faraway expression, I sensed the rest of the story even before he went on.

"Dinah couldn't have kids, Mayor. Not after she lost the first one, a year after we were married. It was a boy. He died inside her not long before the due date. It almost killed her, getting that dead baby out. They managed to save her, but not—you know. She was pretty botched up inside. So that was it. She couldn't have any more babies. Ever. I tried to help her, but I'm a working-man, Mayor. I've always worked two jobs so that my wife wouldn't have to."

I nodded sympathetically and told him how sorry I was about their loss.

"It was a long time ago. But," he said, inhaling deeply with the air of one who has long ago accepted his lot, "my wife started running around on me after that. And I started drinking. Although, you know, if you ask me which happened first, I'd have to say I don't remember. It's like the chicken and the egg, you know?"

"Mr. Leary," I said after an appropriate pause, during which he glanced at the screen, where the Patriots were moving in to score as the half ticked away second by second. "What was the relationship between your wife and Mr. Calvino at the time of his death?"

"It was over," he said promptly, his gaze flicking away from the television as the half ended and the game was replaced by a commercial.

"How do you know?"

"When I got sick a few weeks ago, we had a real scare. The doctor told Dinah that unless I changed my ways, I wouldn't be around much longer. She started crying, saying she didn't want to lose me. So I told her I'd change my ways—you know, with the drinking—if she was there for me a hundred percent, the way a wife should be there for her husband. I never mentioned her affair with Calvino."

"Do you think she knew what you were talking about?"

He shook his head. "She never knew I knew. She went to too much trouble to make sure I didn't find out—always sneaking around, making up stories. I think she thought I would go nuts if I knew she was sleeping around."

"So," I prompted, "she broke it off with Angelo Calvino."

"Yes, she did."

"How did he take it?"

He shrugged. "How should I know? My guess is, not good. Have you ever seen my Dinah?"

"Not . . . in person." I found myself looking at a framed photo, on a nearby tabletop, of the woman in question standing in a provocative pose, cleavage proudly on display.

"Yup, that's her," Leary said, following my gaze. "She's really something, isn't she?"

"She really is."

"I'd say a man would have to be pretty upset to lose a woman like that. I know I would be," Leary told me.

"But you didn't lose her," I said pointedly, watching him carefully to see whether he betrayed any hint of a lie—anything that would point to his having killed Angelo Calvino in a rage of jealousy.

"Nope. Dinah and me have had our ups and downs, Mayor, but we're together for the long haul." Everything about him spoke of straightforward honesty.

Still, you never know.

"Mr. Leary," I said directly, "where were you on the night Mr. Calvino was killed?"

"That's easy," he said, nodding. "Last Monday night? Dinah and me was celebrating our fortieth anniversary. It was a few weeks late—I was in the hospital on the actual day, but we figured it's never too late to celebrate."

"And . . . where were you?" I repeated, keeping my voice level.

"On the Staten Island ferry. That's where we met," he said. "Dinah grew up in Port Richmond, and I met her when I was on my way to visit a friend there. You should have seen how nice Port Richmond was back then, in the fifties, before those malls took business away from downtown."

"I'm sure it was," I murmured. "So you two were riding on the Staten Island ferry last Monday night? And what did you do when you got there?"

"Turned around and came right back again. We musta rode that ferry three or four times, round trip."

"Did you speak to anyone?"

"Nope. You know, you and the cops ask a lot of the same questions. You just do it in a nicer way, Mayor."

"Oh?"

"You don't make me feel all nervous the way those detectives did when they were here. They made me feel like I was hiding something. And, Mayor, I got nothing to hide. I had nothing to do with Angelo Calvino's murder. And neither did Dinah."

"Where is she this afternoon?"

"She went out to do some Christmas shopping on Canal Street."

"Any idea when you expect her?"

"When my Dinah's shopping, Mayor, there's no telling when she'll be back." He chuckled softly and shook his head. "She's some woman."

I smiled faintly.

I had every reason to believe that Gil Leary was still madly in love with his wife after all these years.

But everyone knows that being madly in love can do strange things to a normally sane person.

And though I was tempted to cross Gil Leary off my mental list of suspects in the Calvino murder, something made me hold back.

It was still pouring outside, but my bodyguards had radioed for my car, and it was waiting right in front of the building. I was about to get in, when a pastry shop across the street caught my eye.

I've never met a New Yorker, Italian or not, who doesn't love cannoli—crisp pastry tubes filled with a light, sweet ricotta cheese mixture.

And no visitor to Little Italy should leave without visiting one of the neighborhood's many small cafés. They are, invariably, crowded, brightly lit rooms with tile floors, ceiling fans, and the kind of small tables and chairs one would find in an ice cream parlor.

I was eager to get back uptown, but I simply couldn't resist.

I had to tell my driver to wait, and I had to cross the street and go into that pastry shop, where I greeted the pleasant, smiling woman behind the counter and asked her to please select a half-dozen cannoli.

"Do you want them in a bag, or in a box with string?" she asked as she slid open the glass case with its mouth-watering contents.

"In a bag, please—they're going to be eaten right away," I told her.

No, they weren't all going to be for me. I figured my driver and bodyguards deserved a treat. And anyway, so did I. Though I had indulged in potato latkes and brisket yesterday at Pat's, I had passed up the rich, buttery hamantaschen and rugelah, sticking with a bowl of fresh fruit for dessert.

As it turned out, it was fate that my willpower decided to

crumble at that particular point in time, prolonging my visit to Mulberry Street.

With my white bakery bag of cannoli tucked under my arm, I headed, flanked by my bodyguards, back across the street toward my waiting car. I was about to get into the backseat, when I happened to notice a woman on the sidewalk nearby.

She was a redhead, carrying several shopping bags, and dressed in a short yellow rain slicker. What had called my attention to her, I realized, was the whistle of a passing man, who had stopped to admire her long, black-stocking-clad legs that ended in a pair of impossibly high heels.

Dinah Leary.

I knew it was her even before she stepped toward the door of the building I had exited not long ago. As she struggled to balance her shopping bags while fumbling in her oversized red leather purse, presumably for her keys, I told my driver to wait and I walked toward her.

"Need a hand?" I asked, joining her beneath the overhang as my ever-wary bodyguards positioned themselves on the sidewalk in the pouring rain.

"No, that's . . ." She trailed off when she glanced up and recognized me. "Oh," she gasped, "Mr. Mayor!"

In her thick local accent, it came out, *Mistah Mayah.*

"And you're Mrs. Dinah Leary."

"How'd ya know that?" She shifted one shopping bag to her other hand as though it were heavy, eyeing me with curiosity—and awe.

"Let me take that for you," I said, removing it and another from her grasp. Judging by its weight, she had been shopping not on Canal Street, but at a gravel quarry.

"Oh, Mr. Mayor, you don't have to—"

"It's a pleasure," I said. "Are you a coffee drinker?"

"Not anymore." She pursed her ruby-lipsticked lips. "I can't enjoy a cup of coffee without a cigarette to go with it, and I gave up smoking a few weeks ago. Believe you me, it's been hell—pardon my language."

"You're pardoned. How about coming across the street with

me anyway, to that little pastry shop? I hear they have excellent cannoli."

She looked hesitant. I watched as she carefully ran a hand over her hair, as if to smooth it. That was utterly unnecessary, as it was teased and sprayed so that it barely moved in the driving wind.

She finally shook her head, her long gold earring jangling faintly, and said, "Mr. Mayor, I'm a big fan of yours and all, but—I'm a married woman."

I nodded, fighting back a smile. "I'm aware of that, Mrs. Leary. I merely wanted to ask you some questions about the Calvino murder."

"Oh—*oh.*" She looked flustered, and her face paled beneath the liberal smears of rouge on her cheeks. "I should have known— I mean, I did read that you were working on the case. But . . . I don't have anything to tell you that I didn't already tell the cops. I don't know who killed Ang—Mr. Calvino. I don't know anything about it."

"But you did know the victim fairly well," I said pointedly.

"Who told you that?"

"Why don't we talk in the pastry shop?" I suggested. "My bodyguards are getting drenched on the sidewalk."

She cast a glance at the brawny men who stood patiently in the downpour, and her expression softened.

"All right," she agreed. "But not for long. My Gil is expecting me back upstairs to get his supper."

My Gil.

My Dinah.

The Learys certainly gave every appearance of being a loving, affectionate couple. But was it genuine? Or a carefully contrived image to cover up a murder one of them had committed?

After I had persuaded her to stash her shopping bags in my car for the time being, we splashed across Mulberry Street to the pastry shop.

The dark-haired woman behind the counter smiled and said to me, "Back already for more? My cannoli are truly delicious, aren't they?"

I smiled and nodded, aware of Dinah's perplexed expression but choosing not to offer an explanation. I simply asked for a large cup of coffee for myself and invited her to order whatever she wanted.

"I really should watch my figure, but I suppose one biscotti wouldn't hurt," she decided after surveying the delectable contents of the vast bakery case.

When we were seated at an empty table in the small, crowded dining area—my bodyguards positioned around the room, looking not just vigilant, but hungry—I sipped my coffee and smiled at Dinah to put her at ease.

"This is so weird," she said nervously, nibbling on the edge of her chocolate-covered biscotti.

"What is?"

"Me sitting here, with you. I wish Gil could see me . . . although, he might not think it was so great."

"Why not?"

She hedged, then admitted, "I guess you'd say he's the jealous type."

I nodded and waited for her to go on.

She didn't.

So I asked, "Was he jealous of you and Angelo Calvino?"

She nearly choked. "Mr. Mayor!"

"I'm fully aware of the facts, Mrs. Leary. You and Angelo Calvino had an affair that ended not long ago, when your husband became ill." I kept my voice low enough that only she could hear me. No need to spread gossip unnecessarily.

She looked so taken aback that for a moment she didn't reply. Then, her voice taut with tension, she said, "Mr. Mayor, I did not kill Angelo Calvino."

"Any idea who did?"

"No. The night he was killed, I was with my husband, just like I told the police. I know it sounds strange, but we were riding the Staten Island ferry to celebrate our fortieth anniversary. It's where we met, and . . . well, Gil has always been a romantic." A slight smile touched her lips before she pursed them and looked me in the eye. "I swear I didn't kill Angelo, Mr. Mayor, and neither did Gil."

"Did he have any enemies?"

"Not that I know of."

"What about your husband?"

"My husband? He doesn't have an enemy in the world. Everyone loves Gil."

"No," I said patiently, "what I meant was, would you consider your husband an enemy of Angelo's?"

"No! Gil has always liked Angelo. We've been neighbors for years . . ."

"But you said yourself that Gil is the jealous type. So when your husband found out you were sleeping with your neighbor, wasn't he angry?"

"He never found out."

"Are you sure about that?"

"Of course I'm sure."

But she wouldn't look at me, just stared at the barely touched biscotti clenched in her hand.

I watched her, and it suddenly struck me that for a woman who seemed to favor flashy makeup, clothing, and jewelry, she curiously lacked the polished—most likely, scarlet—manicure one might expect. Her fingernails were unadorned—and, I saw, bitten down to raw nubs.

I also noticed that the small round table was vibrating enough to slosh my coffee over the rim of the mug, and realized she was nervously tapping her foot against the pedestal.

"Look, Mrs. Leary," I said, leaning toward her, "I'm not saying you or your husband is a suspect in this case. But I do know that you are one of the few people who knew the victim . . . intimately. And as such, I hope you will provide me with as much information as you possibly can, so that the true murderer can be caught and punished."

"But I don't know who the true murderer is."

"Can you think of any possibility? No matter how far-fetched it is?"

"No," she said after a moment's thought, her round green eyes meeting mine directly. "I'm sorry, Mr. Mayor. Believe me, if there was anyone I could possibly think of—anyone at all—I would tell you. I would love to get the focus off me and Gil once and for all. But Angelo was a simple guy. I can't imagine why anyone would want him dead."

"What did he like to do in his spare time?" I asked. "Any hobbies?"

"Not really. Oh—except chess," she told me. "He used to play chess in the park once in a while. And he liked to listen to those call-in radio talk shows. He never called any of them himself—I don't think he had strong opinions about anything, you know? But he always got a kick out of listening to what other people had to say. Oh, and he liked to feed the pigeons. He made a bird feeder every winter, and he always kept it hanging on the fire escape outside his kitchen window. He used to like to watch the birds while they ate."

"He sounds like a harmless, nice man."

"Angelo was a real peach," she agreed, shredding the edge of a paper napkin into a narrow fringe without looking down at it. "I'm really going to miss him—as a friend, of course," she added hastily.

"Of course."

"Mr. Mayor . . ."

"Yes?"

"I know it's a little late to ask, but . . . you won't tell anyone . . . about what we've talked about today? My marriage is better than ever, and I can't afford to screw things up now."

"I assure you, Mrs. Leary, that I will do everything I can to keep what you've told me confidential. You wouldn't know where I could find Angelo's daughter, would you?"

"Her? Nah. She's too snooty to stay down here in the old neighborhood. Ever since she went away to that fancy girls' college in New England, she changed. Ended up marrying some rich older businessman and moving to Arizona with him. She hardly ever came home to visit Angelo. It broke his heart."

"That's a shame."

"Yeah. If I were you, I wouldn't waste my time talking to her. She won't be able to tell you anything about her father. She barely knew him over the last ten years or so. Then again, who am I to tell you how to solve the case? I'm no detective. That's up to you. I just really hope you'll find someone for the police to arrest soon."

I tried to catch her eye again, but she refused to meet my gaze directly. I sensed the conversation was over even before she took a last nibble on her biscotti, then abruptly rose and informed me that her husband would be worried about her and she had better get home.

We retrieved her packages from my car, I thanked her for talking to me, and I asked her to call me if she thought of anything else that might be important. She said she would, but I knew she wouldn't.

As I watched her scurry toward the door of her apartment building, I thought about what she'd said about her husband. She had no idea he had been aware of her affair, and she obviously didn't want him finding out now.

Mrs. Tucci had said that when Dinah told him their affair was over, Angelo had threatened to tell Gil Leary about it. Had Dinah been paranoid enough to guarantee his silence . . . by killing him?

The motive was certainly there.

And as for the alibi—riding the Staten Island ferry was pretty flimsy. But there was no way to prove they hadn't been there.

As I got into my car, Dinah Leary joined her husband at the top of my list of suspects.

A message from Barnaby Tischler was waiting for me when I returned to Gracie Mansion late Sunday afternoon. He had left his home number and asked that I please call as soon as possible.

I did—after changing out of my damp clothing and fixing myself a preventative mug of Glugol Muggle. With my vacation to Barbados right around the corner and my usual feverish schedule for the coming week leading up to my departure, the last thing I wanted was to get sick again.

Then I settled in my study, where a fire was blazing on the hearth, and I dialed Barnaby's number at home in Great Neck.

His wife, Wanda, answered on the second ring. After a brief exchange of small talk, during which we both conscientiously avoided mentioning the murder, she called her husband to the phone.

"Ed," he said warmly, "it was good of you to call back."

"Is everything all right, Barnaby?"

"Things have been better, but they could be worse. No new developments on this end. I just wanted to thank you for putting in an appearance at the store on Friday night. I know that you're busy and it meant a lot to me that you would go out of your way like that."

"Actually, it wasn't so much out of the way," I said honestly. "I had shopping to do, and, Barnaby, Ramsey's has always been one of my favorite department stores in the city. Besides, I'll admit that your extended weekend hours were very convenient for someone like me."

"I wish more people felt that way," he said bleakly. "Hardly anyone took advantage of the round-the-clock hours. Although, I have to admit that Saturday night was a slight improvement over Friday, thanks to you."

"I'm glad to have been of service, then."

"Likewise. It's funny—just a few days ago I called you in there to talk about Highview Meadows and how it was ruining my business. If I'd had any idea what was coming . . ."

"You couldn't have known."

"No. But I thought that mall was the worst thing that could ever threaten my store."

There was a pause.

Then Barnaby asked cautiously, "Er, Ed, do you think you could pop in again tomorrow? Say, at high noon? And bring some press along with you?"

"Barnaby, I can't do that—"

"I could really use some positive publicity, though, Ed. I've been trying like crazy to get a shipment of Henrietta Hyena puppets—every store in the city is sold out—but even if I do get them in, it won't do me as much good as having the mayor show up to shop."

"I can't do that," I repeated, "because I have the rehearsal for the tree-lighting ceremony."

"Oh. That," he said glumly. "I was supposed to be there, Ed, as part of the program. I was going to introduce the Ramsey's Santa, and he was going to sing some carols with the Special Olympics kids for that production number. But the producers called me last week and told me to forget it. They gave our Santa the ax too."

I winced at the mental image conjured by *that* particular phrase.

"Did they say why?" I asked.

"Why do you think? Ed, I really wish you would find time to stop in at the store tomorrow . . ."

"Barnaby, I told you—"

"I know, I know. The rehearsal. And anyway, it would be wrong for you to manipulate your political position that way, right? Still, it would be so good for business . . ."

"So would catching the murderer," I pointed out. "I'd rather put myself to use that way, Barnaby."

"You're right . . . have you made any progress?" he asked, his voice brightening.

"Actually, some."

"Suspects?"

"I've got a few possibilities. I interrogated some of the victim's neighbors and came up with a couple of leads. Nothing concrete, but I'm checking into them."

"That's more than the police seem to be doing. So far, they haven't come up with anything. Or if they have, they aren't telling me. What about Simon Weatherly?"

"What about him?"

"Have you spoken to him yet, Ed?"

"As a matter of fact, I tried. I stopped by the store just this afternoon on my way home to see if he was in, but he wasn't there."

"That's no surprise. He's probably holed up somewhere, plotting to take over my store building."

No use arguing with a vengeful Barnaby.

"He has an alibi for the night of the murder," Barnaby pointed out glumly. "And it checks out. But that doesn't mean he didn't hire someone to kill Calvino for him. He's not the type who would want to get blood on his hands anyway. If he's behind it, I'm getting more and more convinced he used a hit man, Ed."

I nodded thoughtfully.

All I said was "I'll try and catch up with Simon as soon as I can, but I can't promise you anything. My schedule this week is hectic. The President is coming to town on Thursday, and then I'm leaving for Barbados next Sunday."

"I know, I know . . . And believe me, I'm not holding you

responsible for solving this case, Ed. It's not your job. But I can't help feeling that if anyone can come up with something, it's you."

"I'll do my best, Barnaby."

"Thanks. I just hope it's soon."

"Barnaby . . ." I said in a warning tone.

"Sorry. It's just . . . patience has never been one of *my* virtues. I can't even handle waiting in line at a supermarket."

"Well, this is a little different."

"I know. I'll let you get going now. But . . . Ed?"

"Yes?"

"Uh, if you remember any other last-minute gifts you need . . . we're having a terrific one-day sale on Tuesday."

SEVEN

Monday dawned cold and clear, promising to be the kind of rare December day when the sun sparkles brilliantly in a deep azure winter sky.

I spent the early morning hours working from home, where I managed to make serious progress on the stacks of letters, memos, reports, and charts that needed to be read, signed, initialed, or approved.

I was interrupted once by a phone call from my niece, Melissa, who wanted to know if I could get my hands on a Henrietta Hyena puppet for Schuyler.

"It's all she talks about, Uncle Ed," she said. "Remy and I are at our wits' end. Every store in the city is sold out, and so is Highview Meadows."

"You actually went there?"

"We're desperate, Uncle Ed. Schuyler keeps talking about how Santa is going to bring her Henrietta. She'll be so disappointed if we don't find one for her."

I bit back the impulse to point out that countless children in this city are forced to do without food and decent clothes and a place to live, and that privileged little Schuyler is a tad bit spoiled anyway.

Instead, I said, "I hear that Ramsey's is expecting a shipment of Henrietta Hyenas any day now. Maybe you'll be able to pick one up there."

"I already told you, Uncle Ed . . . I don't feel safe going into that store. Can't you pull some strings somehow and get your hands on a Henrietta for me? After all, you're the mayor."

"Surprising as it may be, being the mayor of New York City doesn't allow instant access to elusive giggling puppets, Melissa," I pointed out dryly.

After hanging up with my disappointed niece, I watched the local morning news broadcast, and witnessed the lovely and eloquent Tommi Tremaine blasting me from the Queens Boulevard gutter she calls home.

"The mayor has no right to tell me what to do."

The woman was bleeped by the network's censors so often that it was a bit frustrating to piece her entire statement together as she rattled on. But I got the gist of it, which was that she hated my guts and intended to make me pay for what I had done.

Which, essentially, was save her life.

The lawyers who had taken her case—pro bono, of course— had been in contact with the city's legal counsel over the weekend, and I knew they were going ahead with the lawsuit.

As far as I was concerned, it was a waste of time for all concerned.

Tommi Tremaine, and not the Ramsey's murder, was primary on my mind as I headed down to Rockefeller Center in rush-hour traffic just past nine o'clock.

But when I stepped out of the car in front of the enormous pine tree that had recently been shipped to Manhattan from a woodsy backyard in northern Westchester County, the murder took a sudden leap to front and center.

There, mingling with the Rockettes and several television production types, was the elusive Simon Weatherly.

The rehearsal, held on a platform just above the famous Rockefeller Center ice skating rink, went as smoothly as one would expect, considering that we were outdoors in the middle of midtown with curious passersby staring down at us from the perimeter of the rink. I had a few minor tiffs with the director over what I considered a cheesy canned monologue they had kindly provided on cue cards for me.

When I protested for the tenth time that I was perfectly capable of ad-libbing my own clever quips, the executive producer—Martin St. Martin, a longtime friend of mine—was called in to mediate.

He pulled me aside and said, "Just read the script, Ed. It's a hell of a lot easier."

"I don't like the script. It doesn't sound like me. I have a very distinct way of speaking, Martin. I would never say something like 'Here now are the Rockettes, to put the jingle into your jangle.' What does that even mean?"

He frowned. "I have no idea."

"So you see what I'm saying?"

"Okay, cut the jingle and jangle," he called to the director, who threw up his hands and looked exasperated.

Then, to me, Martin said firmly, "But the rest of it has to stay, Ed. The show is tonight. There isn't time for the writers to come up with a new script."

"Fine," I said abruptly, deciding that since the show would be live, there was no sense in arguing now.

When the time came for me to take center stage, I would simply be myself, ignore the cue cards, and speak the way I normally do. That was the only way I could guarantee a decent performance as master of ceremonies.

We got through the rest of the rehearsal, including the part where Simon Weatherly came onstage to introduce the Weatherly Brothers Santa, who sang "Up on the Housetop" and "Jolly Old Saint Nicholas" with the Special Olympics children.

Wait until Barnaby finds out about *this,* I thought, watching Simon gloat from the steps overlooking the rink.

As soon as rehearsal was over, I made my way through the throng of children and technicians and Rockettes, locating Simon as he made his way toward a long black limo parked nearby on Fiftieth Street. He was a tall, gaunt figure in a long black coat that whipped around his legs as he strode along the sidewalk.

"Simon," I called, hurrying after him with my bodyguards hurrying after me.

Either he didn't hear me, or he ignored me, because he failed to turn around.

I sidestepped a bell-ringing Santa, who greeted me with an upbeat, "Hey, ho, ho, ho, Mr. Mayor."

"Simon!" I bellowed again.

He stopped, turned, and his angular face registered nothing more than mere recognition. "Yes?"

"Can I have a word with you?"

"About tonight's program?"

"No."

"I'm a busy man, Mr. Koch," he began, glancing first at his watch and then at his car.

I cut him off with a snort and a curt, "Believe me, so am I. This won't take long."

He sighed, looking resigned, and said, "What is it?"

Out of the corner of my eye I noticed a camera-toting reporter bearing down on us.

"Let's go into that café," I suggested, pointing across the street. "We can talk more privately in there."

"I'm perfectly comfortable right here."

"Well, I'm not." I distinctly disliked the man, which was going to make it difficult to be objective.

I led the way across the street to the small French café chain, which was nearly deserted at this hour of the day. I ordered a large coffee and signed an autograph for the congenial young man behind the counter.

Simon, sulking, declined to order anything.

We easily found seats at a small table in a corner.

"What are they doing?" Simon asked, eyeing my bodyguards, who, as usual, had positioned themselves nearby.

"They're my security team. They're keeping an eye on me."

"Who would want to assassinate you?"

"I'm flattered you think so highly of me, Simon," I said, deciding to take it as a compliment. I removed the plastic lid from my coffee and took a sip, then said, "Unfortunately, there are people who might wish to harm me, impossible as that may be to believe. I never go anywhere without my bodyguards."

He nodded, seeming to have lost interest in the subject.

"What is it that you wanted to talk about?" he asked impatiently.

"I didn't realize you were scheduled to appear in tonight's program."

"I wasn't, originally."

"Oh?"

He shifted his weight in his chair and toyed with the cuff of his coat. "After the rather unfortunate mishap involving the Ramsey's Santa Claus, I replaced Barnaby Tischler, and the Weatherly Brothers Santa replaced—well, you know."

"Whose idea was that?"

"I happened to run into Martin St. Martin outside the gym last Tuesday afternoon. Knowing he would be in a bit of a bind, I volunteered the services of myself and our Santa."

"I see." Tuesday had been the day after the murder. "That was kind of you."

"Nobody is more full of the Christmas spirit than I am, Mr. Koch."

I nearly choked taking a gulp of my coffee. Simon Weatherly radiates about as much mirth as Ebenezer Scrooge and the Grinch rolled together.

"It was a tragedy, the Ramsey's murder," I said, watching him over the rim of my cup.

He merely nodded.

"Who would have committed such a dastardly crime?" I mused, rubbing my chin.

"An utter idiot, that's who," Weatherly pronounced.

"What do you mean?"

"Why would anyone kill somebody right in the store, where anyone could have come along and witnessed the crime? The old coot lived alone—"

"Who lived alone?" I asked, intrigued that Weatherly would call a murder victim an old coot.

"Calvino."

So Weatherly had no respect for the late Ramsey's Santa. But I had to remind myself that a lack of taste and compassion didn't make him a killer.

"And . . . ?"

"If someone was so hot to bump him off, it would have made more sense to do it more privately. Like at his apartment."

"Unless . . ."

"Unless what?"

"Unless the very reason that he was killed was that he *was* in the store. Maybe the motive was simply to kill the Ramsey's Santa, not to kill Angelo Calvino."

"That's sick," Weatherly muttered.

"It is sick," I agreed. "But it makes sense."

"Why are we talking about this?" he asked abruptly.

As if he didn't know.

I cleared my throat and said in my straightforward way, "I was going over, in my head, the people who might have a motive to kill not Angelo Calvino, but the Ramsey's Santa. And you, Mr. Weatherly, came to mind."

"That's preposterous!" he sputtered, starting to rise.

"Sit," I said calmly, aware that the few other customers in the shop were eyeing us with curiosity. "Unless you want to cause a scene."

He sat.

"I had nothing to do with that murder," he said vehemently, leaning toward me across the table, his voice low and menacing.

"I didn't say you did. Only that you, as manager of the store's foremost competition, are one of the people who might conceivably have a reason to generate some bad publicity for Ramsey's."

"You are obviously not aware, Mr. *Mayor*," he said, snidely stressing my title, "that the foremost competition for Ramsey's—and for Weatherly Brothers—is Highview Meadows, the new shopping mall over in Jersey. Why don't you go over and harass the mall manager instead of wasting my time?"

"Because the mall manager doesn't have any intention of moving his business to the Thirty-fourth Street building occupied by Ramsey's," I told him. "You do."

"Where did you get a crazy idea like that?"

"Simon, I'm not a fool. I happen to know that there is only so much midtown real estate to go around. And the historic Ramsey's building is one of the city's finest properties—in terms of both the department store itself and the location."

"What do they have that I don't have? My store is a stone's throw from Ramsey's," he said, attempting to dismiss my point with a wave of his bony hand.

"Your store is inferior, and it's in the middle of the block. Ramsey's is much bigger and has far more architectural appeal, and it has ample display windows not just on Thirty-fourth Street, but on the avenue. Stop playing games, Simon. You would jump at the chance to get ahold of that building and move in there, and we both know it."

"I wouldn't kill for the chance, Mr. Mayor," he said icily. "If you had done your homework, you would know that the police have already questioned me and checked out my alibi for last Monday night."

"I did know that," I said crisply. "You were having dinner at Smith and Wollensky . . ."

"Where I saw at least a dozen people who know me very well, including the waiter who served my table. Any of them would be glad to vouch for my whereabouts, as I told Detective Lazaro."

I nodded. If he *had* hired someone to commit the murder and he *were* consciously trying to establish an alibi, what better means than by dining in one of New York's most popular and crowded restaurants?

"What about the bomb threats?" I asked abruptly, shifting gears.

He looked startled. "What are you talking about?"

"You don't know?"

"Know what?"

"About the bomb threats?" I asked, and he shook his head.

"That's funny," I said. "I was under the impression that it had been in all the papers. And your store is right down the block on Thirty-fourth Street, so how could you not have noticed that Ramsey's has been evacuated several times because someone has been phoning in bomb threats?"

"Oh. That. Maybe I did hear something about that. Now, if you'll excuse me, and you really have nothing important to discuss, I have to be going, Mr. Koch."

As I said, I was doing my best to remain objective about the man. But I couldn't help wondering if Barnaby was right about him after all.

It wasn't hard to imagine Simon Weatherly phoning in a bomb threat to Ramsey's Department Store.

And it wasn't hard to imagine him engineering a cold-blooded murder either.

The tree-lighting ceremony went off without a hitch.

Well—almost.

Shortly before we went on the air, the Weatherly Brothers Santa hadn't yet shown up. The television people were in a furor, trying to come up with an alternate plan for the Special Olympics segment.

Though I didn't want to see one of the big production numbers ruined, I'll admit that I did get enormous satisfaction out of watching Simon Weatherly pace and fret and place agitated calls on his cellular phone, trying to track down the missing Santa.

Finally, he showed up just before the production got under way. You didn't have to be standing right next to him to smell that booze on his breath. The guy reeked of it.

Even so, no one in the live audience seemed to notice that the Santa was slightly off balance and off key during his production number, or that he nearly tripped over a little boy in a wheelchair.

And no one—except, perhaps, the director, who took on a panic-stricken expression every time I took the mike—seemed to mind that I was neglecting to read the cheesy scripted lines from the cue cards. If I do say so myself, my snappy quips and ad-libs went over very well, even stopping the show for big laughs on more than one occasion.

And when I asked my trademark question halfway through the show—"How'm I doing?"—the crowd went nuts, shouting and clapping and whistling like crazy.

At the Rainbow Room gala afterward, the director gave me the cold shoulder, but Martin St. Martin came up and clapped me on the back.

"You were brilliant, Ed," he said jovially. He was wearing a red Santa cap and sipping a bright red cosmopolitan in a martini glass.

"Thank you, Martin. It was a lot of fun."

"I think we showed everyone who was watching across the country that New York City hasn't lost the holiday spirit. It's a shame about the Ramsey's Santa though. This bozo made a poor substitute."

I followed his gaze to the bar, where the Weatherly Brothers Santa was bellying up for another shot of what looked like straight whiskey. His fake white beard was askew, and his nose, true to the famed poem about him, was as red as a cherry.

"Where's Simon Weatherly?" I asked, realizing I hadn't seen him since the show's finale.

"I have no idea. He left right after the show was over. Probably too embarrassed to show his face here, after he went out of his way to put his Santa into the production."

"He should be embarrassed." I noticed that the drunken Weatherly Brothers Santa was in the process of making some kind of remark to a young woman I recognized as one of the stars of a daytime soap filmed here in New York. She promptly looked insulted, made an angry retort, and stormed away.

Nearby, I noticed, was my pal Sybil Baker, who was watching and wearing a thoughtful expression that meant she was filing away a tidbit for tomorrow's column.

I managed to catch her eye, and she waved and made her way over just as Martin excused himself to speak with Marcus Dorman, one of the Radio City honchos.

"Ed, you did a beautiful job as emcee," Sybil said, greeting me with a hug. She was dazzling in a shimmering, bright emerald-colored cocktail dress with rubies at her ears and throat.

"You're looking festive in red and green," I told her. "But why are you all dressed up?"

The reception was casual. I had on a tuxedo, of course, but I had been master of ceremonies for the show. Most of the technicians, who seemed to be mingling mostly with the Rockettes, were in jeans.

"Oh, I'm on my way to that opening night party for *Rudolph*," she informed me. "Are you going?"

Rudolph—a film about the notorious fictional reindeer—was the latest computer-animated feature that was sure to be a Christmas blockbuster. It was being produced by Byran Wells and Nicholas

Marino, the brilliant Hollywood screenwriting team responsible for the *Star Passage* film trilogy that was such a smashing success in the late eighties.

Tonight's premiere party, to which I had been invited, was going to be held at Tavern-on-the-Green, which is magical year-round, but especially at Christmas, with the millions of little white lights and its pastoral Central Park setting.

"I hadn't planned on going," I told Sybil. "I really need to get back home. I've got an early breakfast in the morning with the governor, and then I've got a meeting with the corporation counsel."

"About the Tommi Tremaine fracas?" Sybil asked.

"What else?" I grumbled.

"What do you think?"

"What do I think?" I snorted. "Ridiculous! The whole thing is ridiculous!"

"Then you won't be pleased to know that the latest off my Hollywood pipeline is that she's talking to movie producers about selling the rights to her story."

"You're right, Sybil. I'm not pleased, and I'm not surprised either. The woman's nothing but a—"

"Don't get all worked up, Ed," Sybil cautioned me. "Why don't you come to the *Rudolph* party with me? It'll be fun—not to mention a memorable event. In fact, everyone's been talking about it."

"Why?"

"Oh, the producers are pulling out all stops to make it a huge PR success. I hear they hired a snowmaking machine so that the park grounds outside Tavern would be a winter wonderland even if Mother Nature didn't cooperate—which she hasn't."

I had heard about the snowmaking machine too, of course. The arrangements had required all kinds of string pulling, paperwork, and a special permit from the city's Parks Department. Seemed excessively time-consuming, expensive, and extravagant, even for Wells and Marino.

"They certainly don't need all the hoopla to guarantee a hit," Sybil went on. "Everything Wells and Marino touch turns gold.

Look at what happened with that fiasco a few years ago when they were making that pirate film."

"*South Seas Swashbuckler,*" I said, nodding. "That was the one where the three Jamaican extras drowned in the Caribbean during the shoot."

"Right. And then Marino's brother Dante, who was an assistant director on the film, was actually arrested for smuggling heroin into the country on some of the ships they were using for the set. . . ."

"And two of the stars walked halfway through the filming, and they were way over budget and blew the production schedule by almost an entire year," I remembered. "Did anything go right with that movie?"

"Absolutely, Ed. When all was said and done, it made a fortune at the box office. One of the highest-grossing films of all time. That, my dear, simply proves what I've told you all along—particularly last year, when you were investigating the Matthews murder."

"To which words of wisdom are you referring, Sybil?"

"That ultimately, any publicity is good publicity. Nearly every celebrity scandal I have ever reported in my column has resulted in giving the personality in question an exceedingly high profile. And if they play their cards right and take advantage of the media exposure, a celebrity can turn a potential disaster into a financial and professional triumph."

"That may be true. But I, as a celebrity of sorts, am not interested in finding out firsthand how that works. And as I was saying"—I glanced at my watch and nodded at my bodyguards—"I hate to disappoint you, but I've really got to get home, Sybil. It's been a long day."

She shrugged and threw up her hands in a what-can-I-say gesture. "You're probably the only person who was invited to this thing tonight who's not going to show, Ed. It's a hot ticket. Word has it that Simon Weatherly has been trying to finagle his way onto the guest list."

"Then I *really* don't want to be there," I said conclusively. "I've seen more than enough of him today."

"Well, I'm sorry you won't be joining me, Ed, but I suppose

that with you, work has to come before pleasure. Luckily for me, in my field, work *is* pleasure.''

"Believe me, Sybil, I usually consider my work pleasure too. But lately things have been pretty stressful. I'm really looking forward to that vacation next week.''

"Bimini, isn't it?''

"Barbados.''

"Oh, that's right. Claude and I were just there last spring. The scuba diving is spectacular.''

Did I mention that Sybil is the most athletic, adventurous sixty-something woman I've ever met?

"I wasn't planning on scuba diving, Sybil, but thanks anyway for the tip. All I want to do is relax and forget about nasty weather, Tommi Tremaine, and . . . the Ramsey's murder. Hopefully there'll have been an arrest by the time I leave.''

She looked intrigued. "Are the police closing in on a suspect? I haven't heard anything about it.''

"I don't know about the police,'' I told her, "but I've got three potential murderers on my list, and I'm about to narrow the field and figure out which one killed Angelo Calvino.''

"Can I quote you on that?''

"Absolutely not. Don't you breathe a word of this in your column, Sybil.''

"I won't,'' she said, sounding resigned. "But I want an exclusive the moment an arrest is made. Deal?''

"Deal.''

I couldn't possibly have known that at that very moment, the Ramsey's case was growing far more complicated than anyone could have imagined.

A howling winter storm blew into Manhattan in the wee hours of Tuesday morning. Sleet beat steadily against the windows of Gracie Mansion and the wind caused the sprawling old place to creak and shudder.

Snuggled beneath my warm blankets in the cozy master bedroom, I found myself wide awake at three A.M., and wondering why. Storms certainly don't bother me; I've always found it comforting to be lulled to slumber by the familiar sounds of rain and wind.

I didn't have to be up for a few more hours, and I had been so exhausted when I'd tumbled into bed just before midnight that I had drifted right off. But now here I was, staring into the dark, my whole body tense, as though something were about to happen.

And it did.

Just before five o'clock, when I had finally decided I might as well get up and beat the alarm, I heard quiet footsteps outside my door.

There was a soft knock.

"Who is it?" I asked promptly, slipping out of bed and tying on a robe.

"It's Ted," said one of my aides, who usually wouldn't be at the mansion at this hour.

I hastily opened the door.

"Oh . . . did you already hear?" he asked, looking surprised to see how alert I was.

"Hear what?"

"Oh. I thought maybe since you were up—but you don't know, do you?"

"Know what?"

"That another Ramsey's Santa was murdered last night at the store."

EIGHT

It was well past noon by the time I had met my morning obligations: breakfast with the governor at the Cafe Pierre at the Pierre Hotel, the meeting with Erik Dolk and associates concerning the Tommi Tremaine lawsuit, a briefing with my financial advisers to prepare for the upcoming meeting with the President to discuss my proposed budgetary support, and my usual eleven A.M. press conference.

The press room at City Hall was awash with reporters who wanted to know what I knew about the latest Ramsey's murder. At that point I presumably had less information than they did, and I told them precisely that.

What I didn't mention was that I had tried to gain access to the crime scene early that morning, and was refused. Detective Lazaro told me over the telephone, in no uncertain terms, that he was in charge of the investigation and intended to strictly limit access to the scene.

I could have made a big stink about it; I could have called my police commissioner, Harris Bayor, and insisted that I be allowed to visit the scene.

But the reality is that my first and foremost priority must always be to stay on top of my mayoral responsibilities.

And this morning I was simply too busy with the governor and other city business to get involved in all the red tape that getting special permission would involve.

So the bare-bones facts, as I relayed them to the restless reporters at the press conference, were as follows:

The body of Marlon Killdaire, sixty-five, of Sunnyside Gardens in Queens, was found on the store premises shortly before eleven o'clock last night, dead of a single gunshot wound to the back of the head.

That was all I knew.

Hardly mollified, the press moved on to an equally distressing topic: the Tommi Tremaine lawsuit.

The day was not off to a good start.

Following a brief lunch break at a nearby diner with my first deputy mayor, I managed to reach Barnaby Tischler, who was in seclusion at his home in Great Neck.

"Ed . . . thanks for calling . . ." He sounded too distraught to say more.

"Barnaby, I was upset when I heard what happened. Do you have any idea how . . . or why?"

"All I know is that someone got into the store with a gun somehow, and they were lying in wait for Marlon when his Wonderland shift ended."

"Where was the body?"

"Behind a row of lockers in the employees' locker room, not far from where Calvino was found."

I shook my head, bemused. "What about all the extra security you hired?"

"Ed, what can I tell you? I have metal detectors at every entrance we use, for crying out loud."

"Every entrance you use?" I asked, my ears pricking up.

"To save some expense, I had one of the small Thirty-fourth Street entrances and the employees' entrance that faces the alley locked."

"What about the loading dock?"

"That's guarded by a full-time security team, and they check out every delivery person who comes and goes."

"But someone could have smuggled a weapon in that way."

"It wouldn't be impossible, but highly unlikely. What delivery person would want to murder Santa Claus?"

"A delivery person might not want to commit the murder," I pointed out patiently, "but he or she might be persuaded to smuggle a weapon into the store for whoever *did* commit the murder."

"Like Simon Weatherly," he said, his voice flat.

I was about to protest that Weatherly wasn't the only suspect, when I was struck by a sudden, profound realization that would have come to me earlier if not for my hectic morning agenda.

My other two suspects—Gil and Dinah Leary—had motives to murder Angelo Calvino. But why would either of them want to kill this Marlon Killdaire?

The case had taken on an entirely different angle.

It now seemed fairly obvious that the two Santas had been killed simply because they *were* Ramsey's Santas. Which most likely ruled out the Learys as suspects.

Leaving *only* Simon Weatherly as a suspect.

Unless . . .

"What am I going to do, Ed?" Barnaby was saying, sounding morose. "This is going to ruin me."

Something Sybil had told me just last night ran through my mind.

Any publicity is good publicity.

Because of the murders, Ramsey's Department Store was front-page news—not just locally, but across the country.

The immediate result had been a loss of business. But when the dust had settled, would Ramsey's business be stronger than ever before?

And who would directly benefit from that?

Barnaby Tischler.

As he went on talking about how distraught he had been ever since the police had summoned him to the store late last night, my mind was reluctantly trying to grasp this new perspective on the case.

It seemed not just unlikely, but impossible that Barnaby could be responsible for taking the life of a human being. *Two* human beings.

I felt my stomach shift with an unsettling queasiness at the mere notion.

But a good investigator doesn't let emotion stand in the way of common sense.

And common sense told me not to rule out anyone as a potential suspect.

Reluctantly, I added my old friend to my mental suspect lineup—just behind Simon Weatherly, who, after all, was a far more likely candidate and would remain at the top of the list.

And I turned my full attention back to the conversation, asking brusquely, "Barnaby, were you at the store when the murder was committed?"

"No, Ed, I just told you I had left to drive home at about eight last night. The police called me just past eleven-thirty, when the body was found, and I rushed back to the store. I was there until a few hours ago. I haven't slept a wink."

Naturally, the last thing I wanted to do was alert him to my suspicions, so I had to think carefully before phrasing my next question.

"Did you happen to catch the tree-lighting ceremony on television?" I asked as casually as possible.

"Oh . . . no. No, I missed it."

"Didn't get to leave the store in time?"

"No, that wasn't it—"

"Wanda wanted to watch something else?"

"No, Wanda was out at a Garden Club Christmas banquet last night."

"So you had the house to yourself? What about the house-keeper?" I pressed.

"She had the night off. What's this about, Ed?" he asked, suddenly sounding cold. "Are you trying to make sure I have an alibi for the time the murder took place last night?"

When I didn't answer promptly, he exploded, telling me that I had some nerve to accuse him of murder.

"I didn't accuse you of anything, Barnaby," I pointed out, managing to sound utterly reasonable. "But you must know how the police are going to look at this. They're going to want to know where you were and what you were doing last night. Are you prepared to—"

"Why would I kill two of my own employees? Why would I deliberately destroy my store's busiest sales season and ruin our reputation?"

I didn't say a word about my earlier speculation that publicity was a possible motive.

I simply said, "You *wouldn't* do that. It would be ridiculous for anyone to consider you a suspect, wouldn't it, Barnaby? But the police will want to investigate every angle, just as they did with Calvino."

"They never made me a suspect in that. And they aren't saying I'm a suspect now, Ed."

At least, not publicly, I thought grimly.

"Just hang in there, Barnaby," I told him. "You've been through a lot. You have to get through this one day at a time, and I'll do everything I can to help."

"Yeah. Sure." He sounded curt.

"Barnaby—"

"I have to go, Ed. There are a few phone calls I need to make."

I started to say good-bye, but the line went dead with an abrupt click.

The first thing I did after my last meeting late in the day was place a call to Darius Jones, my friend at the coroner's office.

"What can you tell me about the Killdaire murder?" I asked after engaging in a few moments of small talk during which we both pretended to be unaware of the real reason I was calling.

"Ed, you know I'm not supposed to discuss it. The autopsy hasn't even begun."

"Darius, like I said before, it's all going to come out in the press sooner or later. Why shouldn't I get a jump on the public? I am the mayor, after all."

"You are really something, man. You don't give up."

"Not when we're talking about two dastardly murders in my city."

"Yeah, I get where you're coming from. What do you want to know?" he asked, sounding resigned.

"Cause of death?"

"Looks like a single gunshot wound to the back of the head, close range—same as before. Nine-millimeter pistol, same as before. The body was found where it dropped. No sign of a struggle."

"What time?"

"Officially, between eight-thirty and eleven. I'd expect the final estimation to put it at ten o'clock, ten-thirty . . ."

"Same as before."

"Exactly."

"Anything else you want to tell me?"

"Nope. That's all I know, Ed. But that's some pretty sick dude out there, gunning down guys in Santa suits. I hope somebody catches him soon, before this happens again."

Before this happens again.

Darius's words had lit yet another bulb in my mind.

What if the motive behind the killings wasn't greed or publicity or vengeance?

What if the motive was simply . . . to kill?

As in, some psycho serial killer on the loose?

Sick as it was, I personally felt that that particular scenario was more plausible than the theory that Barnaby Tischler had committed the murders.

And I saw in the evening papers that I wasn't the only one who was considering the serial-killer possibility.

The Daily Register headline screamed "NO SANTA IS SAFE!"

There were reports of panicky department store Santas and sidewalk Santas quitting their jobs across the city. Costume shops were reporting countless cancellations by people who had reserved Santa suits.

And there seemed to be a mass exodus of shoppers leaving New York to visit Highview Meadows. The shuttle lines were jammed and there were record numbers of automobiles heading for the New Jersey mall via the Lincoln and Holland tunnels and over the George Washington and Verrazano bridges.

I noticed that Highview Meadows had added a new line to their usual two-page advertisement in our papers: "Feel sure and secure as you shop in the safety of suburbia."

Ridiculous! I scoffed, crumpling the ad and tossing it aside every time I came across one.

I carefully perused every newspaper account for a mention that there had been more than one Santa on Ramsey's payroll at the time of the murder, but there was no hint that the media was aware of that fact. The Ramsey's employees and Santas who were in on the secret were clearly honoring their confidentiality statements.

The papers were, however, full of details about the unfortunate Marlon Killdaire.

He was described as having been "incredibly brave to step into the Ramsey's Santa suit after his predecessor had been so violently killed"—no clue that he had been working at Ramsey's as one of the many rotating Santas *before* Calvino was killed.

Marlon Killdaire, it turned out, was a city cop moonlighting at Ramsey's while out on a short-term disability leave. It seemed he had been injured a month before in an accident when the brakes on his patrol car had failed.

His family and friends had convinced him to apply for the job as Ramsey's Santa. According to Barnaby Tischler, Killdaire had originally been selected as an alternate and was called to duty when Angelo Calvino was killed.

This outright lie in the press had me questioning Tischler's integrity once again.

Still, lying to reporters to hide a business secret was one thing.

Killing two men in cold blood was quite another.

I still wasn't convinced Barnaby was capable of the heinous crime.

Then again, I wasn't convinced that he wasn't.

Wednesday dawned deceptively warm and bright, and Fifth Avenue seemed dazzling as a warm April day as we headed downtown to City Hall early that morning. People strolled along with their jackets unzipped and sunglasses on. The breeze blowing in the window of my car was positively balmy, and sweetly scented with a hint of springtime.

But according to the papers, the sunny reprieve was cruelly temporary. By tonight the temperatures would plunge into the twenties, and a monster of a snowstorm would power its way up the East Coast. Metropolitan New York could expect high winds and anywhere from six to twelve inches of snow.

"That's a hell of a lot of snow," my bodyguard, Tony, said from the front seat, where he sat beside my driver, listening to the weather report on the radio.

"Three feet is a lot of snow," I conceded, scanning the forecast in the morning newspaper. "One foot . . . that's a different story. That's just twelve inches. With twelve inches, people can still get around fairly easily—at least in Manhattan. We can handle it. It doesn't affect the subway here."

Tony, who had grown up in southern California, just looked dubiously at me.

"I said *fairly* easily," I pointed out. "It's not a piece of cake out on the streets. You have snowshoes, Ambrose?"

"Snowshoes?"

I had to laugh at the horrified expression on his face.

Personally, I was hoping for a miracle. With any luck, the storm would reach New Jersey, hang a hard right, and blow right out to sea.

Do you know what it costs to deal with one to three feet of snow in New York City? I'm talking about salt for the roads, and equipment, and hours of overtime for everyone involved. And then there's the Metropolitan Transit Authority, which must do its best to keep public transportation running around the clock, and then there are the schools and businesses that shut down because people can't get around, or *think* they can't, and . . .

I shuddered to think of what lay ahead.

I flipped the page of the newspaper and my gaze fell on an image of a smiling man surrounded by what appeared to be a loving family.

"Marlon Killdaire, center, celebrating his thirty-fifth wedding anniversary with his wife, Alva, and their children and grandchildren three years ago," read the caption beneath the photograph.

I studied the victim. He was a handsome man, with a tousled head of white hair, and bushy eyebrows and a full mustache to match. I couldn't help noticing that his eyes were as twinkly and his dimples as merry as Santa's in the proverbial Clement Moore poem. No wonder his family had urged him to apply for the job as Ramsey's Santa.

His wife, by contrast, was a plain woman who wore a serious expression. Her straight gray hair was pulled severely back, emphasizing a nose that was too long and eyes set too close together.

But, looking closely at the photo, I saw that her hand was clasped in her husband's, and their shoulders were companionably close together. There was true affection between them; it was obvious even in the grainy newspaper photo.

Their children, according to the article accompanying the photo, included two sons, David and Michael.

David, the older of the two, seemed to have inherited his mother's drab features and somber expression. He stood slightly apart from everyone else in the picture, unsmiling and appearing almost uncomfortable.

His brother, Michael, seemed to have their father's congenial countenance. He wore a broad grin and had one arm slung casually over Marlon Killdaire's shoulders, and the other around a petite woman who was, quite obviously, very pregnant. According to the article, the woman was his wife, Anne, and all three young children in the photo belonged to them.

The family had refused to comment on Marlon's death, and a resident of their Sunnyside Gardens neighborhood had told reporters that they were "utterly devastated."

I shook my head and scanned the rest of the coverage. Nothing new.

Fellow cops in Killdaire's precinct described him as "an all-around wonderful guy"—"a dedicated police officer"—"a true family man with a heart of gold."

Mohammed Johnson, one of my bodyguards and a New York cop with the same precinct, had told me that he recalled Killdaire, remembering him as "the kind of no-nonsense cop with a fierce sense of justice, who wouldn't take any crap from anyone."

The police officers who had been on the scene refused to comment about any link between Calvino's and Killdaire's death, but there was speculation by the media that the fact that Killdaire was on the NYPD force would make solving his murder an immediate priority—as though solving *any* murder wasn't a priority for New York's Finest, I thought, disgruntled.

Barnaby Tischler could not be reached for comment, and hadn't been seen at Ramsey's since before the murder. The store had been closed on Tuesday and Wednesday but was scheduled to reopen early Thursday.

Detective Lazaro of the homicide squad said only that the police were investigating several leads. He asked that anyone with any information about the murders contact him at a special eight hundred number that had been set up for that purpose.

"Here we are, Mr. Mayor," announced my driver.

I glanced up from the newspaper to see that we had, indeed, arrived at City Hall.

"Another busy day, huh, sir?" Ambrose said as he opened the back door of the car.

"Every day is a busy day, Ambrose," I told him, feeling frustrated.

I wanted to take some time to look into the latest murder. But with the President due in town first thing in the morning, and a jam-packed schedule from the moment I would welcome him at the heliport on the west side until he left on Friday at noon . . .

There would be no time to investigate this week.

And I was scheduled to leave for Barbados on the weekend.

Unless . . .

What if . . . ?

No.

No!

I dismissed the irritating thought the moment it nudged into my consciousness. No way was I going to cancel my well-earned and long-awaited vacation.

No way.

If the case wasn't solved by the NYPD before I left town, I would simply have to leave it in their capable hands.

A light snow was already falling by the time I got back to Gracie Mansion late Wednesday evening. I wasn't in the best of moods after a particularly trying day—due, for the most part, to Ms. Tommi Tremaine.

The woman had begun the day as a guest on a live local morning talk show, where she proclaimed me an enemy of New York's homeless. She confirmed to the somewhat befuddled host that yes, she was talking to producers about selling the motion picture rights to her story. In fact, she would be flown out to Los Angeles this coming weekend, where she would presumably be wined and dined by Hollywood's most shameless opportunists.

When I left City Hall at about noon, late for a diplomatic lunch meeting uptown near the U.N., I encountered a protest by several hundred homeless people—organized by none other than Tommi Tremaine, with the assistance of the New York Civil Liberties Union. From what I gathered, as my security guards whisked me toward my waiting car, they intended to resist my standing orders that they be removed to the city's homeless shelters in inclement weather.

"Do you have any comment, Mr. Mayor?" asked a reporter on the scene.

"Just one." I turned toward the angry throng, cleared my throat, and said succinctly, "For your sakes, I hope that the temperature stays above freezing and that not another snowflake falls in this city for the remainder of the winter, because the streets will be deadly otherwise."

Now, here we were, a scant twelve hours later, with flurries that seemed to ominously foreshadow the big snow that had been falling along the lower eastern seaboard all afternoon and evening. According to the latest forecast, the storm was headed straight for New York.

I shivered as I walked from the car toward the porch, thinking of all the protesters I had encountered that afternoon, who foolishly intended to spend the night on the streets, thanks to Tommi Tremaine.

As I stepped into the warm house, my housekeeper greeted me with the news that there was an important call for me.

As I strode toward my study to answer the phone, I expected it to be about the homeless situation, since I had asked for regular updates.

Instead, I was caught entirely off guard when I heard Barnaby Tischler's terse greeting over the line.

"What is it, Barnaby?" I asked, instinctively bracing myself for bad news.

Could there possibly have been another murder?

"Ed, I'm in trouble," he said, despair edging into his shaky voice.

"What is it?" I asked, though I knew before he told me.

"You were right when you warned me about . . . they've been questioning me all day, Ed. They think that I killed Calvino and Killdaire."

"Who's been questioning you?"

"Detective Lazaro, mostly. I can tell he doesn't believe me, Ed. I swear on my great-grandmother's grave that I had nothing to do with this. Why would I kill two of my own employees? My business is in ruins because of it. The store's been closed, and at this time of year . . . Ed, I need help. Please." His voice rose in desperation.

"Okay, Barnaby," I said, clutching the receiver and perching on the edge of a leather wing chair, still wearing my wool overcoat. I pulled a pad and pen across the desk and told him, "Calm down."

"How can I stay calm when I'm a suspect in a murder case? Poor Wanda's a wreck too. I can't believe this is happening."

"If you're innocent—"

"I *am* innocent!" he thundered. "Don't you dare—"

"Barnaby, be quiet and listen to what I'm saying," I snapped. "If you're innocent, you have nothing to worry about. Don't get all worked up. It's very important to keep things in perspective at a time like this, so—"

"In perspective? Here's perspective for you. I don't have an alibi that can be checked out, remember? I was at home, alone. Wanda was out with her Garden Club and the housekeeper had the night off, so there's no one to—"

"What about neighbors? Wouldn't anyone have noticed that your car was there?"

"You've obviously never been to my house," he said wryly. "Let's just say I have a lot of property."

Having visited wealthy friends in Great Neck, I got the picture.

Barnaby didn't exactly live in a block-party-and-barbecue type neighborhood, where houses are close together and neighbors can freely indulge in nosiness.

More likely, he lived on a woodsy private drive, on an acre or more of prime real estate, behind high walls and hedges.

"I can't prove that I wasn't at the store when the murder took place, Ed."

"But you were home when they called to tell you what had happened."

"The time of death was between nine and ten, Ed, roughly the same as last time. I got the call at about eleven o'clock. That would have barely given me time to commit the murder and get out here to Long Island, but I know what they're thinking. That it wouldn't have been impossible, especially if traffic was cooperating."

"And did it cooperate that night?"

"You mean when I left the store at eight?"

"Yes."

He paused just long enough to make me set down my pen and frown, waiting for the reply.

"Well, just between you and me, Ed, there was a big accident on the Long Island Expressway in Queens, just before it meets up with the Van Wyck."

"And . . . ?"

"And I heard about that on the car radio right after I got on the road, heading for the Midtown Tunnel . . ."

Another pause.

"Keep talking, Barnaby," I said tersely.

"It's just that . . . well, you know how jumpy I am, Ed. I'm impatient. I hate to sit still. It's just the way I've always been, you know?"

"I know," I said, thinking, *get to the point.*

"So I headed uptown instead, and I took the Triborough Bridge. I went up through the Bronx on the Bruckner Expressway, and then I came back down across the Throgs Neck and took the Cross Island Expressway. That way, I figured I would overshoot all the traffic from the accident. But it probably took me twice as long anyway, since the bridges were all jammed up."

That was certainly a roundabout route to Great Neck, which is at the western edge of Nassau County, just over the border from Queens, a straight shot from midtown if you took the Queens Midtown Tunnel and the Long Island Expressway.

Barnaby's route had taken him *way* out of the way. I scribbled a note on my pad to check with the highway department to confirm the Monday-night accident on the L.I.E. near the Van Wyck. Knowing what a rush-hour accident can do to snarl New York traffic, I figured his story wasn't impossible to believe. And he *had* mentioned recently that patience wasn't one of his virtues.

Still, it wouldn't hurt to check the facts, I thought, before asking him, "Why is this just between you and me, Barnaby?"

"Because I didn't mention it to the police."

"What? Why didn't you?"

"Because they wouldn't buy it, Ed. It sounds made up. They would wonder why anyone would take that convoluted route from Manhattan to Long Island. They would be suspicious."

"Barnaby, I can't believe this. Why didn't you just tell them the truth?"

"I know, I should have. But I guess I panicked. I just kept thinking about how crazy it would sound—"

"It does, but it's the truth, isn't it?"

"Of course it's the truth!"

"Well, the truth is always important when you're giving an alibi for a murder, Barnaby!" I said, exasperated.

"I swear, Ed, I was in my car for almost two hours, stuck in traffic, and then I was at home watching television until I got the phone call."

I sighed. "What about the parking attendant? Can he vouch for the time that you took your car out of the garage?"

Barnaby snorted. "You would think so. But they had some new guy on duty who barely speaks English. When they finally got through to him, he said he didn't remember seeing me."

"That doesn't sound good, Barnaby."

"Tell me about it, Ed. The kid had to be high—I remember thinking that he seemed like he was on something, the way he drove my car up to the entrance of the garage. And he was wearing one of those portable CD players with the headphones. He seemed all wrapped up in the music. He barely looked at me.''

"That doesn't sound good," I heard myself repeating.

"No. But according to the police, even if the guy could vouch for the fact that I left the garage at eight o'clock, it technically doesn't prove anything. As far as they're concerned, I could have taken my car out of the garage, driven it around the city, and then double-parked it somewhere on the street nearby while I ran back to the store and committed the murder before making my get-away.''

He—rather, the detectives—had a point, one that didn't seem any more far-fetched than some of the other scenarios I had envisioned.

"Ed," he went on, "I'm telling you, they think I'm guilty, and I swear to you that I'm not. I didn't do this. I *couldn't* do it. I'm not capable.''

I wanted to believe him.

And for the most part, I did . . . except for a barely there mental reservation motivated by my cynical side, the part of me that has seen it all.

Over the years, as an attorney and politician, I've learned that virtually nothing is too far-fetched to believe, and that very few people are one hundred percent honest one hundred percent of the time.

Barnaby would have had, quite frankly, not just the motive, but the means and the opportunity to kill both Angelo Calvino and Marlon Killdaire.

Still, so would Simon Weatherly—who had been conspicuously absent from the post–tree-lighting party Monday night at the Rainbow Room.

I wondered now whether he had been at the Wells and Marino premiere party at Tavern-on-the-Green, and made a mental note to call Sybil and find out.

It was intriguing to recall that he had, according to her, been trying to finagle a spot on the guest list for the party—one of the most high-profile social events of the season. Another deliberate, ironclad alibi . . .

If Simon was really behind the murders.

If he wasn't . . .

For Barnaby's sake, I did my best to sound optimistic as I assured him that I would do what I could to help him.

But after I hung up the phone, I bleakly reminded myself that I wouldn't have a moment to spare with tomorrow's presidential visit.

_____NINE

For the second time that week, I awoke before dawn to the sounds of a storm battering Gracie Mansion. Climbing out of bed, I made my way to the window and peered out into whirling white nothingness.

An hour later, in my study, I hung up the telephone and sighed. The city was virtually paralyzed, with half a foot of snow on the ground and more on the way. Though the plows and salt trucks were doing their best, it was coming down faster than they could clear it away.

According to the Metropolitan Transit Authority, the subways were running but the commuter train lines expected extensive delays, with buses and ferries expected to fare even worse. The airports, of course, were closed, and so were the schools, as well as most businesses and stores.

I issued a statement advising anyone who didn't absolutely have to be out in this weather to stay put, restricting traffic within the city limits to emergency vehicles only.

I then spoke to the President, who reported that he was snowbound at the White House, and obviously would have to reschedule his trip. Since he was leaving for the Middle East on Friday, it wouldn't be until sometime next month.

"Stay warm and dry, Ed," he told me in parting. "If you ask me, this is the worst storm the East Coast has seen in decades.

Even that nasty blizzard of ninety-six doesn't hold a candle to this one. It's going to take quite a while for things to get back to normal when this passes."

"Looks that way," I agreed as the fierce wind rattled the windowpanes behind my desk.

I telephoned Sybil, who sounded grumpy when she came to the phone after I insisted that her housekeeper wake her.

"This is the one morning that everyone in this city is allowed to go back to bed and sleep until noon without guilt," she informed me. "Why are you tearing me away from my sweet dreams? This had better be good."

"I can promise it'll be quick," I told her. "Tell me, did you see Simon Weatherly at that Wells and Marino party on Monday night?"

"No, I didn't. In fact, I checked with the doorman when I went in to see if Weatherly was on the guest list, and he wasn't."

"What made you check?"

"Oh, you know me, Ed. I get a real kick out of knowing that people I dislike are forbidden to attend fabulous events to which I'm invited."

"You would go so far as to say that you dislike Simon Weatherly?"

"Who wouldn't? The man's a slimy cretin." She yawned. "Is this about the second Ramsey's murder?"

"Mmm."

"Any leads?"

"Mmm-mmm," I said noncommittally.

"Is Simon Weatherly your chief suspect?"

"Did I say that?"

"You didn't have to. Don't worry, I won't print a word until an arrest is made. And then I get—"

"I know. An exclusive." I sighed. "I have to go, Sybil. Get back to your sweet dreams."

"I'll try. You're not actually going out in this abominable weather, are you?"

"I haven't decided yet."

"You are a dedicated mayor, Ed."

"Feel free to print that."

"Nah. Not exciting enough." She yawned again. "I'm going back to bed."

After a breakfast of grapefruit and two mugs of steaming coffee, I came to the conclusion that it would be best not to venture down to City Hall, since driving all the way down there on snow-clogged, slippery streets promised to take up a big chunk of the morning.

Instead, I spent an hour-long conference call with my deputy mayors and various commissioners, some of whom had made it to City Hall and reported that it was a virtual ghost town.

We briefed each other, juggled our schedules, and resolved various storm-related issues. To my relief, I learned that most of the homeless who had been approached by human services workers on the city streets overnight had allowed themselves to be moved to the extra shelters we had set up because of the storm, despite their orders from Tommi Tremaine and the New York Civil Liberties Union.

With my telephone meeting taken care of, I tackled a mountain of paperwork that had been waiting for my attention, finishing all of the most pressing documents by late morning.

Then it was time to evaluate the rest of the day.

I could stay in my study and take advantage of being snowbound by going through the rest of the paperwork right down to the mundane but necessary items at the bottom of the stack.

Or I could pack the paperwork in my suitcase and bring it along on the plane to Barbados, which was what I had originally planned to do.

If I opted for the latter, I would find myself with a free afternoon.

An afternoon that could be spent investigating the Santa murders.

First stop: Sunnyside Gardens, Queens, via the subway. It had been a while since I had been on the number seven train, which goes across Forty-second Street in midtown Manhattan, then under the East River, emerging aboveground in Queens with stops from Long Island City to Flushing.

Though the snow was still coming down at a furious clip, I was pleased to see, when the train ventured out of the tunnel into broad daylight in Queens, that the tracks and platforms were being kept relatively clear. There were no delays.

Though the car was fairly empty, and I rode unnoticed for most of the trip, a group of young teenagers boarding at Queensboro Plaza did a double take when they spotted me sitting at one end of the car.

"Yo, it's the mayor!" one of them said excitedly.

"Yo, Eddie!" called another.

I waved and called, "How'm I doing, fellahs?"

"You rule, Koch!" I was told.

It's not often that an elected official hears such an unabashed compliment, and I was still grinning broadly when my bodyguards and I got off the train, walked down the steps, and found ourselves on Fortieth Street and Queens Boulevard. The borough's main thoroughfare was eerily hushed and drifted over with blowing snow.

We walked north up Fortieth Street, through a pleasant neighborhood that consisted mostly of large, boxy walk-up apartment buildings and two-story row houses. The streets were deserted except for a smattering of kids playing in the snow and one or two grim-faced adults picking their way along the snowy sidewalk.

I was bundled in a heavy parka with a hood, a scarf covering my entire face except for my eyes.

Still, I heard somebody calling, "Hey, Ed! Ed, is that you, Ed?"

I turned and saw an elderly man—a man I had never before seen in my life—waving with one arm as he used the other to sweep snow off the stoop of a small brick house across the street.

The strange thing about being mayor of New York is, people will recognize you under any circumstances. It never ceases to amaze me.

The old man called, "So when are the plows going to get to us?"

"As soon as they can," I promised. I had authorized overtime for all the snowplow operators, but in a city this size, with the snow still coming down hard, it would be a long time before all the streets were cleared.

We crossed tree-lined Skillman Avenue, then turned right and headed east for a few blocks until we came to a neat redbrick two-family row house that bore Marlon Killdaire's address.

The upper apartment, I knew from newspaper accounts, was vacant. The tenants, a Korean family, had moved out on the first of the month, and couldn't be located for comment on the murder of their former neighbor.

I opened the outer storm door to block the wind, and was about to ring the bell for the first floor apartment, when I clearly heard voices inside.

"Don't leave, David. At least stay with me tonight. You shouldn't go out in this storm."

"I'll be fine. The subway's running."

"Then stay for me, David. I don't want to be alone," a female voice pleaded.

"Let Mike stay with you, then, Ma. Look, I have to get out of here."

"Michael can't be here, David. Anne is overdue, and she needs him at home with the little ones—"

"Ma, I'm sorry, but I've got to get going. I didn't plan to stay even this long."

"But I don't want to—"

"You'll be *fine*, Ma. I don't have time for this. I'll call in a few days."

There were a couple of brief footsteps on the other side of the door, and then it jerked open.

I found myself face-to-face with a scowling young man whom I recognized as Marlon Killdaire's elder son. Despite the frigid temperatures, he wasn't even wearing a hat over his long, shaggy dark hair, which half hid a long, pale face. His dark eyes were shadowed by bushy brows, and they narrowed suspiciously when he glanced from me to my bodyguards.

"Yeah?" he growled.

I got right to the point, sensing he was about to bolt. "Are you David Killdaire?"

"Yeah."

"I'm Ed Koch . . ."

"Yeah . . ."

Apparently, his vocabulary consisted of only one word, I thought.

"I'm very sorry about your dad. Can I ask you a few questions about him?"

"Nope," he said promptly, and my theory crumbled.

"It will take only a minute or two—"

"No." He flung that over his shoulder as he headed down the sidewalk, plodding through the shin-deep snow. I watched as he crossed Skillman Avenue, turned right, and strode off down Forty-third Street, back toward Queens Boulevard.

"What do you want to talk to my son about?"

At the sound of the voice, I looked up and saw a woman standing in the doorway, her hand on the knob. I knew she was Alva Killdaire.

Her hair was pulled straight back from her plain face the way it had been in the newspaper photo I had seen. She was dressed in a black, long-sleeved dress that hung on her thin frame, and chunky-heeled black shoes.

"Mrs. Killdaire, I'm Ed Koch . . ."

She nodded. The expression in her weary, red-rimmed eyes wasn't hostile, as her son's had been, but it wasn't particularly welcoming either.

"I'm terribly sorry about your husband."

Her thin lips tightened and she nodded slightly. I noticed that she clutched a white hanky in her fingers, and that her hand was trembling. She was the very picture of a grieving widow, and my heart went out to her.

"May we come in?" I asked.

She looked hesitant, and I realized that she was looking my bodyguards over.

"They're my security team," I informed Alva Killdaire.

"I worked for a while in your husband's precinct. He was a great cop and a great guy," Mohammed Johnson spoke up.

She made a choked little sound and nodded. Then, without further prodding, she stepped back, holding the door open, and gestured for us to come in.

As I wiped my snowy boots on the small rubber mat in the tiny foyer, I glanced around. The place was dark, with old-fashioned rust and gold striped wallpaper that had to date back to the early seventies.

Alva Killdaire recovered her voice and said, "Come in."

Her heels made tapping sounds along the parquet floor as she led the way into a small, shabbily furnished living room. It contained your standard middle-class urban trappings—couch and recliner, television and stereo, framed family photos on the walls. There was an artificial Christmas tree loaded with tinsel, and shiny, multicolored old-fashioned metal ornaments.

Ultimately, nothing very unusual or even particularly eye-catching . . .

Then I noticed an old upright piano jammed into the far corner, behind a boxy end table and a rickety-looking old floor lamp.

"Do you play the piano?" I asked Mrs. Killdaire as I sat on the sofa. My bodyguards remained in the doorway, just outside the room, though they kept watch.

She shook her head, lowering herself to sit somewhat stiffly in the chair a few feet away. "Marlon does. He loves music. All kinds of music. Wanted to become a concert violinist when he was a little boy, but his parents couldn't afford the lessons. He taught himself the best he could as he was growing up."

"Taught himself? On what?"

"He has a violin. His grandfather brought it over from Europe years and years ago. He has always treasured that instrument. When I met him, he had been accepted to a music conservatory in Europe. He had planned to go . . . but he didn't."

"Why not?"

"Because we got married instead," she said quietly. "We had a baby on the way, and—I would never have stood in his way, but he made a choice, and he chose me and our family."

"I'm sure he never regretted that choice, Mrs. Killdaire."

"He didn't. But anyway," she said with a sigh, "Marlon still hopes—*hoped*—to take lessons someday, even though he knew he would never play professionally, with a symphony orchestra."

"That's an ambitious goal."

"He had a lot of big plans a long time ago, before the boys started growing and needing—well, there are always expenses when you're raising children," she said in a faraway voice. "But Marlon was happy being my husband and their father and a policeman. He really was content. And the boys never knew what he gave up for his family. They don't even know he played the violin, or that he has one."

"Why not?"

"That's just how Marlon is," she said with a shrug. "I think that for him, it's part of another life. It's waiting there for him, for retirement, and he won't pick it up until he knows he won't have to put it down again. He's very good at the piano though. It was in the apartment when we moved in years ago—the tenants couldn't get it out because the hallway had been narrowed at some point. Marlon was thrilled. He taught himself to play piano too. He's very good at it. He can pick out any tune on that keyboard."

I couldn't help noticing that she spoke of her husband in the present tense, the way so many newly widowed spouses do when the loss hasn't yet sunk in.

"Just the other night, he was sitting there playing Christmas carols while I decorated the tree," she said in a hollow tone. "He loved Christmas. He loved being Santa for all the kids at Ramsey's. . . ."

"How did he happen to get the job?" I asked her.

"My son suggested it."

"David?"

"Michael. He had worked at Ramsey's as Christmas seasonal help in the toy department for quite a few years, and he always thought Marlon would be the perfect Santa Claus. This year, when my husband had his accident and went out on disability, it was right around the time when they started that big Santa search. And my son brought my husband an application."

"I see."

"The extra money was nice, and so was the discount he got at the store," she said. "We were planning to get Michael's kids a big wooden toy train set for Christmas this year—the kind with all those different bridges and tunnels and fancy equipment. They would have loved it. But now . . . oh, I dread the holidays. I dread every day without him. . . ."

She trailed off, choked up.

I leaned forward, reached out, and patted her thin, bony hand that clenched the arm of the chair. I noticed the yellow-gold wedding ring on her fourth finger and again felt a pang of regret.

I tried to phrase my next question gently. "Do you have any idea who would have had reason to have harmed your husband, Mrs. Killdaire?"

She made a high-pitched, strangled sound, biting her lip and clenching my fingers. The woman was emotionally anguished—that much was obvious.

I paused, then said quietly, "I know this is difficult for you, Mrs. Killdaire, but it's important that we catch whoever committed this crime."

Her eyelids fluttered closed and she bent her head. "I really don't want to talk about it anymore, Mr. Mayor. Please . . . I've already told the detectives everything I know. . . ."

"Would you mind going over a few things with me again?" I pressed. "I want to help you, Mrs. Killdaire."

"Aren't you—" She stopped, shook her head as if puzzled, and started again. "Aren't you here just to say you're sorry? Isn't that what the mayor does—visits the families of police officers who are killed?"

"I do that, yes," I said, nodding, thinking of all the sorrowful widows and widowers I had comforted over the years, not just as a dutiful mayor, but because my heart went out to them.

I went on. "In your case, I'm not here just to pay a sympathy call, Mrs. Killdaire. I'm here to assist with the investigation into the murder of your husband, and anything you can tell me would be helpful."

She bit her trembling lower lip and finally nodded.

"You said you told the police what you know," I told her gently. "Does that mean you know something?"

She shrugged and said faintly, "Marlon was a cop, Mr. Mayor. A lot of people don't like cops—especially upright ones like my husband."

"He had enemies?"

She tilted her head. "Everyone has enemies. As a politician, you should know that. Look at you—you can't make a move without being followed by all those bodyguards." She gestured at the somber-faced men gathered in the doorway, and added bitterly,

"But nobody protects police officers, Mr. Mayor. I wish to God my husband had had his gun on him the night he was killed. . . ." Her voice broke and she pressed a fist to her mouth.

"Had anyone threatened your husband?"

"Threatened? Not that I know of. But he wouldn't have told me. He knew I worried constantly about him as it was."

Something in her expression made me pursue the angle. "If there weren't direct threats, was there anything specific that made you concerned about his safety?"

"Every wife and husband of every law enforcement official is concerned about their safety."

"I'm aware of that. It goes with the territory. But your husband . . . did anything ever happen to him that made you wonder if he was in excessive danger?"

"There were a few hang-up calls late at night several months ago," she acknowledged, sounding reluctant. "But there's no reason to think it was because of Marlon's police work. In fact, I'm fairly certain it wasn't. . . ."

"What else could it have been?"

She shrugged. "My son—he lived with us until a year ago. He used to get phone calls at all hours of the night. Maybe somebody was trying to reach him . . . I don't know."

"Your son . . . David? The one who just left?"

She nodded. "He lives in New Jersey now."

"Why did he move out?"

"Why does any adult move out of his parents' house?" she asked, meeting my gaze and lifting her pointy chin.

But something, some sixth sense, told me she was hiding something.

"What was your son's relationship with your husband?" I asked her.

"Marlon was a wonderful father. He spent a lot of time with the boys as they were growing up. Used to take them to Coney Island and to the movies . . ."

"That's not what I asked, Mrs. Killdaire. I was curious about David's relationship with his father. His *recent* relationship with him."

"Why do you want to know about that?"

"Just curious. They didn't get along, did they?" It was a statement, not a question, and I could tell by the flicker of anger in her eyes, even as she started to shake her head, that I was right.

"What father and son get along perfectly?" she demanded.

I noted that for a fleeting moment her glance shifted to the wall behind me before skittering away again, back to her hands in her lap.

I turned and followed the direction her gaze had taken.

There, I saw a large, framed snapshot of Marlon Killdaire and a young man I recognized as his other son, Michael. They had their arms slung casually around each other's shoulders and looked as though they had just finished laughing heartily together at some private joke.

"Your husband got along with Michael, didn't he, Mrs. Killdaire?"

She nodded. "They were always together. Two peas in a pod. Loved to do the same things. Michael wanted to be a cop like his dad, but he couldn't get into the police force."

"Why not?"

"He was hit by a city bus when he was a little boy. His right leg was badly mangled and had to be amputated. He has a prosthesis."

"That's a shame. What does he do?"

"You mean, for a living?"

I nodded.

"Michael works wherever he can find it. He has his hands full with three jobs these days. His wife, Anne, is expecting their fifth child."

"Five children?"

"We're good Catholics, Mr. Mayor," she said calmly. "Children are a blessing from God. If I could have had more, I would have, but . . ." She trailed off and shook her head, renewed pain reflected in her eyes.

"It can't be easy to raise a large family in New York these days," I observed. "Or anywhere else, for that matter."

"They're struggling financially, but my son is determined to provide," she said proudly.

"What about David?"

"What about him?"

"What does he do?"

She hesitated only for a moment, but long enough for me to realize that she was reluctant to answer the question. "He's a musician," she told me.

"Oh . . . ?"

"Yes."

"Does he play the piano like your husband does?" I asked when she didn't elaborate.

"He sings," came the terse reply.

"Where?"

"Excuse me?"

"Where does he sing?" I inquired pleasantly. "Is he in a band, or does he perform solo?"

"He used to have a band, quite a few years back, when he was in high school. Lately, he's solo. . . ."

But she sounded unsure of herself.

"How does he make a living?"

"How does any aspiring artist make a living?" she asked, sounding defensive again. "He works here and there to pay the bills."

"Here and there?"

"He's done some bartending. And . . . he was a salesman at Ramsey's for a while. . . ." She trailed off, and I surmised that she had pretty much summed up her son's job history.

"Is he married?"

"No—"

The sudden ringing of the telephone made both of us jump, startled.

"I have to get that," Alva Killdaire said, rising and hurrying into the next room.

I heard her say hello, and then, "Oh, Michael, is it Anne? . . . No? Well, how is she? . . ."

There was a pause, and she said, "No, he just left . . . I don't know where . . . No, he wouldn't . . . Michael, it's all right. I'll be fine . . . No, you have enough to—Michael, you just go home to Anne and the kids after work. Don't worry about me. Listen, I have company right now . . ."

With that, she lowered her voice and I couldn't hear the rest of the one-sided conversation.

Minutes later, she reappeared in the living room. "I'm sorry about that, Mr. Mayor," she said, the brief interruption having erased the faint mistrust that had been in her eyes moments earlier.

"That's all right," I assured her. "It was your son?"

"Michael," she said, nodding. "He told me to tell you whatever I knew so that you could help to solve the case. And he said that he'd like to talk to you as well."

Intrigued, I said, "How can I reach him?"

"He's at work right now—he's a janitor at Con Edison. His shift doesn't end until late tonight. He asked me to give you his home number and ask you to call him early in the morning. Maybe you can talk to him before he leaves for his other job—he does morning deliveries for a bakery in his neighborhood."

"Which neighborhood is that?"

"Long Island City."

"So he stayed close to home," I said, nodding. "It must make you happy to have your grandchildren nearby."

"It does. Marlon . . . he doted on those babies. They're so young . . . they're never going to know—" Her voice broke and she wiped her eyes.

I cleared my throat. "I realize this is a very difficult time for you, Mrs. Killdaire . . ."

"It is . . . I really need to be alone. Please, Mr. Koch . . ."

I hesitated, a small part of me tempted to continue with my questioning. Still, I could see there was very little chance that the fragile woman would be able to carry on a conversation at this point. She had told me very little that I hadn't already read in newspaper accounts of the crime. Gathering more facts would be painstaking, and seemed unfair under the circumstances.

My humanitarian instincts won out, and I stood and buttoned my overcoat. "I've appreciated your assistance, Mrs. Killdaire," I told her. "I'd like to talk to you again. And if there's anything important, anything you've forgotten to mention or feel that I should know, please call me at any time." I handed her a card with my private telephone number on it.

She took it and brought it over to a large gilt mirror hanging on the wall between the two windows. She wedged the corner of the card carefully into the crack between the frame and the glass, then smiled faintly at me.

"I won't lose it that way. I've been so forgetful these past few days . . . last night I forgot to turn off the stove after I made a cup of tea. I had taken the sedatives my doctor prescribed for me. . . . If it wasn't for David being here, I could have burned the place down."

"You really shouldn't be left alone at a time like this, Mrs. Killdaire," I pointed out. "Couldn't one of your sons stay with you for a few weeks—or a few more days, at least?"

Her smile faded and she shook her head. "I'll be fine. But thank you for your concern. I've always liked you, Mr. Mayor. So did Marlon. We both voted for you every time."

"Thank you. Please call me if there's anything I can do."

"I will."

She seemed about to say something else, but her mouth remained closed.

I waited.

She started walking toward the door, and I knew our visit was over.

I took the number seven train back to Manhattan, getting off at the Fifth Avenue and Forty-second Street stop. The main branch of the New York Public library is located on that corner, and it was open despite the still-falling snow. White drifts had nearly obscured the famous stone lions guarding the main entrance.

The place was virtually deserted, which allowed me to go about my research in peace.

Less than two hours later, I emerged into the stormy winter dusk with several weighty books, along with photocopied articles, statistics, and reports.

"Where to now, Mr. Mayor?" called Ambrose above the blowing wind and sifting sound of grainy snow. He blew on his gloved hands as we plodded carefully down the slippery steps to the deserted sidewalk.

"Gracie Mansion," I decided. "I have a lot of reading to do tonight."

"I take it you're not talking about snuggling up with a bestselling novel," Lou Sabatino said ruefully, eyeing the volume of research material I was toting along.

"You take it right," I agreed, leading the way along the street toward the bright green globe that marked the subway entrance.

In the hours that lay ahead, I planned to learn everything there was to know about serial killers.

___TEN

Friday morning dawned gray and blustery, the snow had abated to light flurries, though the city was, for the most part, utterly buried. Over thirty inches had fallen in the metropolitan area, with more in the northern and western suburbs.

It promised to be another slow day as most New Yorkers hibernated indoors, with only a few hardy souls venturing to dig their way out from beneath the vast white drifts that had buried stoops and sidewalks, cars and curbs.

I fully intended to head down to City Hall, though I was still deciding whether to take the car or subway, when I received a call from Helen, one of my deputy mayors, who had already made the trip.

"Don't bother," she said, and went on to inform me that there had been a problem with the heating system overnight. Pipes had burst, the place was freezing, and I should stay home, since there was no reason to witness the disaster firsthand. They would operate on a skeleton staff until they got some heat.

"I'll be down later to check the damage," I informed her.

"But why, Ed?"

"Because I'm the mayor," I said simply. "If there's a problem at City Hall, I'm going to be there in person and see what I can do about it."

146 / Edward I. Koch

I then telephoned Michael Killdaire in Long Island City. The phone was answered on the fourth ring.

There was a clattering sound indicating that someone seemed to be banging the receiver against a hard surface.

I frowned.

Then . . .

"Heh-wo?" came the voice of a very young child.

I had to smile.

"Hello, is your daddy there?" I asked, clearly enunciating every word.

Another clattering sound, this time as if the receiver had been dropped.

I winced and held the phone away as I heard the child holler, "Da-addy! Teh-wa-phone."

A moment later a man picked up the line with a weary "Yes?"

"Is this Michael Killdaire?"

"Yes . . ."

"This is Ed Koch, Mr. Killdaire."

"Oh! Mr. Mayor, I'm real sorry about that . . . I was getting ready to leave for work and my wife was changing a diaper, so we asked our three-year-old son to get it. . . ."

"He was charming," I assured him. "And very competent."

"Yeah, well . . ." He sounded embarrassed. "What can I do for you?"

"As you know, I was at your mother's home yesterday. I'm looking into your father's murder. Your mother mentioned that you might be willing to talk to me about it."

"Definitely. I'm very eager to help with the investigation in any way I can," he said grimly.

"You mentioned that you were on your way to work. . . ."

"I am. I do morning deliveries for a local bakery. After that I have to go to my other job—"

"At Con Edison?"

"Yeah. I'm a janitor there."

"Would you have time to talk tomorrow?"

He hesitated. "I've got a weekend job . . . I'm working Saturdays and Sundays in a sporting goods store over on Steinway Street from now until Christmas."

"What time?"

"Normally ten to six, but it's ten to ten tomorrow because one of the guys was fired yesterday."

"I see."

It seemed that Michael Killdaire's schedule was even more hectic than mine.

"How about Sunday?" I asked. I hated to wait that long to talk to him. Still, I was flying to Barbados at one o'clock that afternoon, and I had to go through Queens on my way to the airport anyway, so—

"I work from twelve until eight that day," Michael Killdaire informed me. "But I'm a eucharistic minister at our church, and I have to serve on the altar at ten o'clock mass."

I pondered that and made a decision. "How much time do you have today between your bakery job and Con Ed, Michael?"

"Less than an hour. It wouldn't be enough time for me to come into Manhattan and—"

"No, but if I came out to Queens, it would be enough time for us to sit down and talk, wouldn't it?"

"I guess so."

"Then that's what we'll do."

He seemed to hesitate, then asked, "Where do you want to meet?"

"How about Asta?" I suggested promptly, naming one of my favorite Greek diners in the city, located beneath the elevated N train on Thirty-first Street, on the border between Long Island City and Astoria. Ambrose, who had grown up on Ditmars Boulevard in Astoria, had recommended it several years ago.

They have the most delicious Greek salad I've ever tasted, and I was in the mood for something light, having indulged in the meat loaf, mashed potatoes, and gravy Lucien had made last night. He's very big on comfort food, particularly on stormy winter days.

"Asta would be great," Michael Killdaire said, sounding relieved. "That's halfway between my house and Con Ed."

"That's what I figured."

"Can you, uh, come alone, Mr. Mayor? Because I really want this to be between you and me."

"I'll come alone," I told him. "Well, except for my body-guards."

There was a pause. "Bodyguards?"

"I can't go anywhere without them. But don't worry. They're trustworthy and discreet. In fact, they're all members of the NYPD, and one of them knew your father. He thought very highly of him."

"Oh . . . that's great."

He sounded edgy.

"So what time do I need to be there, Michael?"

"Are you sure you want to do this? I mean, it's so far out of your way, and we can just talk another—"

"No," I cut in, "I will be there. You just tell me when."

After arranging the time to meet, I hung up and spun around in my swivel chair. My gaze fell on the stack of books and papers on a table by the reading chair beside the fireplace. It was there that I had spent the better part of the previous evening, poring over pages of information about serial killers.

While it was likely that the same person had killed both Angelo Calvino and Marlon Killdaire, I was reluctant to buy into the theory that the murderer was a crazed stranger who had committed the crimes primarily for the sport of killing.

I had learned that the vast majority of serial killers are influenced by deviant sexual behavior, which seemed to have no bearing in the Ramsey's case.

Furthermore, I had discovered that some killers are motivated by the pleasure of hunting and killing, and they tend to abduct and torture their victims. Others seek power, power that is stoked by the fear of their victims. They, too, abduct and torture their prey.

Both Calvino and Killdaire had been ambushed from behind and shot within a matter of seconds, and chances were that they never knew what—or who—hit them. This was entirely out of keeping with the methods used by most serial killers.

But then again, the Santa slayings had managed to throw the world's most visible metropolis into a media-fueled turmoil. One would be hard pressed to find a single New Yorker—or, more likely, a single *American*—who hadn't heard about the grisly murders at Ramsey's Department Store on those two consecutive bloody Monday nights.

And my research had revealed that many serial killers, with their maniacal egos, feed off the anonymous notoriety.

It was conceivable, then, that whoever had killed Angelo Calvino and Marlon Killdaire lurked now in our midst, chuckling to himself over the multitudinous press accounts of befuddled detectives, distraught children, and panicky New Yorkers . . . and that he planned to continue the grisly game.

After inspecting the damage at a chilly City Hall and being assured that everything would be up and running again by tomorrow, I found myself with over an hour to kill before meeting Michael Killdaire.

I decided that it wouldn't hurt to drop by the scene of the crime, and instructed my driver to head back uptown to Thirty-fourth Street.

The snow had finally stopped falling, though the skies over New York remained a milky gray shade that mirrored the vast drifts blanketing the streets and sidewalks. Lower Manhattan seemed to be showing signs of gradually stirring back to life, and by the time we reached midtown—slow going, thanks to slippery, snow-clogged roads—a smattering of pedestrians and traffic had reappeared, though not nearly at a normal level for a Friday afternoon during the Christmas season.

The sidewalk in front of Ramsey's Department Store had been shoveled down to the bare concrete, and enormous signs at the Thirty-fourth Street entrance trumpeted a new shipment of Henrietta Hyenas, the elusive laughing puppet coveted by children far and wide.

Even that amazing feat didn't seem to have generated much inspiration in the few passersby on the street. It wasn't that they didn't notice the store, because they did.

In fact, as I stepped out of my car I saw several knots of people standing on the sidewalk, gawking at Ramsey's as though the bodies of the two dead Santas were graphically displayed in the vast plate-glass windows.

But no one seemed willing to venture inside, past the security guards and metal detectors that were plainly visible from the street.

No one except me.

Trailed by my own security team, I pushed through the revolving door. The Ramsey's security team hustled to attention as though they were eager for something to do.

"Hello, Mr. Mayor," said one of the men. "I'm sorry, but I have to ask you to step through this metal detector."

I recalled that the last time we had been in the store, my security team had been allowed to sidestep the device, and I had been invited to do the same.

"No problem," I assured the guard, passing through the detector. "I'm always glad to follow security procedures."

My bodyguards—who are, of course, armed—stepped around the metal detector.

Then we all ventured into the expansive, seemingly deserted first floor of the store.

Jaunty holiday music was playing in the background, and there were fresh greens, red velvet bows, and white lights everywhere you looked. Still, the festive trappings did little to erase the eerie sense of desolation in the nearly empty store.

"Ed?"

I turned at the sound of a vaguely familiar voice that virtually echoed in the cavernous space. There, waving from behind a counter laden with ladies' hats and earmuffs, was the saleswoman I had met last weekend.

"Hello," I called, waving back.

She fiddled with the chain that held her glasses around her neck, then settled them on the bridge of her nose. "I thought that was you!" she exclaimed.

"It's me." I made my way toward her.

She reached up to pat the white curls into place on top of her head as she said, "I'll bet you don't remember my name."

"Of course I do. It's Dotty."

She broke into a pleased smile. "Oh, my, how did you remember that?"

I shrugged. "How could I forget you?"

"Are you here to buy more presents for your family?" she asked eagerly. "Because we just got in the most delightful poinsettia caps—"

"Maybe I'll take a look at them in a few minutes," I told her, leaning closer and lowering my voice slightly—not that there was anyone lurking nearby to eavesdrop. "You weren't working the night of the murder, were you?"

Her smile faded faster than a tan in December. "You mean the second murder?" she asked, looking grim.

When I nodded, she said, "You bet I was. That was a terrible night for me, what with all the commotion from the shoplifter and all. . . ."

"What shoplifter?"

She sighed. "Oh, some young punk who thought I wasn't sharp enough to notice him sticking five leather handbags under his coat."

"*Five* handbags?"

"They weren't even designer bags—we keep those locked in the display cases. Why a *boy* would want to steal empty purses is beyond me, although you never know these days."

"No, you never do," I murmured. "When did this happen?"

"Just before closing," she said. "I remember that I hadn't eaten dinner and I was terribly hungry. I was planning to go over to that deli down the block on my way to the subway and get myself a Reuben and a cream soda—do you like cream soda, Ed?" she interrupted herself to ask.

I nodded and started to ask her another question about the shoplifter, when she went on. "I don't like it myself. Not usually. But for some reason, on Monday night I felt like having a cream soda. I'm just that way sometimes. For example, I never could stand fish, but once in a while I'll march over to the pub in my neighborhood and I'll order a fish and chips to go. And do you know what?"

"What?" I asked helplessly.

"I eat it. Every bit of it," she said solemnly. "I even put vinegar on the chips—that's what they call french fries over in England, did you know that?"

"I—"

"Why do you suppose that is?"

"I don't—"

"Never been to England," she mused. "Have you?"

Exasperated, I nonetheless admitted, "I've been there a few times."

"Well, you're a mayor. Mayors travel. My brother was a shoe-maker. But he went to England. In fact, he died in England. He and his wife were there for their fortieth wedding anniversary, and he dropped dead of an aortic aneurysm right in front of Bucking-ham Palace. I don't even know if he ever had a chance to taste the fish and chips over there before he died, poor thing. His name was Louie, but everyone called him Loony. We were quite a pair when we were growing up." She giggled. "Dotty and Loony."

I couldn't think of a thing to say to that.

"So I was planning to get a Reuben and a cream soda"—amazingly, she picked up her story exactly where she had left off—"and then I saw this shoplifter out of the corner of my eye. He was the worst shoplifter I've ever seen. Looked guilty, like he was sneaking around. And there were purse straps hanging out from underneath his coat."

"So what happened?"

"I picked up the phone and called security. One of the plain-clothes guys came walking over, and the kid took off running. But you know what he did? He went right for the escalator, and he ran *up* the down escalator."

"Why wouldn't he try to leave the store?"

"I think he got confused and panicked," Dotty said. "Or maybe he figured he couldn't get past the security guards at the exits—even though they were only keeping an eye out for people who were trying to get *in.*"

"What happened to the shoplifter?" I asked thoughtfully.

"It was quite a scene. Several security guards chased him up the escalator, and a couple of cops came running in from the street, and they were chasing him too. They caught him on the fourth floor, hiding under a bed in Fine Linens. And I was so shaken up by the whole thing that I never did get my Reuben or my cream soda. In fact, I took a cab home right after that, instead of the subway, and I made myself a can of Campbell's Chicken and Stars soup, but I barely touched it."

"That's a shame," I muttered, frowning. "What time did you say this shoplifter was in the store?"

"Right before closing," she said. "At about ten to ten, maybe five to ten."

I pondered that. Marlon Killdaire had been murdered right around that time.

Could the shoplifter have been responsible?

For the first time in a long time, I felt that I had stumbled upon a true lead.

I told Dotty that it had been nice talking to her, then hurried off to my appointment with Michael Killdaire.

"Have you ever eaten here before?" I casually asked the young man seated across from me in the crowded Asta diner.

He looked nervous and I found myself wanting to put him at ease—and not only because it would be easier to question him if he were relaxed.

It was just that Michael Killdaire was one of those people that one can't help liking on sight. Just as Simon Weatherly is one of those people you can't help strongly disliking the moment you meet him.

Marlon Killdaire's younger son had an easygoing demeanor despite the pronounced limp in his walk and the dark circles under his eyes, which seemed to betray sleepless nights and profound grief.

At my question about whether he had ever been to Asta before, Michael glanced up from his menu, which he held clenched in slightly trembling hands that, I noticed, were terribly chapped. I had noticed that he wasn't wearing gloves when he came in, and that the cuffs of his green down jacket were frayed.

"I was here once, a long time ago. My wife and I don't get out to eat much now that we have the kids," he confessed, looking slightly embarrassed. "But I hear the food is great. Have you ever been here, Mr. Mayor?"

"A few times. And lunch is on me, so order anything you want."

"What do you recommend?"

"The moussaka," I said without hesitation. "It's out of this world."

"Is that what you're having?"

"Nope."

He glanced up, looking slightly startled, and I chuckled. "You must be the one New Yorker who doesn't know that I'm watching my weight. I'm just having the Greek salad and maybe a plain pita pocket on the side."

Oh, who was I kidding? I had conveniently forgotten, until then, about all the feta cheese, olives, and oil packed into a heaping Asta Greek salad, making it about as slimming as a bowl of Häagen-Dazs.

"So you won't mind if I ask you some questions?" I asked Michael when the amiable waitress had taken our orders and chatted endlessly with me, Michael, and all of my bodyguards, who were strategically grouped around the place, keeping an eye on our table.

"That's why we're here, isn't it?" he asked, sipping from the small glass of ice water in front of him. He still looked pretty nervous, though the discussion about food and the waitress's banter had been a momentary distraction.

"But before I say anything, I need to make sure this is just between you and me," he told me.

I nodded.

"And I don't want anyone to overhear us, so keep your voice down, okay, Mr. Mayor?"

"Absolutely. Nobody can hear a thing with all this racket anyway," I said, glancing around the jam-packed diner. People were chattering, dishes were clattering, phones were ringing—you couldn't hear a conversation in the next booth.

Still, I saw Michael Killdaire cast a long, wary glance at my bodyguards. "They don't have you bugged or anything, do they? You know, so they can eavesdrop on your conversations?"

"No. And they can't hear us from where they are, so don't worry," I assured him, thinking he was extremely paranoid and wondering why. He clearly had something very sensitive to reveal to me.

He fiddled with the scalloped edge of the paper place mat on the table in front of him.

Before he could change his mind about talking to me, I placed my elbows on the table and leaned toward him.

"Do you know who killed your father, Michael?" I asked point-blank.

He shook his head. "I don't *know.*"

The way he emphasized the word made me pause, watching him carefully. I rephrased the question.

"Do you have any theories about someone who might have had reason to kill your father?"

He glanced around, then at me, and leaned across the table. "There are a few people who weren't overly fond of Pop, if you know what I mean."

"One being your brother, David."

His eyes widened and he sat back abruptly. "Who told you that?"

I shrugged. "Do you think your brother was capable of killing your father?"

"I can't believe David would do something like that." He shook his head, his voice just above a whisper.

"That's not what I asked you. I asked you if he was capable. If he *could* have done it."

Michael Killdaire's slight hesitation was all the answer I needed, but I didn't reveal a thing as I watched him, waiting.

"My brother has always been screwed up," he said at last. "He was always in trouble with Pop. When we were kids, he was the one who thought up all the things I knew we shouldn't do, and I usually backed out. But he never did. He always went through with the stupid stuff. And he always got caught. You would think he would have learned, but he never did."

"What kind of stuff did he do?"

"Just kid stuff, but way before any of the rest of us thought of it."

"Like what?"

"Like the time he stole cigarettes from the deli across the street and smoked them—he was barely eight. And the time he cut school to take the subway to Times Square and sneak into those peep shows—he was twelve. David wasn't afraid of anything," he told me, shaking his head and wearing a faraway expression. "Not even afraid of Pop."

"You were?"

"Everyone was. My father was a big man. He was a cop. You didn't screw around with him."

"But you got along with him?"

He nodded, and when he looked up and met my gaze directly, I saw tears glistening in his eyes. "I loved my father, Mr. Mayor. He was my best friend in the world. I just . . . I can't believe he's gone."

"Your brother doesn't seem too broken up over it."

"Yeah, well"—he lifted his chin and swallowed hard, composing himself—"David and Pop never got along, like I said. Especially lately."

"Ever since David moved out." It was a statement, not a question.

He nodded. "They haven't talked to each other ever since that."

"Why did your brother move out?"

"Pop kicked him out," he said, looking surprised I didn't know that.

"Why is that?"

"Because . . . my mother didn't tell you, did she?" That, too, was a statement and not a question.

"No, she didn't."

"She wouldn't. That's how she is."

"What happened?"

"David hit her."

"I see."

"He wanted her to give him some money—I guess she had been slipping him money all along. He never held down a job, you know? He was always mooching. I got so sick of it that I put myself on the line a few years ago and got him hired at Ramsey's as Christmas help in the men's furnishings department. I thought maybe he would turn himself around. He got caught stealing his second day."

"Stealing what?"

"Cash, what else? Right from the cash register. He was so

desperate, he wasn't even sneaky about it. I guess it was because
. . . my brother had a gambling problem."

"He was in debt?"

"Always. That was constantly a huge thing between him and
my father. Pop made him pay rent to live at home—a lot less than
David would have paid in an apartment, but Pop refused to give
him any handouts, and he had told my mother not to. Not that
she listened. She always spoiled my brother, from the time we
were kids."

"Why is that?"

Michael shrugged. "Maybe she felt sorry for him. David never
really had any friends, and he was always getting into trouble. . . .
Besides, she was his mother. She wanted to protect him. That's
what mothers do, isn't it? My wife is the same way. One of our
kids does something wrong, and right away she's making excuses
for him."

"So what happened with your brother?"

"This one day, when David asked Ma for some money, she
either got fed up, or she didn't have any cash for him. She said
no, and he smacked her. With his fist. In the face."

"And your father found out? Did your mother tell him?"

"I did."

"Were you there when it happened?"

"No. But I showed up right after that, and Ma was crying and
had an ice pack on her face, and my brother was slamming things
around in his room, cursing her out. I figured out what was going
on. It wasn't hard."

"Did either of them admit it?"

"Are you kidding? But that didn't matter. I know what had
happened, and Pop knew what had happened. He threw David
out that night, and that was it."

"So who killed him?" I asked matter-of-factly. "Was it your
brother?"

He looked me in the eye. "No."

"You're sure of that?"

"Not a hundred percent . . ."

"No?"

"But ninety-nine-point-ninety-nine percent sure," he said hastily.

"What about your father's life insurance? Did he carry anything in addition to what his police job provided?"

"Actually, he did take out an extra policy. He always said he wanted to make sure Mom was taken care of in case something happened to him. She's not a very strong woman. She wouldn't be able to go out and work or anything."

"Did he have anything else? Besides the insurance policy, I mean?" I was thinking of the violin, the family heirloom that Alva Killdaire had said his sons didn't know he had.

I happened to know that heirloom violins can be worth quite a bit of money—particularly the prized Stradivarius.

"Pop did have a savings account," Michael confided. "He was always putting money away, saving for retirement. I always said, 'What are you saving for, Pop? You going off to see the world?' And he would laugh, because he wasn't the type who liked to travel. The farthest he's ever been from home is Albany. I think that deep down inside, that's what he was looking forward to after he retired. I think he thought maybe he would take my mother and the two of them would just set sail for someplace. . . ." He trailed off and cleared his throat.

I thought about the Marlon Killdaire his wife had revealed, the man who secretly yearned to learn to play an instrument he'd kept locked away for all those years.

"It's such a waste," Michael mused. "He was always saving for the future, my father. Now he doesn't have a future . . . and all that money is sitting there in the bank, when he could have been enjoying his life."

"Does your mother inherit the money your father left, then, Michael?"

"Most of it. He said he was leaving some to me, to help with the kids, and some to my brother. And I was the executor of the will."

"Do you know how much—"

"Here we go, fellahs," interrupted the waitress, who breezed over, plunking down Michael's moussaka and coffee and my salad and diet Coke.

Naturally, she felt compelled to stick around and chatter some more. The diner was filled to capacity, and you would think she had other tables to attend to, but she leaned against the coatrack beside our booth, her arms folded across her pink uniform as she made conversation like she had all the time in the world.

When she finally bustled back to the kitchen, I picked up my fork, held it poised over the heaping bowl in front of me, and addressed Michael Killdaire once again.

"You think, that with money as a possible motive, your brother David *might* have killed your father?" I prodded.

"No," he said once again. "I think it was someone else."

"Who?" I sensed that he was hedging, so I popped a big forkful of salad into my mouth, as though I wasn't hanging on his every word.

Still, he hesitated. "My mother doesn't know anything about any of this. . . ."

"Any of what?"

"Any of what I'm going to tell you. She was squeamish about Dad's being a cop anyway, and he didn't like to worry her any more than she already worried. But something was going on with Pop on the job."

"What is that?" I reached for my glass and took a swig of soda.

"You know he had a little car accident a few months back with his patrol car?"

I nodded. My interest piqued, I fought the urge to set my fork down. I continued eating, yet I watched him, waiting.

"That was no accident," he told me.

"What happened?"

He glanced around the restaurant, seeming to be particularly watchful of my bodyguards, before saying quietly, "Somebody sabotaged my father's car."

"Why would somebody do that?"

"Because Pop had found out something that somebody didn't want him to know."

"What was that?"

His eyes grew shadowed. "Pop was pretty sure that some of the cops in his precinct were on the take."

"What made him think that?"

"I don't know. He must have stumbled onto it. And believe me, my father wasn't the type of guy who would overlook something like that. He had a great sense of justice. That's why he went into law enforcement in the first place. He was trying to figure out what was going on, when he had the accident."

"So you think somebody found out that he was on to them, and tried to get rid of him by making it look like an accident?" I clarified.

"That's what I think." He took a small bite of his moussaka, not hungrily, but as if he needed a distraction. "That's what Pop thinks too—I mean, that's what he *thought.*"

I speared a large black olive and put it into my mouth, munching as I thought over what Michael was implying. "Did your father tell anyone what was going on?"

"Besides me? Nah."

"How do you know that?"

"He said he didn't. And he wasn't the type to go around blabbing about anything. Pop did things on his own. Said that was the only way to get things done."

"Why did he tell you?"

"Because he knew he could trust me."

"He just came out and told you this one day?"

"No. I asked. I knew something was worrying him, and I kept bugging him about it until he gave in and told me. And I think he was worried that something was going to happen to him too. I think he wanted someone to know what was going on so that if something *did* happen—which it did—whoever got to him wouldn't get away with it. He knew I wouldn't let that happen. Which is why I'm talking to you, Mr. Mayor. Until I found out you were at my mother's house that day, asking questions about the murder, I was trying to figure out what to do. I didn't know who I could trust."

"What, exactly, did your father tell you about the corruption he had uncovered?"

"No details. Nothing about who was specifically involved, just that they were officers in his precinct. He just said that he was planning to get all the information he needed as proof, and then take it straight to the commissioner."

"Did you tell any of this to the detectives looking into the investigation, Michael?"

The expression in his eyes gave me my answer before he spoke. "I told you, I didn't know who to trust. For sure, not them."

"You didn't trust them? They're trying to find out who killed your father."

"They're cops, Mr. Mayor. Do you know how many corrupt cops there are out there?"

"You're asking *me* that question?" I smirked, thinking about how my administration had fiercely cracked down on police corruption over the past few years.

"I'm sorry . . . I guess you do know," he said, looking a little sheepish before he put both of his hands, palms down, on the table in a no-nonsense pose. "But look, Mr. Mayor. I have a wife at home, and four kids. I don't know who to trust—besides you. If those detectives working on my father's murder happened to be connected in any way to what was going on in Pop's precinct, and if they thought I knew too much, who's to guarantee that somebody wouldn't decide to get rid of me—or maybe shake me up a little by getting to my wife and kids?"

I could see his point.

"So you think that your father was murdered by someone within his precinct."

He leaned back, took his hands off the table, folded them across his chest. "That's what I think."

"Any idea who?"

"No. All I know is— oh, hey!" he suddenly exclaimed, jumping up, all agitated.

"What? What is it?" Concerned, I watched him fumbling around, like he was looking for something.

My bodyguards had approached us at Michael's sudden movement and now hovered, looking highly apprehensive as he reached into his pocket.

But Michael merely pulled out a beeper and looked at it.

I breathed an inner sigh of relief.

"It's Anne," he blurted out. He reached up to the coat tree for his jacket and slid his arms into it. "She must be in labor.

That's the only thing we use this pager for. God, it's about time. She's way overdue."

Labor. He had another baby on the way.

Now, of all times.

"I realize this is urgent," I found myself protesting, "but can you hold off just another minute while I ask you a few more quick questions?"

He was already on his way to the door. "Sorry, Mr. Mayor," he called over his shoulder. "This is baby number five—it's probably going to come fast. We barely got to the hospital with the last one—she was born on the way to the delivery room. I've got to go right now."

With that, he was gone, leaving me with two barely touched lunches—and a lot to think about.

Predictably, I had a pile of messages when I got back to Gracie Mansion. I knew I would be spending the rest of the day on the phone conducting city business. There would be very little time to devote to the Ramsey's case today.

As I flipped through the pile of messages, I came across an urgent one from my father. Concerned, I went right to the study and quickly dialed the number.

He answered on the first ring. "Hello?"

"Pop?"

"Eddie? Is that you?"

"Of course it's me. I just got back. What's wrong? What happened?"

"Who said something happened?"

"You left me a message marked urgent."

"Oh, that. I figured if you were busy, you might not call me back until tonight, and I needed to talk to you right away, while your mother's out at mah-jongg. I have to go out before the stores close."

"Before the stores close?" I sat down on a chair, sensing this wasn't going to be a quick, simple, or urgent conversation. "Why is that, Pop?"

"Because I have to go out and get something for your mother, and I'm not sure what to get."

"You mean, she left you a grocery list and you can't understand it?"

"A grocery list? What do you mean?"

I fought back frustration. "I mean, she wanted you to go get something for her at the grocery store, and you're not sure what it is? Is that it?"

"Eddie, you're not making sense. Why would your mother leave me a list for the grocery store? She just sent me there with a long list this morning, as soon as they shoveled the sidewalk out in front of our building. I should go to the grocery store twice in one day?"

"No, you shouldn't, Pop."

"That's right, I shouldn't. Who has time for that? I have to go uptown to buy your mother a Hanukkah gift. All week I meant to go and take care of it, but I couldn't. Yesterday there was the snow. Such snow, Eddie. Did you see it?"

"It was hard to miss, Pop."

"The day before, I had my pinochle game. The day before that . . . what was the day before that?"

"It's all right, Pop; I see what you're saying. . . ."

"The day before that was the day we drove out to Long Island to visit your mother's niece Selma. Such a trip, that trip. So much traffic, and your mother started yelling at me when we got to the toll booths at the bridge, telling me to go into a longer line. I said, 'Why would I want to do that, when there's hardly anyone waiting in this line?' And she said—"

"Pop, that's because the shorter lines were for people who have EZ-Pass," I cut in.

"What are you talking about?"

"You don't have EZ-Pass."

There was a pause. "What's that?"

"It's a way to pay tolls electronically," I said, marveling at my own patience. It was as if we had never before had this exact same discussion. "If you have EZ-Pass, you don't have to take the time to slow down and stop at a booth and hand over cash or a token."

"Well, why didn't your mother say so?"

I was sure she had tried, but for some reason my parents don't communicate as efficiently with each other as they do with the rest of the population—which is *really* frightening, if you think about it.

All I said to my father was "Maybe she forgot to tell you about it."

"How could she forget?"

I sighed. "I don't know, Pop. Sometimes people forget."

"Your mother, she doesn't forget a thing. If it's so great, why don't I have this EZ-Pass, Eddie? Why didn't my son the mayor come to me before now and tell me all about it?"

So he was going to get into the my-son-the-mayor routine. I headed him off with a resigned "I don't know—I guess I've been busy, Pop."

"Where do I sign up for this EZ-Pass, Eddie?"

"I'll take care of it for you, Pop. I promise. The next chance I get."

"Good. Because I don't like to wait in traffic. It's a long enough trip out there to Levittown as it is without . . ."

Pop's voice faded in my ears as I was struck by a sudden realization.

Why hadn't I thought of it before?

I hurriedly interrupted my father, asking him why he had called in the first place about the gift for my mother.

He said he wanted to know what he should get her as a Hanukkah present.

With growing impatience, I said jewelry.

"Why jewelry?" he wanted to know.

"Why not?" I returned absently, flipping through the Rolodex on my desk until I came to the T's.

"Your mother has enough jewelry. How about a nice porcelain vase?"

Every year my father gets my mother a nice porcelain vase for Hanukkah.

Every year my mother tells him that she loves it.

And every year she complains to me that it's not her taste and she has no place to put another vase, and why doesn't he just get her jewelry instead?

"I don't know, Pop," I told him hurriedly. "Doesn't she already have a nice porcelain vase . . ."

. . . or twenty?

"Sure, she does. But you can never have too many vases. You know how your mother loves *chatchkes.*"

"Well, she loves jewelry too," I pointed out. "How about a nice bracelet?"

"When would she wear it?"

"When you go out, Pop. She would wear it when you go out."

"Where we go, no one needs to wear fancy-schmancy jewelry, Eddie. That would just be asking for trouble, if you know what I mean."

I didn't, but I wasn't about to ask.

"It doesn't have to be fancy, Pop," I said, checking my watch. "Just something simple."

"Like what?"

"I don't know . . . a gold bangle?"

"A bangle? What the heck is a bangle?"

I gritted my teeth. "You know what, Pop? Now that I think about it, you were right. I bet Mom really would like another nice porcelain vase."

"See? What did I tell you? You should listen to your father, Eddie. A father always knows."

As I dialed Barnaby Tischler's number after hanging up, I prayed that my mother never found out that Pop had consulted me about her present this year.

And I vowed to buy her the most extravagant bangle I could find for Mother's Day.

And flowers.

Lots and lots of flowers, I thought grimly, picturing all those nice porcelain vases.

It was late when Barnaby Tischler finally called me back, just as I was about to wrap things up in my study, head upstairs, and turn on the eleven o'clock news.

"Sorry I didn't get back to you sooner, Ed," Barnaby said, sounding anxious. "Wanda and I were out to dinner. What's going on?"

"Something occurred to me about your alibi for the murder,

Barnaby. About how we can prove that you were where you say you were."

"So you believe that I'm innocent, then?"

I wanted to. Oh, how I wanted to. And if what I had in mind actually worked, I would be able to knock him off my list of suspects.

I avoided answering his question by posing one of my own.

"Do you have EZ-Pass, Barnaby?" I asked.

"Do I . . . ? Not yet. Why?"

My glimmer of hope faded. "Because I thought that if you had EZ-Pass, which documents all toll activity for your car, we could use it to prove that you went through the toll booths on the Throgs Neck Bridge at around the same time the murder was committed on Monday night. But if you don't have it . . ."

"No, I don't—"

"Wait a minute!" I exclaimed. "You went over the Throgs Neck Bridge!"

"Yes . . ."

"The toll booths on that bridge are under video surveillance, Barnaby!" I said triumphantly.

There was a pause as this information sunk in.

"You mean," he asked slowly, "that there might be—that there *is* a video out there somewhere that shows my car driving through the toll booths on Monday night? And we can show it to the police and prove my alibi?"

"That's exactly what I mean."

"How do we find it?"

"I'm the mayor, Barnaby," I reminded him cheerfully. "Just leave it up to me. And while I'm doing that favor for you, would you mind doing one for me?"

"Not at all, Ed. Anything."

"Can you please check your records and see if Marlon Killdaire was working the night Angelo Calvino was murdered?"

"Sure, I can check, but it'll have to wait until tomorrow, when I'm back at the store. I don't have access to that information at home. Why do you need to know?"

"We'll talk when I call you back about the videotape," I promised him.

I wasn't going to let Barnaby in on any of my speculation until I had cleared him as a suspect once and for all.

Of course, the matter wasn't necessarily as simple as it seemed.

Even if I did prove that Barnaby couldn't have committed the Killdaire murder because he was in his car someplace in the Bronx when it occurred, it didn't mean he couldn't have hired someone else to do the actual killing . . . just as I had speculated that Simon Weatherly might have done.

But I had to take the common-sense angle into consideration.

And it simply didn't make any sense for Barnaby Tischler to have involved another person.

He would have had access to every inch of his department store, and would know, better than anyone, how to kill someone on the premises and get away with it.

With that in mind, I decided that if I found video evidence of Barnaby driving over the Throgs Neck Bridge on Monday night, as he had claimed, I would clear him of all suspicion.

ELEVEN

Mentally and physically exhausted as I was, I somehow managed to toss and turn for several restless hours on Friday night.

I kept going over every possible angle involving the double murders, trying to come up with answers.

If what Michael Killdaire had said was true, then his father really had been killed by a corrupt police officer who didn't want Killdaire going to the commissioner with whatever it was that he knew.

But then . . .

What about Calvino?

Using the Michael Killdaire theory, the first Santa killing could be explained only one way.

Whoever had murdered Calvino had meant to murder Killdaire. It was obviously someone who didn't know there was more than one Santa working for Ramsey's, and he had simply pounced on the first person who happened along wearing a red and white Santa suit: the hapless Angelo Calvino.

I also knew that the killer most likely had some knowledge of the layout and behind-the-scenes operation at the department store. After all, he had to know where to find the employees' locker room, where to lie in wait for the victims, and where to hide the body to allow enough time to make an escape before it would be discovered.

Which meant that possible suspects included delivery persons and employees—including former employees.

David Killdaire had once briefly worked for Ramsey's Department Store.

And so had his brother, Michael.

That fact kept zooming back at me, much as I wanted to ignore it.

I didn't want to place Marlon Killdaire's favorite son on the list of suspects. After all, Michael was a likable family man, the father of four children—probably five by this time, I amended, remembering that his wife had gone into labor.

Besides, he had been willing to help me with the investigation—in fact, it had been his idea to talk to me.

But what if that cooperation had simply been a calculating move of a cunning killer, a killer who had committed one of the most heinous crimes there is: patricide.

Michael Killdaire *had* been intensely nervous throughout our meeting at the diner.

That could be attributed to the fact that he possessed some highly sensitive information about police corruption and his father's death.

Or it could be attributed to the fact that he was guilty and was trying to deflect my suspicion away from the real killer.

Either Michael himself.

Or his brother David—who, Michael had admitted in so many words, had been violent toward their mother and was estranged from their father.

So.

Both Killdaire brothers could be seen as suspects.

And both would have had a simple motive for killing their own father.

Money.

Had one of them found out about or stumbled across the heirloom violin and decided that perhaps it was worth a lot of money?

Or had one of them discovered that their father had a substantial amount of money in his savings account?

I knew that both David and Michael were experiencing severe financial difficulties.

David, the compulsive gambler, was heavily in debt, most likely to loan sharks, and might very well have found his own life in danger.

Michael, the overburdened husband and father who was forced to work three jobs to make ends meet, was expecting yet another mouth to feed.

But he and his father adored each other, I kept reminding myself. I couldn't help remembering the framed photo of father and son that I had seen in the Killdaires' living room, the photo that had seemed to radiate genuine warmth and affection—just as Michael himself did when he spoke of his father.

Yet I had to remember one of the most basic rules of crime solving: Appearances could be deceiving.

With that in mind, Michael Killdaire could very well be a cold-blooded killer, much as I hated to believe it.

Which meant that the information he had provided about his father having uncovered police corruption within the precinct was either a deliberately planted red herring . . .

Or the most significant lead I had received.

First thing Saturday morning, even before I got off my stationary bike, I got a telephone call from Toby Fitzsimmons, my contact at the Throgs Neck Bridge.

"Hey, Mr. Mayor, how's it goin'?"

"So far, it's going just fine," I said, a little breathless from my workout.

"Well, allow me to make a good day even better, because I've got it, Mr. Mayor," he announced triumphantly in his thick Bronx accent.

"You've got . . ."

"I've got the videotape you asked for. And not only have I got the tape, but I've got the footage that shows that car you wanted to find. A black Lexus, last year's model, and it went through the toll booth at . . . let me check my notes . . . at nine fifty-nine P.M. last Monday evening."

"You're sure this is the car? You're positive that it matches the license plate I gave you?"

"It matches the license plate, and there's a decent shot of the driver."

I couldn't ask for anything more.

Relief coursed through me as I mentally removed Barnaby Tischler from my list of suspects.

"Listen, Toby," I said, my mind racing. "I'm going to send a messenger to pick up that videotape. Until someone gets there, you guard it with your life."

He promised that he would, and told me to stop by his office for a cuppa joe and a doughnut the next time I crossed over the Throgs Neck Bridge.

"I'll do that," I told him. "In fact, I'll bring the coffee and doughnuts myself."

"Hey, that would be great. Just for the record, I like the pow-dered-sugar kind with red raspberry jelly inside. A *lot* of jelly, not skimpy."

"You and me both, Toby."

I hung up, called to arrange for the messenger, and then called Barnaby Tischler at home. His wife, Wanda, told me he had left for the store bright and early today and should be there already.

"Can I just ask . . . is it good news, Ed?" she said tentatively before we hung up.

"It's good news, Wanda."

She let out a shaky sigh, and I could hear the joyful sob in her voice as she thanked me.

I was smiling when I reached Barnaby in his office.

"Ed!" he said, sounding incredibly nervous. "Did you have any luck?"

"I have proof that you were where you told me you were on Monday night, Barnaby."

He let out an enormous sigh of relief and said in a shaky voice, "Oh, thank God. Thank God."

"Don't thank God, thank me," I told him, and he did. Pro-fusely.

"Now all you have to do," I advised him, "is tell Detective Lazaro that you weren't quite honest when you told him your story the other night. Just tell him what you told me—that you were panicky and thought nobody would believe that you had taken such a roundabout route back to Long Island. I'll back you up."

"You will?"

"Sure. I'll tell him that you're the most impatient human being I've ever met, and that it makes perfect sense to me that you'd drive all those miles out of your way just to avoid sitting in traffic."

"It's just that I like to keep moving, Ed, you know? I hate sitting still. . . ."

"I know, I know. And then, Barnaby, we'll turn the videotape over to the detectives as soon as I get my hands on it, which should be soon. And you'll be cleared of suspicion."

"You're a real friend, Ed. A real friend. And in return, I have the information you asked for. Marlon Killdaire *was* working the night Angelo Calvino was shot. He punched out about five minutes before Calvino did."

Mmm-hmm. Just as I thought.

"Is that all you needed to know, Ed?"

"No. There's something else. Did you happen to hear anything about a shoplifter who tried to take several handbags on Monday evening at your store?"

"I know there was a shoplifting incident, yes. They always inform me about them, but believe me, lately, petty thefts are the least of my worries."

"An arrest was made in this case, wasn't it?"

"I don't remember off the top of my head. Hold on while I find the file, Ed."

I could hear him whistling and papers shuffling in the background.

"Okay, here it is. Now let me check . . . okay. I've got it."

"Tell me what you've got."

"It was a fourteen-year-old kid. His name was Joey Santiago, and he was taken down to the local precinct by the officer who was on patrol in the area when the shoplifting occurred."

"Which officer?"

"I know that several responded to the radio call and gave chase here in the store. But I have the arresting officer listed as John Panopolous."

I thanked him for that information and told him I would look into it and let him know what I discovered.

"You think the shoplifting and the murder are somehow connected, don't you, Ed?"

"They happened at around the same time, Barnaby. The shoplifter could have been planted, to cause a commotion and allow the murderer to slip past security."

"But the police thought of that already. They questioned my security staff about it. The guards assigned to the entrances said they never left their posts while the shoplifter was being chased through the store, and I believe them."

I pondered that until Barnaby asked, "Can you stop by the store later today, Ed? Maybe you could come in and buy a Henrietta Hyena puppet or something. It would be good publicity for us, and we need that desperately, Ed. We're really hurting."

"I know, Barnaby. I wish I could help, but—"

"If you really want to help, come over and put on a Santa suit. We've got only one guy left in the Wonderland—the rest of them quit after what happened to Killdaire, and I can't say I blame them."

"I wish I could help," I said again.

He sighed heavily. "It's all right. I guess we don't need more than one Santa anyway these days. The store is just about empty. People are too afraid to come in."

"I'm so sorry, Barnaby. It's a terrible shame."

"When people think of New York at Christmastime, Ed, they think of Ramsey's. As I've been telling people all along, this isn't just a tragedy for my store, it's a tragedy for the entire city. And you're the man in charge of the city. It's up to you to do what you can to make things better."

What could I say? He was right.

But there was only so much I could do in the next twenty-four hours, unless I cancelled my vacation.

And I really didn't want to do that.

I desperately needed this vacation.

I had been *living* for this vacation for so many weeks, months . . .

I couldn't cancel it.
I really couldn't.

I had received the videotape and sent it over to Detective Lazaro by early Saturday afternoon, after calling him to explain what I had discovered.

He didn't seem at all pleased to hear from me, and he certainly wasn't thrilled to hear that Barnaby Tischler had lied about his alibi.

However, he agreed that Tischler would be ruled out as a suspect—just as soon as Lazaro had viewed the video evidence.

Apparently, he wasn't going to take my word for it, and that was fine. Nobody knows better than I do that a good detective is a thorough detective.

I was in my office at Gracie Mansion just after one o'clock, conducting a lengthy and unpleasant telephone meeting with the chairman of the City Planning Commission, when I was interrupted by the first of two emergency messages.

This one was delivered in person by Carmine Bello, one of my deputy mayors, who appeared in the doorway of my office looking anxious and gesturing wildly that something was up.

"What is it, Carmine?" I asked him after putting my call on hold. Hopefully, it was good news. I could have used some right about then, since my conversation with the chairman hadn't been going well at all.

"A body was found out on Queens Boulevard early this morning, when they were plowing the sidewalk."

Uh-oh.

It doesn't take a genius to figure out that finding a body is never good news.

Curiously, though, Carmine didn't seem particularly upset.

In fact, he looked almost . . . pleased?

"Whose body was it?" I asked, perplexed.

"A man who went by the name of Angel Smith."

"Angel Smith?" It meant nothing to me. "And this is relevant because . . . ?"

"Angel Smith was homeless, Ed. He was also a good friend of Tommi Tremaine's. Such a good friend that he went along with her orders to protest being taken to a shelter. He spent the past few nights on the streets."

"In the snow."

"In the snow," he affirmed, nodding. "The man froze to death, Ed."

"That's a terrible thing."

"For him it's a terrible thing. For you it's not so terrible."

I frowned.

"Don't look at me like that, Ed," Carmine said. "Don't let your emotions get the best of you. You have to be realistic. This is a very momentous development in the lawsuit against the city. It proves that Tommi Tremaine was wrong to convince people to resist being taken to shelters. No one can deny that her case is going to fall apart as a result of this guy's death. She's lost, Ed. You've won."

"I've won," I said hollowly. "All because a man named Angel was found dead in the snow. Yippee, Carmine."

"Don't look at it that way. Don't get cynical. Don't get caught up in the details. Think about what this means for you and for the city."

"I can't help it, Carmine. A dead body is never good news, no matter what it stands for."

I couldn't help feeling somber as I returned to my phone call with the chairman of the City Planning Commission, which had grown increasingly unpleasant as we locked horns over a proposal for federally funded housing units. It was slated for a section of Staten Island that I didn't think was suitable, and I wasn't hesitating to tell him why not.

We picked up our argument where we had left off.

Less than five minutes passed before there was a second interruption, which I will confide that I initially welcomed.

This time it was a call from Harris Bayor, the recently appointed police commissioner.

"Ed, I'm sorry to disturb you," he said, "but I thought you'd want to know—"

"Know what?"

"They've found a body—"

"I already know. Angel Smith. In Queens," I told him. "It's a terrible shame."

There was a pause. "That's not what I was going to say."

"You weren't?" I blinked. "Then which body were you talking about?"

"A young black man named Guy Drummond. He was found in Brooklyn just a little while ago. Ed, he worked for some charity down there. He was collecting donations on a street corner, when someone shot him in the back of the head. And, Ed? He was dressed in a Santa Claus suit."

I canceled my flight to Barbados just before holding a noon press conference at City Hall.

I had concluded that there was no way I could leave my beloved New York in the middle of an escalating crisis.

Sure, the Guy Drummond murder might have been a fluke, totally unrelated to the earlier Santa slayings. But what if it wasn't? What if there really was a crazed killer on the loose, determined to gun down Santas all over the city?

During the press conference, I assured reporters that everything possible would be done to find the murderers of Guy Drummond, Angelo Calvino, and Marlon Killdaire.

"Murder*ers*, Mr. Mayor?" a reporter asked dubiously. "Don't you mean murder*er*?"

"Isn't it obvious that the three killings are linked?" called someone else.

"I'll let the police commissioner comment on that," I said, and turned the microphone over to Harris Bayor.

No, detectives hadn't yet established a link between the latest homicide and the deaths of the two Ramsey's Santas.

And no, they weren't releasing any details about possible suspects in any of the murders. But anyone with any information about any of the crimes was asked to call a special eight-hundred number set up by the NYPD.

After the press conference, Harris Bayor and I met privately in my office, where he informed me that robbery may have been a motive in the Drummond case. The charity money the victim had been collecting in a tin container was missing.

"With that in mind, I doubt that we have a serial killer targeting people in Santa suits," he confided. "This appears to be an isolated incident."

"Is it possible that the Brooklyn murder might have been a copycat crime?"

"It's possible. But aside from the fact that all three were dressed in Santa Claus suits and shot in the head from behind, the circumstances with Drummond's case were different. It happened way out in Brooklyn. A different type of gun was used. And he was robbed."

I nodded and pondered what he had told me.

I had been debating whether or not to tell him about my meeting with Michael Killdaire.

If Killdaire really was guilty, then it would be wise to bring my suspicions to the attention of the police.

Then again, what if he had been telling the truth? What if his father really had uncovered police corruption?

It wasn't that I didn't trust Harris Bayor. I trusted him implicitly; why else would I have appointed him police commissioner?

But if I brought Michael Killdaire to light as a suspect now, then I knew it would be up to Harris to have him investigated promptly.

Michael Killdaire's father had been murdered less than a week earlier, and his wife had just had a baby.

If he was innocent, why put him through an investigation—and probable media circus—that would be devastating at this incredibly stressful time in his life?

He had entrusted me with his father's secret, and I had promised not to reveal it to anyone. He would never forgive me for betraying him, and I wouldn't blame him . . . *if* he was innocent.

If he was guilty—well, he wasn't going anywhere. He had a wife and five children, and besides, he didn't know I was suspicious.

I concluded that it couldn't hurt to wait another day or two while I looked into Killdaire's allegations.

"What's going on in that brain of yours, Ed?" Harris asked, watching me.

"I'm just wondering what's going on with the Calvino and

Killdaire cases at the moment, Harry." I leaned back in my leather armchair. "Has the homicide squad uncovered anything new?"

"Something *has* come to light," he admitted, and I sat up again. "What is it?"

"I want you to keep this confidential, Ed."

"Of course."

"We've traced the bomb threat phone calls that were made to Ramsey's Department Store in October and November."

"To whom?"

"Simon Weatherly."

My jaw dropped. . . .

But then, was I really so surprised?

I *knew* the man was harboring hostility toward his own store's rival. I *knew* he had a motive to see that Ramsey's went out of business.

But I seemed to have lost sight of that in the aftermath of my conversations with Alva Killdaire and her son.

I had been focusing my attention away from the theory that the first two victims had been killed simply because they were Ramsey's Santas.

Instead, I had nearly convinced myself that the first murder had accidentally targeted the wrong victim, that Calvino had been mistaken for Killdaire.

"Have you confronted Weatherly with what you know?" I asked Harris.

"Not yet. We're still gathering evidence. There's no denying that he's our primary suspect at this time. However, the fact that he made the bomb threats doesn't mean Simon's behind the murders, Ed."

"No, it doesn't," I agreed. "Does he have an alibi for the night of Killdaire's murder? Because I happen to know that he couldn't get into the Wells and Marino premiere at Tavern-on-the-Green."

Harris nodded. "We are aware that he tried to get himself onto the guest list. He even showed up at the party and tried to convince the doorman that he had been invited."

"What time was that?"

"Between nine and nine-thirty."

"Killdaire was murdered at around ten o'clock."

"From nine-thirty until midnight, he was having drinks and dinner at the Oak Room."

Very clever. One could walk from Tavern-on-the-Green to the Plaza Hotel on Central Park South in about fifteen minutes. And the Plaza's Oak Room, perpetually crowded with see-and-be-seen types, would provide Simon Weatherly with plenty of acquaintances who would vouch for his whereabouts.

If he were behind the Ramsey's murders, I had already established that he wouldn't have done the dirty work himself. It made perfect sense that having hired a hit man to kill both Calvino and Killdaire, Weatherly would place himself in two of New York's most highly visible restaurants on the nights of the two murders.

I voiced my musings to Harris Bayor. "So with Weatherly accounted for both last Monday night and the Monday before that, you would have to assume he had arranged the murders through a hit man or hit men."

"You would have to assume that, yes. Our investigation into Weatherly so far has revealed no ties with organized crime, and nothing that would point to that scenario, Ed."

"Still, I wouldn't put it past him."

"Neither would I," Harris Bayor said grimly.

Then he cleared his throat and said, "There's something else, Ed."

"You're just full of surprises today, Harry."

"This one isn't pleasant. Do you know Alan Jamison?"

I nodded. He was the captain of the midtown precinct that had employed Marlon Killdaire.

"What about him?" I asked Harris.

"This, again, is just between you and me, Ed."

I nodded impatiently. "What is it?"

"Jamison says he received an anonymous typewritten note a few months ago, warning him that one of the cops in his precinct was on the take."

I kept my face poker straight. "What does that mean?"

"We don't know. Jamison has no idea who wrote it, but I had a task force sniffing around, and they did come up with something not long ago. A drug dealer named Nacho Ruiz has been operating in that neighborhood, and he's been claiming on the streets that he's been paying off a cop."

"But he hasn't said who?"

"No. That's all we know, but we're on it. We're trying to locate Ruiz to bring him in for questioning, but so far we haven't found him."

I nodded. "And the connection to the Killdaire murder would be . . . ?"

"Who knows, Ed? Maybe he was the one who wrote the warning. Maybe the corrupt officer found out and whacked him. Or maybe he was the cop on the take, and the dealer had him whacked."

I found the latter scenario unlikely, given what Michael had told me about his father.

Yet the idea of Killdaire himself being involved in unsavory business was unsettling enough to merit further consideration.

"Who knows about this?" I asked.

"Just me, and the captain, and a couple of officers on the task force—that's it. It's top secret, like I said. We can't afford a leak."

Not for the first time, I debated telling him what Killdaire's son had told me.

But I couldn't bring myself to break that confidence.

Not yet.

Not until I had looked into it a little further.

Mohammed Johnson came on duty late Saturday afternoon, and seemed startled when I asked to speak to him privately in my office.

"What's going on, Mr. Mayor? Is anything wrong?" he asked, seated in the comfortable chair opposite my desk.

"No. I just thought you might be able to help me with something, but I need you to keep it confidential."

"You know I will. What's up?"

"Did you ever hear of a patrol officer named John Panopolous?" I asked him.

"John Panopolous?" Mohammed frowned and rubbed his clean-shaven chin. "Yeah. I think so. I think he worked in the same midtown precinct I was in a few years back. . . ."

"He did. Do you remember anything specific about him?"

He thought about it for a minute and then shrugged. "Nah. I think he had dark hair."

"That's all?"

"Not to be disrespectful or anything, but do you know how many cops I've known over the years, Mr. Mayor? They all kind of blend into one face after a while."

"You didn't have any trouble remembering Marlon Killdaire," I pointed out. "Or that pretty blonde we saw at Ramsey's the night of the Calvino murder."

Mohammed grinned. "Yeah, I sure did remember her. But Katrina was, uh, special, Mr. Mayor. Let's just say there aren't a whole lot of cops, male or female, who look like her."

"I'm sure you're right about that."

"Why do you want to know about Panopolous? Did something happen to him?"

"No. I just wanted to ask him a few questions, and I thought I'd check with you before I called him."

"Questions about what?"

"About a shoplifter he arrested at Ramsey's the night of the Killdaire murder."

"You don't think Panopolous was somehow involved in the murder, do you?" Mohammed looked stunned.

"I don't know."

"He and Killdaire worked in the same precinct. Why would Panopolous want to—"

"I didn't say he did," I cut in quickly. "Just that I was curious about him."

And then, feeling as paranoid as Michael Killdaire, I added, "And don't forget that this conversation is between you and me, Mohammed."

"Between you and me, Mr. Mayor," he echoed. "Don't worry. You can trust me."

"I know I can," I said, reminding myself that I trusted Mohammed Johnson to guard my very life.

John Panopolous did, indeed, have dark hair—what hair there was around the fringes of his balding head. He was a rotund middle-aged man with a swarthy complexion and an air of self-importance that came across to me the moment I saw him striding across the precinct station after being summoned by the desk sergeant.

"Mr. Mayor," he said, greeting me in a booming voice that couldn't escape the ears of those nearby, "it's a pleasure to meet you in person. I'm one of your biggest fans."

Everything about him seemed to trumpet, *Hey, look at me! I'm meeting with the mayor!*

"That's always nice to hear," I said, shaking his hand. "Do you mind if I ask you a few questions?"

"Not at all. I was filling out a report, and it's always nice to have a break. People don't realize how much of this job is made up of paperwork. And paperwork is a real pain in the you-know-what."

"Believe me, I know how you feel," I said dryly.

"What did you want to ask questions about?"

"About a shoplifter you arrested earlier this week."

"At Ramsey's?" he asked. "That's the only shoplifting arrest I made this week, Mr. Mayor."

"Why don't we go talk someplace more private?" I suggested, aware of the curious glances in our direction.

"Sure thing." Panopolous led the way past the desk sergeant, through a large briefing room, and down the hallway to an empty office. He held the door open, motioned me and my bodyguards inside, and said, "We can talk in here, since no one's using it right now."

We all filed inside. I took a seat and my bodyguards grouped themselves behind me. I had asked that Mohammed not come along with me to the precinct, unsure of how his status as an officer would affect any information I could uncover.

"Now, what is it that you wanted to know?" Panopolous asked, sitting opposite the cluttered metal desk and steepling his fingers as he looked at me.

"Why don't you tell me what happened the night you arrested the shoplifter?"

"This isn't about the shoplifting incident though, is it, Mr. Mayor?"

"What do you mean?"

"This is about Marlon's murder. I read in the papers that you were investigating it."

"Did you know him well?" I asked.

"Sure. We've both worked here in the precinct together for years. I always liked Marlon."

"But . . ." I prompted, reading his thoughts.

He looked taken aback. "But, what?"

"You always liked Marlon, but . . ."

"I didn't say that. I always liked him. Period."

"Okay," I said, "you always liked him. Why? What was there to like?"

"He was an upright kind of guy. Took his work seriously. Some of the guys around here might tell you he took it too seriously, but is that possible? I mean, for a cop?"

He seemed to be waiting for some kind of approval, so I said, "Of course every police officer should take his work seriously."

"Marlon was the kind of guy who didn't complain about all the paperwork. He didn't complain about the hours. He didn't even complain when you decided to put more cops on foot patrol to make us more visible so people would feel safer—hey, I didn't complain either," he added hastily.

"Good," I said. "Because as you know, ever since my administration took over, crime in this city has been at its lowest rate ever."

"And that's a terrific thing, Mr. Mayor," he said. "Don't get me wrong. I agree with it. I just meant that some officers around here were grumbling. But not Marlon. And not me."

"You don't have any idea who killed Marlon Killdaire, do you, Officer?" I asked John Panopolous.

"I don't know who could have done such a miserable, low-down thing. Although—" He started to lean closer, then broke off and shook his head. "Nah," he said.

"What?"

"I just thought of something, that's all."

"What did you think of?"

He cleared his throat. "What if Marlon was sniffing around where he shouldn't be?"

"What do you mean by that?"

He shrugged. "What if Marlon had something on one of the officers here in the precinct?"

"Had something . . . like what?"

"Like maybe one of the officers was doing something he shouldn't be doing."

"Such as?"

"I have no idea, Mr. Mayor. I'm just speculating."

"You're sure about that?"

"What? That I'm just speculating? Absolutely."

"Was anyone in this precinct particularly close to Marlon Killdaire?"

"Nah. He pretty much kept to himself. Wasn't the kind of guy who would go out for beers with the rest of us. He pretty much liked to get home to his wife. Although . . ."

"What?" I prodded, irritated with his frustrating habit of starting to bring something up and then seeming to consider dropping the subject.

"He and Varinski were close, sort of," he said.

"Varinski?" The name rang a bell.

"She's a female cop here in the precinct."

"Long blond hair?" I asked, remembering the woman I had met with Mohammed.

"That's her. So you've met her, huh. She's gorgeous, but cold as a witch's—"

"Officer Varinski and Marlon Killdaire were friends?"

"Not *friends.*"

"Something more?" I asked, wondering if perhaps Varinski was Killdaire's secret lover, and if she had killed him in a crime of passion.

"No! No way. Killdaire was the kind of guy who wouldn't cheat on an eye exam, Mr. Mayor. I'd swear he was totally faithful to his wife. What I meant by them not being friends is that they were both loners. It wasn't like they hung out together, called each other on the phone. But if there was anyone Varinski talked to, it was Killdaire, and vice versa."

"But they didn't see each other outside of work?"

"I doubt it. He never hung around in the city after work. And she was the type who liked to get right home after her shift was over too. Has a couple of little kids, and she just went through a divorce. Her husband was cheating on her, if you can believe that. I don't know why anyone would look someplace else if he had a babe like her at home. If that were me, I—"

"What about her relationship with Killdaire?" I cut in impatiently.

"I think he used to try to help her out, you know, by listening to her problems."

"I see." I made a mental note to find Officer Varinski and question her.

If Killdaire had discovered corruption within the precinct, I doubted that he would have confided in anyone other than his son—especially not a fellow officer in the precinct.

Still, you never know.

For the time being, though, I had to get back to the matter at hand.

"About this shoplifter, Officer," I said to John Panopolous. "Can you tell me about what happened?"

"Sure. I was on my beat a few blocks away, on Thirty-seventh Street, when I heard over the radio that a shoplifter was being chased by security guards over at Ramsey's. I got there pretty fast—I used to be a high school track star," he added without the least bit of modesty.

"What did you find when you got there?"

"The perp had gone up the escalators and was hiding somewhere on the upper floors of the store. Two other officers answered the call and were on the scene—"

"Who were they?"

"Doug Holt and Bobby Wu."

Doug Holt . . . the name rang a bell, but I couldn't seem to place it.

"We started searching," Panopolous went on. "A bunch of store security guards helped. We all split up."

"How long did you look?"

"At least fifteen, twenty minutes. I was the one who found the guy," he proudly informed me. "He was hiding under one of those platform beds up in the department that sells sheets and stuff like that. The kid thought he was so clever, but I nabbed him."

"His name was Joey Santiago?"

"Yeah. Just turned fourteen."

"What happened after you found him?"

"The usual. Cuffed him. Took him over here. Called the home number he gave me. His mother wasn't around, but his stepfather came right down here. He was really pissed at the kid. Started yelling at him, asking him what the heck he thought he was doing, trying to shoplift a bunch of purses. The kid said he was going to give them to his mother and sisters for Christmas presents. He was all casual about it, like he didn't care what the father thought or what happened to him."

"So what happened?"

"He was a juvie, and it was his first offense. A misdemeanor. So the stepfather took him home. You know the drill. They'll have to appear in court and all that." He shrugged. "Just a routine shoplifting."

I nodded. "Why do you think the kid tried to escape by heading upstairs instead of out of the store? Wouldn't that have made more sense?"

"Did you see all that security they have at Ramsey's now, Mr. Mayor? There are metal detectors and those airport-type machines at the exits, and security guards too. The kid probably panicked and ran in the opposite direction."

"That certainly makes sense," I agreed.

When I left the precinct a short time afterward, it was with the distinct impression that Joey Santiago had been hired as a decoy by whoever had killed Marlon Killdaire.

In the melee that resulted from the chase, a weapon could possibly have been smuggled into the store somehow . . .

Or not even smuggled.

All three of the cops who came rushing in to help find that shoplifter would have had a weapon on him.

Which meant I could add three more suspects to my list: John Panopolous, Bobby Wu, and Doug Holt.

I was almost home, when it suddenly struck me why the name Doug Holt sounded familiar.

He had been the Frito-munching cop at the scene of Angelo Calvino's murder, the one who had tried to get me to stay back from the body.

I made a mental note to see what I could find out about him.

_____ TWELVE

"I hear you canceled your vacation to Barbados, Ed," Barnaby Tischler said over the telephone on Sunday morning, bright and early.

Make that just _early_.

There was nothing remotely _bright_ about the steady drizzle outside my window, or the rapidly melting snow below.

"Believe me, Barnaby," I grumbled, "I would love to be heading for the airport right about now. And if the police make an arrest within the next few days, I'm still planning on salvaging what's left of my vacation by jumping on the first plane out of here."

"Is an arrest imminent?"

"I don't know." I turned away from the window and sat on the edge of my bed. "What can I do for you, Barnaby, before I go make myself a pot of coffee?"

"Funny you should ask . . ."

Uh-oh.

"I was thinking that since you had already arranged to take the time off, Ed, you might be willing to volunteer yourself for a good cause."

"What good cause?"

"My last Santa quit last night after he found out about what happened to that guy down in Brooklyn."

"Guy Drummond?"

"Exactly. The police have told me that they don't think that case was related to the two murders in my store, but that doesn't mean that I'm not still losing employees and customers left and right."

"I don't know how I can help you, Barnaby."

"Well, I do. You can become the new Ramsey's Santa!"

"Ridiculous!" I retorted. "I can't be Santa Claus."

"Why not? You're supposed to be away on vacation this week, which means you have nothing scheduled."

"I can't be Santa Claus," I repeated.

"Why not?" he repeated.

"Because . . . I'm the mayor."

"Which is why you would be perfect for the job, Ed. Santa is the holiday spirit personified. You are New York City personified. If you took over as Ramsey's new Santa, you would be sending out a positive message about the spirit of this city to people all across the country."

"Ridiculous," I sputtered again, refusing to even consider such a ludicrous idea.

I did not give up lying on a sun-splashed tropical beach to sit on a fake throne in a red velour getup with kids crawling all over me.

Yet that was exactly where Sunday afternoon found me.

"How are you doing, Mr. Mayor?" asked Ambrose, who was strategically positioned to the right of the throne in Ramsey's Winter Wonderland.

"This beard tickles my face," I groused.

"I hate to tell you what this leotard is doing to my legs," he shot back.

Okay, so my bodyguards had it worse than I did.

After all, I just had to sit there chatting with New Yorkers in a jolly manner, which is one of my favorite things to do anyway—albeit I'm not usually wearing fake whiskers and a hot, scratchy red suit stuffed with pillows.

However, my bodyguards—much to their dismay—had found themselves posing as elves to my Saint Nick. It was the only way my security advisers would allow me to pull this stunt.

That information hadn't been released to the press, which meant the general public had no idea that the strapping elves in the wonderland scene were actually pistol-packing bodyguards.

You may wonder why I had agreed with Barnaby's outlandish request.

There were actually two good reasons to do it.

The first was that he had a point about how my sitting in for Santa would generate positive publicity.

If New Yorkers saw that I wasn't afraid to don a Santa Claus suit in public, some of their own fears might also subside. After all, the mayor is a role model for the citizens. If I showed everyone that I still had the holiday spirit, it might just catch on.

And then there was the other reason.

In stepping into the role of Ramsey's Santa, I would be stepping into the victims' shoes. I would be allowed insight into the murders from the victims' perspective, at the actual scene of the murders.

I couldn't help wondering if that perspective might shed some light on a case that seemed to be growing increasingly convoluted.

So here I was.

And there were my burly six-foot-plus, five-o'clock-shadowed security team, attired in green leotards, red felt tunics, shoes with curly, pointy toes, and jaunty fur-trimmed caps with jingle bells.

"Mommy, why does that elf look so mad?" I heard a little girl ask from the steadily growing line that now wound through the Wonderland maze.

"I don't know, sweetie. Maybe that's Grouchy."

"Nah. Grouchy's one of the seven dwarfs, not an elf!" the child protested.

I glanced at Ambrose, the elf in question, and decided there was no way on earth that he could ever be mistaken for a dwarf. His straining tunic was the length of a micro-mini, and you could see the crotch of his undersized green tights stretched between his muscular knees.

I couldn't help it. I had to laugh at the glowering expression on his face.

And since I had to laugh, I transformed the laugh into a thunderous, "Ho, ho, ho."

"My turn," said the child at the front of the line, a little boy who had a runny nose and a purple juice mustache above his upper lip. He torpedoed toward me and leapt onto my lap, nearly knocking me from my gold velour throne.

"Hello there, little fella," I said in the booming Santa voice I had been perfecting all afternoon.

"I'm not little, I'm big," he shot back, wiping his nose with his sleeve.

"Of course you are," I agreed. "You must be at least five years old."

"Five! I'm seven and a half!"

"Seven and a half!" I echoed. "What a big boy. So what do you want me to bring you?"

"I typed this list on my computer," he said promptly, pulling several stapled-together sheets of paper from the pocket of his down coat. "It's in order of the things I want the most to the things I want the least. But I definitely want them all."

"I'll see what I can do," I agreed, adding his list to the growing sheaf on the table beside the throne.

This Santa business wasn't so very different from the mayor business, I thought as I watched the kid trot smugly off to meet his mother.

In both occupations, strong-willed people approach you with impossible lists of demands, and you're expected to smile and yes them and keep everyone happy.

"Psst, hey, Ed," came a voice from behind the curtain at my back.

I turned to see Barnaby poking his head through. "How's it going?"

"So far, so good," I told him.

"Word travels fast," he hissed. "People are starting to find out about this. The store is busier than it's been for weeks, and the line for the Winter Wonderland goes all the way through the toy department."

"That's great, Barnaby," I said without enthusiasm as a tow-headed band of squirming, shouting identical triplets made a bee-line for my lap.

★ ★ ★

"KOCH AS KRIS KRINGLE?"

Had I given it much thought, I could have predicted the Monday-morning headline of *The Daily Register*. They're big on alliteration.

So is Sybil, who called me as I was finishing my first cup of coffee. She was in a snit, demanding to know why I hadn't told her I would be sitting in for Santa over at Ramsey's.

"I didn't tell you because I didn't know until a few hours before it happened," I informed her.

"You still could have called as soon as you agreed to do it."

"There wasn't time. I had to get fitted for my suit, and my bodyguards . . . you don't even want to know," I said, shaking my head at the memory of *that* scene.

"I do want to know."

"Okay. Five strapping men, five teensy elf costumes. Use your imagination."

"Oh, my."

"I told you. It wasn't a pretty scene."

"I don't care, Ed. From now on, I want to know everything you do, every move you make—"

"That's ridiculous!"

"You know what I mean. If you're not going to scoop me on the investigation, the least you can do is throw me a juicy morsel about what you're up to now and then."

"You want a juicy morsel about what I'm up to? Fine, here's one. I haven't had a true vacation in over a year, and I canceled a long-awaited trip to the Caribbean so that I could play Santa at Ramsey's by day and play Sherlock Holmes by night. How's that for juicy?"

"Too little too late. But speaking of Sherlock Holmes, how's the case coming along? Is it true that the police are close to making an arrest?"

"Where did you hear that?"

"I have my sources," she said, sounding smug.

"Who do your sources tell you is the culprit?"

"They won't say—most likely because they don't know. But my money's on Simon Weatherly."

"And why is that?" I asked cautiously.

"Who else could it be? What, you don't agree? You have someone else in mind?"

"I didn't say that."

"So you agree that it was probably Simon."

"I didn't say that."

"What *do* you say?"

"I say that I need another cup of coffee, Sybil."

"Well, before I let you go, let me be the first to congratulate you on the Tommi Tremaine case. I hear the lawsuit has been dropped."

"It has. She came to her senses because one of her chums froze to death in a snowbank the other night. The whole thing is a tragedy."

"Well, now people will agree to go to emergency shelters in freezing weather," Sybil said optimistically. "Anyway, I'll see you later on, Ed."

"You will?"

"I'm coming down to the store with a photographer to get the scoop on Hizzoner-as-Santa. Ta-ta to you now."

"And a ho-ho-ho to you," I grumbled, hanging up and refilling my mug.

Sybil wasn't the only reporter at Ramsey's Department Store when I arrived there on Monday morning. The sidewalk on Thirty-fourth Street was mobbed with press.

It was, in fact, just plain mobbed.

So mobbed that the police had been summoned for crowd control.

I stopped just outside the rotating doors at the main entrance to answer a few questions and pose for the cameras with a beaming Barnaby Tischler.

As I looked out over the sea of reporters and onlookers, I spotted two familiar faces among the uniformed officers keeping the throng in order.

One was John Panopolous.

The other was Katrina Varinski.

I had been meaning to get in touch with her since my visit to the precinct on Saturday. Now I turned to Mohammed Johnson, who was at my side and looking glum about the prospect of donning his elf suit, and I motioned him to lean in closer.

"What's up, Mr. Mayor?" he asked, looking concerned.

I asked him if he would mind approaching the female police officer and asking her if she could meet me for coffee someplace close by after her shift ended.

"No problem," Mohammed said, and disappeared into the crowd as I was swept by my other guards through the security checkpoint at the main entrance.

Once we were inside the dimly lit store, which wouldn't open for another half hour, Barnaby turned to me, grinned, and gave me a thumbs-up. "Sales yesterday were up, Ed. Way up. We're sold out of Henrietta Hyena, but I know that's not why so many people came rushing down to the store."

"Oh?"

"I told you this would work, Ed. You're my good luck charm. I really appreciate it. Thanks to you, my business is going to be saved. People see that you're not afraid to be here, and they're all jumping on the bandwagon."

"I hate to rain on your parade, but it's not that simple, Barnaby," I said somberly. "There's still a murderer on the loose someplace in this city, and it's not going to be a happy holiday until that person is caught and punished."

I nearly didn't recognize Katrina Varinski in her street clothes. It was Mohammed who pointed her out to me. She was sitting at a small table at the back of the deli where we had arranged to meet, a can of diet soda in front of her.

She wore jeans and a sweater, and her long blond hair hung loose down her back, still wavy from the rubber bands and pins she used to keep it tied back while she was in uniform.

She smiled faintly and stood when she saw me. I shook her hand and said, "Thank you for meeting with me, Officer Varinski. I know you're probably eager to get home, but I really need to talk to you."

She nodded. "It's not a problem, but I have only about fifteen minutes. I called my baby-sitter and she said she would stay a little longer, but she has a class tonight. She can't miss it."

Knowing Varinski was a recently divorced single mom who probably relied heavily on her baby-sitter, I promised to be brief so that she could get home.

"What is it that you wanted to talk about?" she asked, unwrapping a straw and sticking it into her can of soda. I noticed that her fingernails weren't just short and unpolished the way most female police officers kept them. Hers were bitten down to the quick.

"I wanted to ask you a few questions about Marlon Killdaire," I said in my straightforward way. "I know that you and he were friends, and I thought maybe you could tell me a little bit about him."

I half expected her to correct me when I said *friends*, but she didn't. I wondered about that. Panopolous had specifically told me that Killdaire was a loner, not the type of man to cultivate friendships.

"I've been very upset about Marlon's death," she said, biting her lip and rotating the can of soda between her hands. "I can't believe it—especially after I had seen what happened to that other man, Mr. Calvino, the week before. I keep picturing Marlon lying there in a pool of blood that way. . . ."

"I know, it's very disturbing," I said, patting her hand in sympathy. "You weren't at the crime scene when they discovered Marlon's body, then? I know you're normally on foot patrol in that neighborhood."

"I am, but I wasn't on the scene, thank God," she said, letting out a shaky sigh. "When the call came in about a body being found, I was investigating a hit-and-run accident on Thirty-third Street. Bobby Wu answered the call, and he was terribly upset. He knew Marlon too, of course."

Bobby Wu, I noted, had been one of the two patrol officers who had helped John Panopolous chase down the shoplifter.

Along with Doug Holt . . . but I would get to him in a moment.

"So Wu and Killdaire weren't friends?" I asked Katrina.

"Friends? No, I wouldn't say that."

"Not like you and Marlon."

"No. Marlon looked out for me. He reminded me of my dad, and he was like a father to me in some ways, Mr. Koch. And my ex-husband, the bastard, was just the opposite."

"So you're divorced?"

She nodded.

"That must have been hard on you and the children."

"It was. They're only babies, really. Jenny is three and Andy's only eighteen months."

"They live with you full-time?"

The way she clenched her jaw alerted me that the situation was more complicated than the simple yes she provided.

"What's the matter, Officer?" I asked, concerned, sensing that she was troubled.

"My ex-husband is moving to California with his new bimbo wife, and he wants to take the kids. We've been going through a terrible custody battle."

"Is there really a threat that he could take them away from you?"

She nodded. "I'm a police officer. I work unusual hours. My ex-husband is an accountant. He works from home. And his wife is loaded. She's the heiress to some real estate fortune, but that's not enough for her. First she had to steal my husband from me; now she's trying to steal my kids."

I didn't know what to say to that.

She went on, staring at the soda can she had clenched in her hands. "They live in an enormous house in Rye, with a maid and a huge backyard. My kids go there, and then they come home to the only place I can afford—a dinky apartment in a borderline neighborhood, Mr. Koch. How do you think the judge is going to view that?"

I told her that I completely understood where she was coming from and that I wished there was something I could do.

"There's nothing," she said bleakly. "I've done everything I could. I scrimped and saved so that we could at least move into

Manhattan—we were living out in Far Rockaway until a few months ago. Now it's easier for me to be there if the kids need me, but still . . . I just know I'm going to lose them to that no-good cheater. It isn't fair."

It *wasn't* fair, and I told her so.

"Maybe your ex will drop the case," I said, though I didn't think there was much chance of that.

She obviously didn't either.

"No way," she said, wiping at a tear that had escaped her eyes.

I reached into my pocket, found a tissue, and handed it to her.

"Thanks," she said, sniffling. "I'm sorry—I don't mean to fall apart. It's just that my husband has always gotten everything he wanted. His parents spoiled him rotten—he was an only child. They weren't rich, but he never worked a day in his life until he got out of college. Me, I've done it all. Every odd job there is. You name it, I've been there. Waitress, token clerk, salesgirl, chambermaid. Before I was accepted into the police academy, I was sure I would spend my whole life making minimum wage."

"Do you enjoy being a police officer?"

"I love it. I used to dream about how great it would be to chase down the bad guys, when I was growing up. I've been on my own since I was sixteen. My father had died a few years before that, and my mother was a drunk who threw me out of the house when she hooked up with a man who didn't like kids."

"That's too bad."

"Yeah. My dad . . . he was a wonderful man. He and I did everything together. But she was a shrew," she said, her voice hardening. "I haven't seen her since. I don't know if she's even alive, and you know what? I don't care. She made life miserable for me, and before that she made life miserable for my poor dad."

"That's too bad," I said again.

"When I met Will—that's my ex—I was too blind to see what he was really about. I guess I just wanted someone to take care of me. And I wanted kids. God, all I ever wanted was to be a mom, you know? A mom and a cop. But as much as I love my job, I live for my kids. I can't stand the thought of losing them, Mr. Koch," she said and her voice broke.

I found myself wondering, as I stared into her big, blue tear-filled eyes, whether she had poured her heart out to Marlon Killdaire . . . and whether he had, in turn, unburdened his own weighty secret.

There was only one way to find out.

"Officer Varinski," I said, and cleared my throat to signal a change of topic, "what kinds of things did you and Marlon talk about?"

She blinked. "Me and Marlon? The usual stuff, I guess—arrests we had made, that kind of thing."

"What about your personal life? Did you ever discuss it with him?"

"Not really. Not all that much. I mean, he knew I was getting divorced, and that my ex was trying to take my kids—but everyone at the station knew that. I've needed a lot of time off lately. They've been good about it. . . ."

"So Marlon didn't tell you anything about what was going on with him either?" I asked, to keep her on track.

It wasn't that I wasn't sympathetic to her personal dilemma, but I knew her time was limited and I had to find out as much as I could about Killdaire.

"You mean personal stuff? He told me some things once in a while. When he looked like he had something on his mind, and I would ask if he was okay."

"Did he always open up?"

"Not usually. Usually, he said he was fine," she said with a shrug. "But now and then he would talk a little bit. A couple of times he would tell me about his son."

"Michael?"

"Him too. But mostly he talked about the other one. The troublemaker."

"David."

She nodded. "You don't know how it broke his heart to have such a rotten son, Mr. Koch. He told me he didn't trust him, and that he thought his son was stealing from him. I think he said once that he was even afraid of him."

"Do you remember exactly what was said, or when this conversation took place?"

She seemed to be thinking back, then shook her head. "Not exactly. It was a few months ago, right before he had that accident with his patrol car. You know about that, right?"

"The brakes failed," I said, nodding.

"Yeah, they just happened to fail."

"What are you saying?" I asked, watching her intently. "That it wasn't an accident?"

She met my gaze head-on. "If it wasn't, I wouldn't be surprised."

"And you think his son was behind it?"

"I wouldn't be surprised," she repeated, and checked her watch. "Oh, my God. I have to go right this minute. My sitter's going to kill me."

She jumped up and reached for the long suede and shearling coat hanging over the back of her chair.

"Nice coat," I commented, thinking that it was pretty extravagant for a single mother who had just confided her money problems.

"This?" She snorted and waved it away with a shrug. "It was a guilt gift my ex gave me for my birthday."

"A guilt gift?"

"Yeah, back when he was sneaking around with Ms. Moneybags and he didn't want me to know. I don't know how I could have been so naive. At the time I thought it was the most beautiful coat I had ever seen. Now I wear it just because it keeps me warm, and it's the only coat I have."

I nodded, feeling sorry for her.

I truly hoped she got to keep her kids, but these days you never know which way a judge is going to go with a custody case.

"Good luck, Officer Varinski," I told her. "Please let me know how things work out."

"I will. I'll be in the neighborhood—Ramsey's in on my beat, remember? So . . . how long are you going to be there? Maybe I'll bring the kids over to sit on your lap."

"I'm not sure how long I'll be there, but I'd love to meet your kids. And again, Officer, good luck. I hope it works out for you."

"Well, good luck to you too. I hope you figure out who killed Marlon, and I hope the SOB rots in jail," she hurled over her shoulder before tossing her long blond hair and scurrying out of the deli.

Too late, I realized I had forgotten to ask her about Doug Holt.

THIRTEEN

David Killdaire's roommate was a wispy, vacant-eyed character who introduced herself as Shell—not Shelly, not Michelle, but *Shell.*

"Shell? Your name is Shell? As in *sea?*" I made the mistake of asking her when I met her Tuesday evening at their shabby Jersey City apartment.

"Huh?" she asked vapidly. "Sea?"

"Never mind."

It was worth noting that Shell was the first person I had met in a very long time who didn't recognize me, despite the fact that I introduced myself using my full name and came trooping into the apartment surrounded by beefy bodyguards.

"You a friend of Dave's?" she asked, dragging deeply on a cigarette.

"You could say that."

"He usually doesn't hang with people who look like you—no offense."

"None taken."

"So Dave's at the club," she announced, drinking from a grimy-looking glass that held either water or straight vodka—and judging from the slur in her voice, I would have bet on the latter.

"Which club is that?" I asked.

"You know . . . the club. That club where he plays."

"Is he playing there tonight?"

"Yeah," Shell said with a snort and a roll of her eyes that told me *yeah* meant *no.* "Right. Dave hasn't had a gig in months. He sold his guitar, remember?"

"Actually, I seem to have forgotten all about that. Why did he sell it, again?"

"Hello? For cash?" she said as if I were the most lamebrained person she had ever met.

"He's pretty strapped then, huh?"

"Yeah. Poor guy." She stubbed out her cigarette. "His folks are loaded, but they cut him off just like that when they kicked him out."

"They're loaded?" I echoed.

As far as I knew, the Killdaires were far from loaded, and their apartment and lifestyle showed no evidence of any hidden wealth. There *was* Marlon Killdaire's retirement bank account—and I wondered exactly how much money was in it.

Then there was the violin. That, too, could be valuable.

Still . . .

"Are you sure David's parents are really all that well off?" I asked Shell.

Out of the corner of my eye I saw an enormous cockroach scurrying up the wall behind the sagging brown couch where she was seated.

"Yeah . . . why?"

"I didn't know his parents were loaded."

"Well, they have plenty of money, but they won't give him any. Can you believe that?"

"Has Dave said anything to you about who might have killed his father?"

"Killed his father?" Her expression became even more blank, if that were possible. "Huh?"

"Didn't he tell you that his father is dead?"

She gulped the clear beverage in her glass and echoed, "His father is dead? Since when?"

"Since last Monday."

"Man, that blows. What happened to him?"

"David didn't mention any of this?"

"Maybe . . ." She appeared to be thinking it over. Then she blinked sleepily and shook her head. "I don't think so."

I watched her, wondering if this was an act, if she was trying to cover up for her roommate.

No. Looking into her eyes, I thought that she seemed genuinely confused, and she was definitely on something. Her pupils were the size of nickels.

"Have you seen David in the past few days?" I asked her.

Again she seemed to be struggling to come up with an answer.

"Probably" was the best she could do.

"Probably?"

"He's in and out all the time, and so am I."

"Then how do you know he's at the club right now?" I demanded, frustrated.

"Because," she said with exaggerated patience, "he's *always* at the club. Everybody knows that."

"Where *is* the club?"

"Near the diner," she said, as if that, too, were something everybody knew.

I exchanged a glance with my bodyguards.

"I think I saw a diner on the way over here," Lou Sabatino volunteered. "About a block or two away."

"Is that the one?" I asked Shell.

"Must be," she murmured, looking as though she were about to doze off.

"Let's go," I said, and turned back to her. "Thank you for your help."

"Huh? What help?" she asked sleepily.

"She can say that again," Mohammed Johnson muttered as we walked out of the apartment.

There was no diner a few blocks away, only a dilapidated sign that read STEAKS 'N CHOPS on the side of a building that looked as though it might once have been a restaurant of some sort. I asked my driver to pull up alongside the curb and peered out into the murky winter darkness.

"Is this the place you meant?" I asked Lou, who was in the backseat beside me.

"Uh, yeah, this is it. I thought it was a diner. Guess I didn't look at it very carefully."

"Guess not," Mohammed said under his breath from the front seat.

I glanced around the deserted street corner. I had never before ventured to this particular section of Jersey City after dark, and it was safe to say that I wouldn't be doing so again if I could help it.

"Mr. Mayor, look over there," Lou said suddenly.

I saw that he was pointing at a green neon sign a few doors down, with half the letters missing. It took me a moment to piece together enough to see that it read THE TURKEY CLUB.

I noticed the Budweiser logo in the window and realized that it was a bar.

And I had the feeling . . .

"Do you think that's the place you're looking for, Mr. Mayor?" Lou asked.

"It might be," I said, opening the door of the car and stepping out onto the sidewalk. "Let's go find out."

It was.

The first person I saw when I walked into the dark, smoky tavern was David Killdaire. He was slouched at the near end of the bar with a draft beer in front of him, staring at the screen of the small television mounted overhead. He wore ragged jeans and a khaki fatigue jacket, and had a baseball cap on backward, with his dark, straggly hair poking out beneath it.

There were a handful of other patrons, most of them sitting or leaning at the bar, which ran the length of the place. All of them appeared to be middle-aged men, with the exception of one woman, who was heavyset, with yellow hair and excessive makeup.

The place was just like every other run-down neighborhood corner dive in the world, filled with sad-looking souls trying to drown their sorrows. There was no evidence of the whimsy that might have inspired the bar's unusual name.

Heads turned when I entered the place with my bodyguards, and I heard someone murmur, "Hey, it's the mayor."

"No way," someone else said.

"Yeah, it's him. It's Ed Koch."

"No kiddin'! Eddie!" called a ruddy-cheeked man who had been standing by the jukebox.

"How'm I doing?" I called back.

"You're doing great! I live over in Brooklyn and I just want you to know I vote for you in every election."

"Well, it's working," I said with a grin, keeping David Killdaire in the corner of my eye. "Thanks."

"No problem. Just keep running, and I'll keep voting," promised my newfound friend and supporter. "Hey, can I buy you a beer?"

"No, thanks," I told him politely, and quickly took three giant steps that landed me squarely in front of Killdaire, whom I had seen slipping off his stool as though he were preparing to bolt out of there.

"Going someplace?" I asked him.

"Yeah."

"Where?"

"I don't think that's any of your business."

"I was thinking maybe I could give you a ride, and we could talk."

"I don't need a ride."

"Fine. Then let's talk right here," I said firmly, sitting on the stool next to the one he had just vacated.

"Talk about what?" He sounded resigned and lit a cigarette, which I took as a positive sign.

"About your father."

His already shadowed eyes grew darker. "I don't want to talk about my father."

"Why not?"

"Hell, would you want to talk about your father if somebody blew his brains out?"

"Maybe. Maybe I would want to get my feelings out. And maybe I would want to help the police solve the case."

"You're not the police."

"No, but I'm the mayor," I said, silently daring him to argue with that logic.

He didn't.

He asked, "How did you find me here?"

"Your girlfriend told me where you were."

"I don't have a girlfriend."

"Shell?"

"That waste case sure as hell isn't my girlfriend. She's just my roommate."

"How did you happen to move in with her?"

"Friend of a friend."

"I see."

There was a long pause. I watched him while he dragged deeply on his cigarette.

"Who do you think did it, David?"

I half expected belligerence again, or at least feigned misunderstanding.

But he sat heavily on the stool again, reached for his beer, and said, "I don't know who did it."

"You don't know anybody who would have a good reason to want your father dead?"

"Besides me, you mean?"

I raised my brows at him.

"Well, that's what you're thinking, isn't it?" he asked sullenly. "You're thinking that I didn't get along with my old man anyway, and that since I'm flat broke and in debt up to my—"

"Can I get you something, Mr. Mayor?" the bartender cut in. He was an elderly man with a shock of white hair and bloodshot blue eyes.

"I'll have a Diet Coke," I told him, and motioned at David Killdaire, who still had a nearly full mug of draft in front of him. "Do you want anything else?"

"Another beer," he said promptly.

That wasn't what I had in mind, but I nodded to the bartender, thinking that whatever would keep Killdaire talking was fine with me.

"So you didn't get along with your father, and you're in debt," I said, picking up where he had left off. "And now your father will never bother you again, and you're going to inherit a whole lot of money."

"Says who?"

"You're *not* going to inherit a whole lot of money?" I asked cautiously.

"My father was a cop, not a doctor. Or a mayor," he added pointedly. "He didn't have any money."

"What about his savings account? For retirement?"

"Yeah," he scoffed, "how much money can he possibly have in there?"

"You tell me."

"Not much," he said glumly. "Not enough to get me out of debt."

"How do you know?"

"I just know, man."

"You know how?"

He shrugged and silently smoked his cigarette.

I tried another tactic. "Do you think your father was killed because he was a cop?"

"Because he was a cop? That doesn't make sense. He wasn't even wearing his uniform. He was wearing a freakin' Santa Claus suit."

"So maybe he was killed by someone who was out to get people who were wearing Santa Claus suits."

"Yeah, maybe. Maybe it was just some psycho freak with a gun." He eyed me, as if searching my face for an answer. Then he looked down at his glass and asked, "Is that what you think?"

"I can't think of any other scenario, David. Can you?"

He shrugged and drained his beer in long gulps, then set down the glass and turned to me. "Look, I know what you're getting at, Mayor. I know you think I killed him. But I didn't."

"I want to believe you."

"You do not. And neither did those detectives that questioned me the other day. You all want to pin this on me. But let me ask you something. Why would I kill that other guy? Calvino?"

"One theory is that whoever killed him thought he was your father."

"That's pretty sick. Some poor old guy gets wiped out because somebody mistakes him for somebody else?"

"That's one theory," I said cautiously.

"Oh, yeah? Is it your theory?"

"It's one theory," I repeated. "Where were you last Monday night when your father was killed?"

"Sleeping at the apartment, man. Just like I told the detectives."

"Can anyone vouch for that?"

"Shell was probably around. She talked to them for me. Said I was home."

I thought about his vacant-eyed roommate with the booze on her breath and her slow, foggy manner of speaking. She wouldn't provide a very convincing alibi, and I figured he knew it.

"Look, Mayor," David Killdaire said. "I didn't kill my old man. If you asked me did I ever *think* about it, the answer would be yes. But that's not the same as taking a gun and doing it. He was my *father.*"

The way he said the final phrase, it was just words. Not the heartfelt tribute one might expect.

I searched Killdaire's gaunt face for emotion and thought I saw a glimmer in his eyes, but it was gone before I could be certain.

Anyway, I thought, some people just aren't given to revealing heartfelt sentiment to virtual strangers.

The fact that David Killdaire didn't get all misty when he spoke of his dead father didn't mean that he had committed patricide.

"How do you know how much—rather, how little—money your father has in his savings account?" I asked him as the bartender set down my soda and his new beer.

Killdaire bent his head so that more hair straggled from beneath the baseball cap to fall in front of his eyes. He muttered something, but I didn't hear what it was.

"Pardon?" I said, and sipped my Diet Coke, watching him.

He glanced up at me. "I *said,* he told me."

"When?"

He lit a new cigarette off the end of the old and inhaled deeply before saying, "About a year ago."

"How did it come up?"

"Because . . . I got into trouble. Big trouble."

"What kind of trouble?"

"With a loan shark," he mumbled.

Just as I had suspected.

"I had some debts," he went on with obvious reluctance, "and . . . you know the story, man. I needed money, fast."

"So you asked your father?"

The way he dropped his eyes to his lap alerted me that the situation wasn't quite that cut and dried.

"No, I didn't ask him. Not exactly."

"What happened?"

"I was . . . going through some papers in the drawer of his night table and—"

"And?"

"And he caught me," Killdaire finally said.

"What kind of papers?"

"Bank statements. I knew he had a savings account. I figured that if I knew how much was in there, I could somehow—I don't know . . ."

"Steal it?" I asked tartly.

"Borrow it."

"I see. But he caught you, and he figured out what you were up to?"

"I told him. I had to. This guy was down my throat every minute, making threats . . ."

"The loan shark."

"Yeah. It was serious life-or-death, man. So I told my father that if I didn't come up with some money—"

"How much money?"

"A *lot,*" he hedged. "I told him the truth. That if I didn't come up with it, he'd be paying for my funeral."

"So he took the money out of his savings account," I summed up. "All the money he had been saving for retirement."

"No."

"No?" I asked, surprised.

"There wasn't enough there to even begin to cover what I owed. Just a few thousand. That was it. A whole lifetime he worked, crazy hours, overtime, and he only had a few thousand in the bank," he said with palpable disdain.

I wanted to shake him, to ask him what *he* had to show for himself, to ask him whether he had ever worked an honest day in his life.

But the last thing I needed was to alienate David Killdaire now, when he was talking freely.

So I kept my expression carefully neutral, and all I asked him was "What happened after you explained your situation to him?"

"He asked me if I could buy a few days from the guy who was on me. I said maybe one, or two at the most. So two days later, my father comes up with the money."

"How much?"

He told me.

It was a large sum of money, especially for a man who only days before had had so little in the bank.

I nodded thoughtfully. "Where did he get it?"

"He wouldn't say. But he got it, and he said he would give it to me. . . ."

"Just like that?"

"Well . . ." He hedged. "He told me that if I ever got into trouble again, I would be on my own. That he wouldn't be able to help me, and he wouldn't even pay for my funeral."

"And so you've been out of trouble ever since."

"Yeah . . . for the most part." He refused to meet my probing gaze.

"Why did you move out of your father's house, David?"

"He threw me out," he said without hesitation.

"Why?"

"I told you, we never got along. Don't pretend you don't know that. The whole world knows." He stood abruptly. "Look, I have to go."

"Let me just ask you a few more questions."

"No. I'm through talking. I told you I didn't want to get into all of this in the first place."

"But you have been talking—"

"Because I'm buzzed and I'm beat and you caught me off guard, Mayor. But now I'm through talking, like I said, and I'm out of here."

With that, he turned and walked out of The Turkey Club, leaving his barely touched beer on the bar.

★ ★ ★

By the time I had returned to Gracie Mansion that night, I was half convinced that Marlon Killdaire's treasured violin had been worth an astronomical sum of money, and that he had sold it to save his son's life.

What that had to do with his murder, I didn't know.

I *did* know that I wasn't sure whether I believed David Killdaire's claim that he had nothing to do with his father's death.

For one thing, his alibi—if it depended on his roommate's word—was murky.

And he had worked at Ramsey's, albeit briefly, which meant that he would know how to get around the areas restricted to employees.

As for the motive—he claimed money wasn't it, that he had virtually nothing to gain by his father's death.

But Killdaire had come up with a lot of money, quickly.

If he hadn't had the money in his savings account, how had he gotten his hands on that much cash?

It all came back to the violin.

That, or . . .

No.

I didn't want to believe it.

I didn't *want* to, but I knew I had to consider the possibility.

What if the late Marlon Killdaire had been the corrupt cop in the precinct, the one accepting dirty money from Nacho Ruiz?

It was hard to believe that an upright family man would toss aside so many years of upholding justice to get involved in payoffs from a slimy drug dealer.

But his son's life was in danger. His son was going to die unless he did something, fast.

So . . .

What had he done?

And how, exactly, had his action led to his death?

Or had it?

Was one thing totally unrelated to the other?

The questions were endless, exhausting.

Ultimately, I realized that instead of shedding more light on the case, my conversation with David Killdaire had served only to make it more confusing.

But there were a number of avenues I had yet to explore. . . . Starting with a telephone call to Killdaire's grieving widow.

But it would have to wait until morning, I realized, glancing at the clock on the mantel.

It was late, and I didn't want to startle the already-fragile Alva Killdaire with a midnight phone call.

Wednesday morning I tried repeatedly to reach Mrs. Killdaire before I left for Ramsey's.

There was no answer.

I also tried to reach Officer Doug Holt down at the precinct, and was told he wouldn't be on duty until that night.

I arrived at the store to find the usual crowd of press and shoppers, and an increasingly glib Barnaby Tischler.

"You have no idea what all this positive publicity is doing for my store," he told me after escorting me up to the employee locker room. "Our sales have skyrocketed in the past few days, Ed. And did you notice that the line for the Highview Meadows shuttle is getting shorter and shorter?"

"I'm glad, Barnaby."

"I passed Simon Weatherly on the street yesterday. He was walking with his head down. Didn't even see me. He must be furious that his plan failed."

"Barnaby—"

"I know he was behind those murders, Ed. I swear he was. It's only a matter of time before the detectives prove it."

I knew he didn't know that the police had traced the bomb threats to Weatherly.

In fact, that detail seemed to keep getting lost in the jumble of information in my own mind.

"You're not afraid, are you, Ed?" Barnaby was asking as he handed me the red plush hat with the white fur trim.

"Afraid? Of what?"

"That someone's going to do to you what they did to Calvino and Killdaire?"

"Barnaby, I'm surrounded by bodyguards at every moment of

my life," I pointed out, glancing over at Lou and Mohammed, who hovered nearby, looking mighty glum in their pointy green felt shoes and jingle-bell hats. "No one is going to ambush me. Besides, you still have all that security at the store entrances, and the metal detectors."

"That's what I wanted to talk to you about. I'm having the extra security removed immediately."

"Why?"

"I can't help feeling as though it's no longer necessary, Ed. People are shopping at Ramsey's again. More people than have been here all year. It seems somewhat unnecessary to keep the extra security around as a reminder of the tragedy that occurred here. I think it would be best if we just move on and try to forget about it."

"Forget about it?"

"You know what I mean, Ed. I just feel that it's pessimistic to assume that anything else is going to happen. And, to be perfectly candid, the extra security didn't keep Marlon Killdaire from being murdered. Somebody still got a gun into the store somehow."

"True."

"But you won't be worried if I remove the security?"

"No. I told you, I have my bodyguards around me. I'm sure that I'll be perfectly safe."

"Yes, I'm sure you will be. . . ."

But something in his expression made me feel vaguely apprehensive.

"What?" I demanded, fiddling with the wide black belt around my pillow-enhanced waistline.

"Nothing."

"Good," I said, pulling the high black rubber boots onto my feet and giving my full white beard a final tug to make sure it was kidproof.

I motioned to my bodyguards, and together we clomped off down the corridor toward the Winter Wonderland.

I did my best to get into a suitably jolly mood.

But the conversation with Barnaby had cast a pall over the day, and as the hours wore on, I found myself growing increasingly uneasy.

It wasn't that I was *afraid*.

Still . . .

The sooner I solved this case, the better.

Alva Killdaire picked up on the first ring when I reached her late Wednesday afternoon, after my Santa shift had ended.

"Has something happened?" she asked, sounding anxious. "Have they made an arrest?"

"Not yet, Mrs. Killdaire. I just had a few questions to ask you. I tried to reach you this morning, but—"

"I went to early mass," she said. "I go every morning. And then I went to visit my new grandchild."

"Oh, Michael's baby. Is everything all right?"

"Yes, it was a boy. He's gorgeous, and they named him after Marlon."

"That's very touching, Mrs. Killdaire."

She sighed. "I only wish my husband had lived to see it. What did you want to ask me?"

"When was the last time you saw Marlon's violin?"

"Marlon's violin?" She sounded taken aback. "Why?"

"Something's come up, and . . . have you seen it recently?"

"No. I've *never* seen the violin, Mr. Koch."

"But . . . how can that be?"

"My husband has always kept it in a safe deposit box down at the bank."

"Do you have any idea why?"

"I don't know . . . because he treasured it, I suppose. As I said, it was a family heirloom brought over from Europe. And he was very private about it, like I told you. The boys didn't even know he had it."

"Was it valuable?"

"Valuable? No . . ."

"Are you sure?"

There was a pause. "To tell you the truth, I never considered that it might be valuable, and he never said. We rarely discussed it, Mr. Koch, over all these years. I had all but forgotten about it until you asked me about his music when you were here last week."

"Do you know what else your husband had in the safe deposit box?"

"No. I suppose there were important documents . . . our marriage license. The boys' birth certificates. Marlon handled all of that, Mr. Koch. He paid the bills, he kept track of our finances—I'm going to be lost without him." Her voice broke, and I heard her sniffle.

I waited a few moments for her to collect herself.

My mind was racing.

I couldn't help wondering whether, if Marlon Killdaire really was investigating corruption within his precinct, he might have placed whatever evidence he had collected into the safe deposit box.

Or, if he were the cop on the take, he might have been stashing the cash there.

I asked Mrs. Killdaire, "Does anyone else know about the violin? Did you tell the police?"

"Why would I tell them about a musical instrument?" she asked, sounding bewildered. "Should I have told them?"

"Did you tell them about the safe deposit box?"

"I didn't think to, no. But maybe I should have—"

"Do you know where he keeps the key?"

"To the box?"

"Yes." I did my best not to sound impatient.

"Well . . . it's probably in the drawer of his nightstand. That's where he kept that sort of thing."

"Can you check, please? I'll hold on while you do."

"All right," she agreed, and there was a clatter as she set the phone down.

A few moments later she was back. "It was there. At least, I'm pretty sure that's what this key is for."

"And is the safe deposit box in both your names?"

"I really don't know."

"Mrs. Killdaire, I need you to find out. And if the box is in both your names, you will need to get a court order to get into the box. Arrangements will be made for a state tax estate lawyer to be present to inventory the box's contents."

"But why do you need me to look in the box? What do you think is there?"

"I'm not sure, but I think it's a good idea to check it out."

I didn't mention that the safe deposit box might very well hold the key to her husband's murder.

FOURTEEN

"Mr. Mayor, it's a pleasure to see you again," said Officer Doug Holt, greeting me at the desk sergeant's desk Wednesday evening. "I'm not sure if you remember, but we met a few weeks ago at—"

"I remember," I cut in, the image of the Calvino crime scene vivid in my mind.

"Oh." He seemed momentarily taken aback. "The captain said you would be coming by to see me. I'm supposed to be out on my beat, but he told me to wait. . . ."

His demeanor was far different from the almost cocky attitude he had shown the night of the Calvino murder.

Now he was distinctly nervous, and his hand had been clammy when I shook it.

"Uh, what can I do for you?" he asked.

"I'd like to ask you a few questions."

"Questions? About what?"

"Can we talk in private?" I asked, conscious of the bustling action surrounding us.

"Oh . . . sure. Sure, come on back."

He led the way past the desk sergeant and down the same hall I had traveled with John Panopolous.

"Finish all your Christmas shopping?" I asked conversationally as we walked.

"Just about."

"Do you have a lot of people to buy for?"

"Besides my wife and three kids? Yeah, but they're the biggest expense. The kids want everything. You know that Henrietta Hyena puppet?"

"I've heard of it, but I've never seen it."

"Who has? You can't find it anywhere, and my littlest daughter, she's crazy for it. She wants it so bad. My wife told me she heard people are selling them for three hundred bucks. You ever hear of such a crazy thing?"

"Never."

"I'm telling you, the holidays cost me a fortune every year. I keep saying we gotta cut back, but my wife, she doesn't seem to get it. She just keeps shopping and charging stuff."

"Running up the old credit cards, huh?"

"Yeah, you know it," he said ruefully.

I filed that away, not that it meant anything.

Yet.

"What about them?" Holt asked, opening the door to the office and glancing at my bodyguards, who were right on our heels.

"They stick with me," I told him.

"Everywhere you go?"

I didn't want to answer that.

"Just forget they're here," I told him.

"If you say so." He took a seat and motioned for me to do the same. "Is this about the Ramsey's murders?"

"Why do you ask?"

"It makes sense. I heard you were helping out with the investigation."

"And you were in the store the nights of both murders."

He visibly flinched. "Yeah, but with the first one, where I saw you, it was only because I was on patrol in the area, and I responded to the radio call, just like all the other cops in the neighborhood did."

"So that was the first time you were ever in the employees' locker room?"

"Nah. I was up there one other time; I guess it was two or three years ago."

My ears perked up at that. "What were the circumstances?"

"Same thing. I was patrolling the neighborhood and I answered a radio call for the department store. Those crazy Dobermans had cornered some guy in one of the offices. I think he was an electrician or something. . . ."

"A computer repairman, maybe?"

"Maybe. You hear about that?"

I nodded, recalling that Barnaby Tischler had told me that same story the night of the Calvino murder, when we heard the dogs barking wildly downstairs.

"And you again responded to a radio call the night of the Killdaire murder," I prompted Holt, moving right along, armed with the knowledge that he, like most of the other suspects, would have some familiarity with the parts of the store off limits to the general public.

"Yeah, but I wasn't called to the store because of the murder that night. That happened later. I was there in the first place because they reported a shoplifter on the premises, trying to evade security. A bunch of us cops who were in the area rushed to the scene. At the time, I had no idea that Marlon was even working there as a Santa Claus that night, or that he had been . . . uh, you know."

"Shot to death."

He winced. "Yeah."

"What was your relationship with Marlon Killdaire, Officer Holt?"

"It was normal. Why?"

"Normal?"

"Yeah, you know . . . we worked together. I didn't know him very well. He kept to himself. Especially lately."

"What do you mean?"

"You know . . . for the past six months or so, maybe longer. He never really socialized with the rest of us in the first place, but he had gotten real quiet lately. Like something was bothering him. And if you ask me, he seemed paranoid too."

"Paranoid? How so?"

"I don't know . . . it was just something about him. Like he was . . . I don't know."

"Yes, you do," I said, sensing that he was reluctant to reveal something. "Like he was . . . what?"

"You know . . ."

All these *you-knows* were getting on my nerves.

"Actually, I *don't* know, Officer," I said tersely. "That's why I'm asking you to tell me. How would you describe Marlon Killdaire's behavior in recent months?"

"Jumpy. He was jumpy. I'm a cop, Mr. Mayor, and I know the signs. Someone acts jumpy, with their eyes shifting around all the time, looking anywhere but into yours, then they're up to something. They're feeling guilty."

"You think Marlon Killdaire was feeling guilty about something?"

"Yeah. I think he was hiding something."

I raised an eyebrow at that. "What would he have to hide?"

"You got me. Maybe . . . maybe he was having an affair." He threw up his hands in a disclaimer. "But hey, that's just me. It's just me talking, telling you what I *think*. Not what I know."

"So he was having—you *think* he was having—an affair? With whom?"

He shook his head. "How would I know? I have no idea."

But the way he said it, and the look in his eyes, told me that he had his theories.

"What about Katrina Varinski?" I asked point-blank.

His mouth fell open. "What? What about her? Why would you say that?"

"They were friends, weren't they?"

"Yeah, or so some people thought."

"Other people thought differently?"

"Yeah. What were they supposed to think? That babe doesn't give any of us the time of day, except for Marlon. Marlon, she talks to. *Talked* to," he amended.

"You think they were having an affair?"

"Just between you and me, Mr. Mayor, yeah. I do. Why else would a young, hot babe like that spend so much time with an old guy like him?"

I shrugged, remembering how I had seen Doug Holt eyeing Katrina the night of the Calvino murder. Even then I had sensed that he had a leering interest in the attractive blond officer. I wondered if he had approached her and been rebuffed, and his ego's way of explaining the rejection was that she was already involved with someone.

Maybe.

Then again, maybe there was something to his theory. Maybe Varinski and Killdaire really were involved.

"Maybe they were just friends," I suggested to Holt, watching him carefully.

"Yeah, and maybe there really is a Santa Claus. Come on, Mr. Mayor. Didn't you see the pictures of Killdaire's wife in the paper? She's not very . . . attractive," he said, as if trying to be delicate about it. "You mean to tell me that with a wife like that waiting at home, you don't think the old guy would want a little action on the side?"

He really was a jerk, I concluded.

But that didn't make him a murderer.

And it didn't mean there might not be some truth to his insinuation about Killdaire and Varinski.

I shifted gears, deciding to wrap things up unless there was something else he could tell me.

"Did you notice anything unusual about the store the night of the murder, Officer Holt?"

"Nope. Except for the fact that it was just about empty. Hardly any customers. But it was close to closing time, so maybe that was why."

"Or maybe people are afraid to shop there because two men were murdered on the premises in the space of a week."

"Yeah, maybe. But hey, Mr. Mayor, I hear you're the new Ramsey's Santa Claus. People are psyched."

"I suppose they are."

"Yeah, you're drawing big crowds. The kiddies love you, and so do their parents. They'll probably even vote for you in the next election. Way to go, and ho-ho-ho, huh, Mr. Mayor?"

He leaned forward and slapped me on the back like we were old chums.

"Ho-ho-ho," I echoed thoughtfully.

* * *

Before leaving the precinct, I asked to see the captain.

While I was waiting for him, I bumped into Katrina Varinski. She wore jeans and a white sweater with holly leaves embroidered across the front, and told me she had just ended her shift and was on her way home.

"How's the custody battle going?" I asked her.

"No decision yet, but I'm hoping to know in a few days," she said, her cheeks all flushed pink and her blue eyes looking, if not happy, then at least not as dejected as they had been in the past.

"You must have a good feeling about it," I said. "You look upbeat."

"I am, Mr. Mayor. I have a hunch that the case is going to go my way. By the way, how's your investigation coming along?"

"Pretty well. You haven't thought of anything else you can tell me that might help me out, have you?"

"I wish I could say that I have. I keep thinking there must be something I'm overlooking, since I spent all that time talking to Marlon. But I can't put my finger on anything specific."

"If you do, will you let me know?"

"Absolutely." She pulled on a navy ski jacket and a pair of red mittens. "I'm still planning on bringing my kids down to the store to see you."

"Do that. I'll slip them an extra candy cane or two."

She smiled, waved, and left just as I was summoned into the captain's office.

It took some finagling, but I finally talked him into giving me the address of Joey Santiago, the fourteen-year-old shoplifter.

And after leaving the police precinct, I headed straight over there.

It was a brownstone on St. Nicholas Avenue up in Washington Heights, a part of Manhattan that doesn't feel like Manhattan. At least, I've never thought so.

For one thing, it's very hilly, with steep, winding streets and sweeping water views that seem more reminiscent of San Francisco than New York. There are acres of parks and gardens, and charming prewar apartment buildings.

And despite the presence of world-renowned museums, along

with the prestigious Columbia-Presbyterian Medical Center and Yeshiva University, I've always noticed that there's almost a small-town feel to the neighborhood, which is primarily Latino.

A bunch of shady-looking characters were hanging out on the stoop of Joey Santiago's brownstone. They scrambled to attention and then rapidly dispersed when they saw my official sedan pull up at the curb, followed by another car containing the rest of my security detail.

The front door of the building was standing ajar, so I walked right in, flanked by Lou and Ambrose and trailed by several other wary guards.

A couple of young kids playing in the first floor hallway greeted me shyly in Spanish, and I answered them in turn, wondering what they were doing up at this hour and where their parents were.

On the third floor, I found the Santiago apartment.

The television set was blaring from inside, and I could tell that it was tuned to a cops-and-robbers action show, because I could hear sirens wailing and gunfire cracking.

The apartment door, painted with peeling maroon paint, was thrown open moments after I knocked.

"Are you Joey?" I asked the young boy who stood there.

"Nah. Joey's not home," he said in heavily accented English. "You a cop?"

"Why do you ask?"

He shrugged, staring at me with round brown eyes fringed by long dark lashes.

"Actually," I said, "I'm the mayor. Mayor Koch. Did you ever hear of me?"

"Yeah, I heard of you," he said, seeming unimpressed.

"Are you Joey's brother?" I asked.

"His half brother. I'm a year older."

"So you're fifteen."

He nodded.

"What's your name?" I asked.

"Donnie."

"Donnie Santiago?"

"Nah. Donnie Ruiz. We don't got the same father."

Ruiz.

The name slammed into me like a subway train.

There must have been thousands of people named Ruiz in the city, particularly in this neighborhood.

Still . . .

"Are you any relation to Nacho Ruiz?" I asked Donnie.

"Nacho? You know Nacho? Yeah, he's my big brother," he said proudly.

My mind whirled.

"He ain't here either though," the boy went on. "I'm the only one home, except my little sisters, an' they're sleepin'. Hey, how do you know Nacho?"

It was my turn to shrug.

"Hey, Mayor, you here to give him an award or somethin'?"

"Why do you ask that?"

"You know, 'cause Nacho, he always helpin' people an' stuff. He always buyin' people presents."

"Sounds like a terrific guy," I said wryly. "You wouldn't happen to know where I could find your big brother, would you?"

"He's workin'. He works nights."

I'll just bet he does, I thought grimly.

"You want me to tell him to call you?" Donnie asked.

"No, don't do that," I said hastily. "Don't tell him I was here, Donnie, okay? I want to surprise him with the award."

"Yeah, sure," he said eagerly. "I won't say anythin' about it."

As I left the apartment building less than five minutes after my arrival, I couldn't help feeling triumphant.

I had been right.

The shoplifter had been a decoy.

Which linked Nacho Ruiz directly to the murder, whether or not he had actually pulled the trigger.

But who had put him up to it?

As I lay in bed that night, I felt as though I were missing something, some clue that kept darting to the edge of my consciousness, then slipping away again.

Hard as I tried, I was too exhausted to pin it down.

Maybe tomorrow . . .

★   ★   ★

The case took two major turns early on Thursday.

I received a phone call at Gracie Mansion just as I was walking out the door. It came from Harris Bayor, the police commissioner, who said there had been an arrest in connection with the Guy Drummond murder.

"The perp was a seventeen-year-old heroin addict. The motive was robbery, just like I thought," Harry told me tersely. "We're positive now that the Drummond case is totally unrelated to the deaths of the two Ramsey's Santas."

"I'm not surprised, Harry. Is the press aware of the arrest?"

"They will be after my press conference in an hour."

"Well, maybe some of the furor over the first two murders will die down now that we all know there's no serial killer on the loose in the city."

"Maybe. But it looks like we're at a standstill with the investigation into Calvino and Killdaire. We can't come up with anything to link Simon Weatherly to the murders. And the police corruption angle hasn't turned up anything yet either. It's a damn puzzle. And we can't find this Ruiz character for questioning."

I almost told him what I knew right then and there—about Ruiz's little brother being the shoplifter, and about what Michael Killdaire had said about his father looking into something underhanded before he died, and about Marlon's violin and the safe deposit box.

In fact, I probably would have told the commissioner everything if he hadn't been abruptly called away from the phone at that very instant.

And so there was nothing to do but walk out the door and head down to Ramsey's, where the murders were in the back of my mind all morning.

I was called away from the Winter Wonderland by Barnaby shortly before eleven-thirty, with the news that there was an important telephone call for me.

It was, of course, Alva Killdaire.

"I went to the bank like you said, Mr. Mayor. I found out that the safe deposit box was in Marlon's name only. They said that

228 / Edward I. Koch

I need to hire an attorney to petition the bank for some kind of certificate that will allow the executor of Marlon's will to open the box. That would be my son, Michael."

I nodded, familiar with the procedure.

"That could take weeks," I told Mrs. Killdaire. "But there is another way to do it more quickly."

"What's that?"

"We can get a court order very quickly. After all, this is a murder case, and your husband's safe deposit box might contain evidence that will help us solve the case."

"How do we get a court order?"

"How? I'm the mayor. Just leave the details up to me, Mrs. Killdaire."

As I had suspected, because Marlon Killdaire's safe deposit box contained possible evidence in a murder case, a court order to open it would be processed far more quickly than usual. Erik Dolk, who had agreed to expedite the matter as a favor, informed me that we could have permission as early as tomorrow morning.

With that in mind, I was feeling optimistic late Thursday afternoon when my Santa shift ended.

I left the Wonderland display, flanked by my watchful giant elves.

Our footsteps echoed as we walked briskly along the narrow, deserted corridor leading to the door that opened into the locker room.

I couldn't help but wonder whether we would have an arrest by this time tomorrow.

Maybe so, I thought, reaching out to turn the knob of the door. It was possible, if Marlon Killdaire's safe deposit box revealed the identity of the crooked cop.

But if it didn't, then—

"Oh!"

"Hello, Mr. Koch!"

"Dotty, you startled me," I said, stopping in the doorway to the locker room and placing a palm over my galloping heart.

The white-haired old saleswoman giggled. "You startled me too. Oh, my." Her bony hand fluttered to her throat.

"What are you doing up here?"

"I'm on my break. I was just coming to find you."

"You were?"

I couldn't help thinking that according to Barnaby, she wasn't authorized to venture down the hallway leading to the Winter Wonderland area. Only employees directly connected with the display were allowed beyond the door she had just opened.

But then, Dotty was an old-timer—she'd been with the store for years and probably knew every inch of it.

Besides, until this year, as Barnaby had said, there had been no need to restrict the Wonderland area, because there was nothing to hide.

Anyway, with her brash personality, Dotty didn't strike me as the kind of person who would necessarily pay heed to rules and regulations.

"I have something for you," she said, and reached into the pocket of her double-knit jacket.

For some reason, a chill crept down my spine.

It wasn't that she had spoken in an ominous way, or that I felt threatened by a little old lady—especially with my bodyguards right behind me.

But I was still jumpy at the way she had popped out at me.

And, too, I couldn't help being spooked by the knowledge that I was standing a few feet away from the very spot where someone had crept up and startled both Calvino and Killdaire in the instant before they had been gunned down in cold blood.

I had to struggle to keep from flinching as Dotty pulled something from her jacket and reached toward me.

"What . . . what is it?" I asked, looking down and seeing that it was a small jar that contained some green, congealed substance.

I was seized by the impulse to let out a huge sigh of relief, which was irritating, because what had I been expecting?

"It's Christmas jelly," she announced, looking pleased with herself. "I made it myself. See the label? I had them printed up professionally."

I rotated the jar and saw a red and white candy-striped label with green lettering that read CHRISTMAS JELLY FROM THE KITCHEN OF DOTTY.

"This is very sweet of you," I told her. "I'll be sure to have some with my breakfast toast tomorrow morning."

I never have toast for breakfast, but she wouldn't know that.

"I'm so glad. I wanted to let you know how thankful I am to you for saving my job, Mr. Koch."

"Well, I—"

"Now, don't go saying you aren't directly responsible for that, because I know that you are. If it weren't for you taking over for those poor dead Santas, I just know I would be out of work by now."

"Oh, I don't know about that." I started walking again, heading toward the locker where I had stashed my street clothes.

"It's true, Mr. Koch. You know, I've been working at this store for years and years. I've seen a lot of crazy things in all that time, but the past few weeks really take the cake."

"I know it's been upsetting for you, Dotty."

"You can say that again. You know, I'm not a young woman, Mr. Koch. Last Monday night just about finished me off, with that shoplifter causing such a ruckus, and then the second murder, that poor nice Mr. Killdaire. . . ."

I nodded, sitting on a bench and pulling the black boots off my feet. They were a size too small, and for a moment I just sat there, pleased to be able to wiggle my toes again.

Dotty chattered on.

"If I found myself out of work after that, I would have truly fallen apart. I count on this job, Mr. Koch. It's everything to me. Why, I'll never forget the day they told me, 'You're hired.' I was so excited, because, you know, it was either work here at Ramsey's or take a job sewing for a seamstress in my building. My eyes have never been good, and I don't have much patience for sewing. And I always did like to get out and work with people, Mr. Koch. I'm sure you do too, being a mayor like you are."

"I do enjoy people," I told her, my mind only half on the conversation.

At Dotty's mention of the murders, my thoughts had drifted to Alva Killdaire, and I found myself wondering if she had told her sons yet about the safe deposit box and the violin. I hadn't thought to ask her not to.

"Back in the old days when I got hired here, Mr. Koch, there weren't a whole lot of jobs out there for women who were people lovers. Most women didn't even work outside the home, and those who did didn't have much choice. Most of them were teachers or nurses. That was it, all there was, for a long time. It's amazing how things have changed."

"That's true," I murmured, wincing as I pulled the fake white beard from my cheeks, feeling the glue I had used to attach it sting my skin.

"You know, my daughter always used to tell me she was going to be a fireman when she grew up," Dotty rambled on. "Oh, I would laugh and laugh at that. I said, 'Girls can't be firemen, Donna.' But you know what, Mr. Mayor? They can be firemen these days, even though it's a dangerous occupation."

"Mmm-hmm." I reasoned that Alva Killdaire probably hadn't spoken to David yet. But Michael—she must have told Michael by now.

"I've seen quite a few women who are firemen," Dotty mused, "and quite a few women who are police officers too. Pretty women even. Like that nice blond policewoman who was here the other night. And you know, when that shoplifter was running loose in my department, he knocked over one of the Christmas trees. I'm the one who picked it all up, because who else was going to do it? A lot of the colored glass bulbs were smashed on the floor, and I cut my hand while I was cleaning up the mess. My goodness, did that ever smart."

"I'm sure it did," I said absently, stripping off the heavy red velour coat and tossing it onto the bench.

"I got blood all over my slacks, you know, from the cut, and the policewoman helped me wash it out. You wouldn't catch a male policeman doing that. Of course, a male policeman wouldn't be in the ladies' room anyway, so I guess that's beside the point. You know, I ate in a restaurant the other night that didn't even *have* a ladies' room. Did you ever hear of such a thing?"

"Not that I can remember." I pulled the down pillows from beneath my T-shirt and tossed them aside, relieved to have returned to my usual girth. It's not easy to get around when you've added a few feet to your general circumference.

"There was just one rest room at that crazy restaurant," Dotty informed me. "It was for men and for women. I told my grandson—I was out to eat with him, in Greenwich Village—that's where he lives. He goes to NYU. Anyway, I told him, 'I'm not going to use a rest room that men use.' And he said, 'Why not, Granny? You do it all the time.' And I said, 'I most certainly do not,' and he said, 'Sure you do. I use the bathroom in your apartment when I visit, and I'm a man.' And do you know what I said to him?"

"Nope." I vigorously rubbed cold cream into my cheeks to remove the rouge, and reached for a box of tissues.

"I said, 'That's different, Gregory. You're not a stranger. I can't use a bathroom that strange men have used, and that's that.' Do you blame me, Mr. Koch?"

"Not—"

"Of course, you're a man, and I can't say that I would mind using a rest room you had used, but you're a mayor, and you're not a stranger. I feel as though we've become very well acquainted over the past few weeks since we met, Mr. Koch, don't you?"

"I do, Dotty, but regardless of that fact, I'm going to have to excuse myself now. I need to take off my pants, and I usually do that in private." I patted the red Santa trousers and raised an eyebrow at her.

"Oh! Of course," she said, actually blushing. "I'll be going. I need to run down to the deli and get a sandwich for my supper anyway. Enjoy the jelly. Oh, I'm a poet and I didn't know it!"

"Excuse me?"

"Deli, jelly," she said in a singsong voice. "Have a nice night, Mr. Koch."

"You too, Dotty."

My mind meandered back to the murder as I finished getting out of my Santa suit and into my street clothes.

Something was nagging at my consciousness, but I couldn't quite put my finger on it.

It wasn't until I was in the car, heading back home to Gracie Mansion, that I figured out what it was.

Rather, I figured out *who* it was.

The murderer.

Could it be . . . ?

Maybe.

Just maybe.

But there was only one way to be sure.

I told my driver to turn around and return to Ramsey's Department Store.

FIFTEEN

I was silent in the car as we headed back uptown toward Gracie Mansion a short time later.

At last I had found the evidence I sought, the evidence I had somehow managed to overlook all along.

It was right there in the locker room, right at the scene of the crime, just waiting to be noticed.

I now knew who had murdered both Calvino and Killdaire.

I knew how, and I knew why.

What I didn't know was how to prove it to the police.

The evidence that had convinced me that my hunch was correct was hardly the kind of evidence you could use to arrest someone for murder.

For that, we would need something concrete.

I was hoping that we would find it in Marlon Killdaire's safe deposit box.

And I was hoping we would be able to get into it first thing tomorrow morning.

If the box didn't contain evidence, I was in trouble.

Unless the killer confessed—something I didn't believe was remotely likely—how was I going to see that justice was served?

There was only one way.

I would have to set a trap.

A trap that would, of course, need to be baited.

And as I stared moodily out the window at the twinkling white lights on the Park Avenue island, I realized what the bait would have to be.

Me.

"Hello, Sybil?"

"Ed! You just caught me. I was on my way out the door."

"Where were you going?"

"To have my hair done for the press banquet I'm attending tonight."

"Did you finish your column for tomorrow?"

"Hours ago."

Disappointment shot through me. I had been counting on the fact that Sybil rarely meets a deadline.

"That's not like you," I told her. "Have you turned over a new leaf? Getting started on your New Year's resolution a few weeks early?"

"Wouldn't my editor love that! No, actually, Claude just got in from London this afternoon, and I wanted to spend time with him. We haven't seen each other in two weeks."

"Oh, well, I guess it'll just have to wait, then," I said with a sigh. "I'll let you go. Have fun to—"

"What will have to wait?" Her keen reporter's savvy had leapt on my comment, just as I had expected.

"I know you're in a rush, Sybil, so don't worry about—"

"What will have to wait?" she repeated sharply.

"I had a scoop for you, but if you've already filed your—"

"It's never too late for a scoop, Ed. You know that. Just wait a second while I grab a pen," she muttered, and I could hear her fumbling around on her end. Then she said, "Okay, shoot. What have you got for me?"

"I promised that I'd tell you first, so . . . I've nailed the Ramsey's murderer. I've got evidence, and I'm taking it to the police tomorrow evening, after my Santa shift is over."

"Why not tonight?" she asked, just as I had anticipated.

"Because I need to pull the facts together in a cohesive way. You know me, Sybil. I like to be thorough."

Lucky for me, she bought that excuse.

MURDER ON 34th STREET / 237

"So who is it?" she asked.

"I can't tell you that. But I will say that the truth is shocking."

"You mean it's not someone who has been previously under suspicion?"

"I can't answer that. But you can expect an arrest to be made by the weekend. The whole city will be able to breathe a sigh of relief. In fact, Barnaby Tischler has already removed the extra security at Ramsey's. No more metal detectors, no more guards at the doors."

"Interesting."

"It's been an interesting case. But it's a relief to have solved it at last."

"And you're telling me this because . . . ?"

"I promised you a scoop, Sybil. I never go back on a promise. Why do you think I've been mayor for so long?"

"Let me ask you something, Ed. If you're not going to the police until tomorrow night, and you're giving me this information now, what do you expect me to do with it? Our paper comes out in the morning. The whole city is going to know about it before you even reveal the suspect to the police."

"Hmm," I said noncommittally. "You do have a point."

"Well, what am I supposed to do with this information?"

"You're a reporter, Sybil. Do what any reporter would do."

I had no doubt that she would.

And as I hung up the phone, I felt both triumphant and apprehensive.

My trap had been set.

Now all I had to do was wait for the killer to step into it.

On Friday morning at nine o'clock, my driver pulled up in front of a large yellow brick bank building on Queens Boulevard.

The number seven train rattled by on the elevated track overhead as I stepped out of the car and walked briskly inside the bank, escorted by my bodyguards.

They seemed even more vigilant than usual, if that's possible. They had been carefully briefed on my agenda for the day.

Winter sunlight streamed through the tall arched windows of

the bank, and filtered across the marble floor. The light seemed to cast a surreal glow over the scene.

Five people waited by the entrance to the restricted vault toward the back of the lobby, where the safe deposit boxes were kept.

Alva Killdaire clutched the arm of her son, Michael, both of them clearly on edge.

Erik Dolk held an official-looking envelope that I knew contained the court order to open Marlon Killdaire's safe deposit box.

With them were two other men, both in suits. They turned out to be Jeffrey Waxman, the Killdaires' attorney, and Asad Dalal, the bank manager.

After brief, polite greetings and introductions, we all passed through the door to the large vault that was lined with safe deposit boxes of various sizes.

"Before we do this," Michael Killdaire said, turning to me, "can I ask you about something?"

I saw that he was holding a folded copy of that morning's edition of *The Daily Register*.

In it was Sybil's column, which trumpeted the news that I had identified the killer of Angelo Calvino and Marlon Killdaire, and would be going to the police this evening with my evidence.

"You know who killed Pop?" Michael asked me.

I nodded.

"Who was it?" Alva's voice trembled.

"I would rather not say until after we have opened the box," I told them. "I'm hoping that once we have examined the contents, you'll be able to see for yourselves."

"You think this box contains the name of the killer?" Jeffrey Waxman asked.

"If we're lucky, something in here will incriminate the killer, yes."

"What if it doesn't?" Michael asked.

"Then I'll have proof before the day is over. Now, let's get down to business, shall we?"

Mrs. Killdaire produced the key and handed it to Michael, who, as executor of his father's will, would have the responsibility of actually opening the box.

Dalal held a second key, the bank's master, which worked in conjunction with the box's individual key.

Michael and Dalal walked over to the wall and took turns fitting their keys into the lock and turning it.

Then Michael pulled a drawer and lifted a large box out of its compartment.

"Here we go," he said nervously.

He set it on a table and we gathered around.

The room was eerily silent as he lifted the lid.

I found myself holding my breath, peering over Michael's shoulder, hoping to see . . .

"Nothing."

The word seemed to echo in the room. I don't even know who said it.

But it was the truth.

Marlon Killdaire's safe deposit box was empty.

"His violin," Alva murmured. "Where is it?"

"He must have sold it, Mom," Michael said softly, confirming my hunch that she had told him about Marlon's prized heirloom. "He sold it."

"But why would he do that?"

"Because David needed money." Michael's voice was bitter and his eyes glinted with anger. "It had to be that. I told you, Mom—"

"But what about our marriage license? And your birth certificates? Why aren't they in here?"

"He kept them in the drawer of his nightstand at home," Michael said. "I thought you knew that."

"I never looked in there," she said. "Not until I needed to find the key the other day. But why did he need this safe deposit box, then? Just for the violin?"

"This is the largest type of box we offer." Asad Dalal spoke up. "People who just need a safe place to keep documents don't generally rent a box this big."

"The violin must have been worth a lot of money, Mrs. Killdaire," I told her. "Your husband must have sold it because he needed to get his hands on a lot of cash, quickly."

She nodded.

I sighed.

I was convinced that Marlon Killdaire had sold the violin to save his son from the loan shark's vengeance, just as I had suspected.

But I still lacked the proof I needed to bring to the police.

And now there was only one way to get that.

By Friday afternoon my face was stiff. Whether it was from smiling, or from the glue that adhered the white beard to my flesh, I didn't know.

"Hey, Santa, where are your elves?" asked the curly-haired moppet on my lap. I couldn't tell if it was a boy or a girl. The child was dressed in jeans and a red sweater, and its name was Jordan.

"My elves? They're on vacation today."

"Vacation? Where?"

"Barbados," I said wryly. "It's the perfect time of year for the Caribbean."

"Shouldn't they be busy at the North Pole, making toys, instead of goofing off on vacation?"

"You know, you're a pretty sharp kid," I said, ruffling the child's curls. "Come back and see me in a few years. I'll try and find a job for you. How would you like that?"

"I'd rather just get a bunch of presents."

As the afternoon wore on, I found myself warily searching the faces of the adults in the line that wove through the Wonderland area, looking for a familiar face—even though I knew I wouldn't find the one I sought there.

The killer wouldn't be brazen enough to be seen.

No, this was a cunning person, a person who knew how to creep through the shadows without being detected.

At precisely three o'clock, I made a big show of stretching as though I were feeling lazy and weary rather than taut with tension.

It was time for Santa to take a break.

Time to slip away from the velvet throne and down the deserted hall that had been the scene of two gory murders.

Time to see whether my trap had worked.

As I left the public area, I called loudly over my shoulder, "See you in a little while, kiddies! Santa needs to take a short rest now."

I opened the door that led to the dimly lit hallway that led to the closed door at the other end, which opened onto the locker room.

It was deserted.

I took a step, pulling the door to behind me. It seemed to close with an ominous click.

I began walking down the hallway, conscious of the closed door halfway down on the right, which led to the storage closet where both Calvino's and Killdaire's bodies had been found.

And as I walked, I sensed that I wasn't alone.

Someone lurked in that closet, just as they had on the nights of the murders.

Someone was lying in wait, clutching a gun armed with a silencer.

It took every ounce of willpower I had to keep walking, silent and alone, just as Calvino and Killdaire had.

But they had been unaware of the fate that awaited them.

I knew what was about to happen.

Still, when it did . . .

When I passed the closet door and it flew open behind me . . .

I swear I felt my heart stop.

Everything stopped.

It was as if, in that instant, time stood still.

I couldn't move, couldn't turn my head to see the face of the person standing behind me.

And then, just as abruptly as the world had frozen, it kicked into an accelerated blur.

The doors at either end of the hall banged open and voices hollered *Freeze.* . . .

A figure dropped from an opening in the ceiling overhead, tackling the person behind me to the ground. . . .

And I whirled to see a scuffle as the armed police officer who had been crouched in the rafters struggled on the floor with the suspect, whose face I had yet to glimpse.

I heard running footsteps as the officers who had stormed the hallway approached from both ends.

"Are you all right, Mr. Mayor?" asked Mohammed, who was suddenly beside me, along with the rest of my team.

"I'm fine," I assured him, stepping back from the fray.

"It's okay, we've got the gun!" one of the officers announced. "Where are the cuffs?"

"Here they are, get them on," someone else said.

And then the officers were getting up, brushing themselves off, stepping back. . . .

Leaving me with a clear view of the killer.

The beautiful, bewildered Katrina Varinski.

"But why did she do it, Ed?" Sybil asked, setting her empty coffee mug on my desk before picking up a notepad and pen.

I quickly moved the mug onto the blotter. My cherished desk once belonged to Fiorello La Guardia, and I hardly wanted to mar the polished surface with a white moisture ring.

"She did it," I told Sybil, "because Marlon Killdaire had caught her accepting a payment from a drug dealer. Nacho Ruiz. For over a year he had been paying her to look the other way. Killdaire found out, confronted her with what he knew, and gave her a chance to turn herself around."

"How do you know this?"

"Once we cornered her, she confessed everything."

"Why didn't Killdaire just turn her in?"

"I've been asking myself that same question," I told Sybil. "I think that as much as he had a strict sense of moral justice, he was also able to understand, and to forgive."

I based this assumption on his handling of the situation with his son David. He could have turned his back on his son, who had been in trouble all his life. Instead, he had saved him, and had given him a second chance.

"Killdaire had befriended Katrina," I went on, "and she confided in him about her cheating ex, her divorce, and the custody battle. He knew she was desperate for money so that she could make life better for her children so that she wouldn't lose them."

"That's no excuse for going corrupt."

"No, it isn't."

"So she killed Marlon to shut him up?"

I nodded. "She first tried to make it look like an accident by sabotaging the brakes on his patrol car."

"When that didn't work, she decided to bump him off at Ramsey's. But why do it in a public place?"

"Because it was the one time he wasn't armed. He didn't carry a weapon in his Santa suit. Besides, she knew the store inside and out. She knew just where to hide and wait for him."

"Because she had worked at the store," Sybil concluded. "That place is a drafty old maze. I worked there in the summer, so I never had anything to do with the Winter Wonderland display, but—"

"But Katrina did. She was an elf for several Christmas seasons before she got married," I told Sybil. "It was one of the jobs she had taken to support herself after her mother threw her out at sixteen."

"You knew she had worked there all along?"

"No. Not until the end, when I realized she was a strong suspect. I went back to the employees' locker room, where there are framed photo group shots taken at the annual Ramsey's holiday party. She was in several of them. That was why she looked vaguely familiar the night I first saw her at the Calvino murder scene. I had been glancing at the photographs and must have subconsciously recognized her."

"But the fact that she worked at the store isn't proof that she was the killer."

"No, it isn't proof. But there were a few details that led me to be suspicious of her right before I confirmed that fact."

"Such as . . . ?"

"She lied to me about an expensive coat she was wearing the day I met her in a deli to discuss the case. She claimed it was a gift from her husband, and that she wore it just because it was the only warm coat she had. But I saw her the other night down at the precinct, and she had on a navy ski jacket. That didn't click with me until it was triggered by something else."

"What was that?"

"Something Dotty said to me yesterday when she came upstairs to give me the Christmas jelly she had made."

"Dotty? Christmas jelly?"

"Long story," I told Sybil. "The short version is that Dotty is a saleswoman who has worked here for years, and she likes to chatter. It's hard to pay attention to what she's saying because she drifts randomly from one topic to another. But she did mention that there had been a female police officer in the store on the night of Marlon Killdaire's murder.''

"Katrina Varinski."

I nodded. "She had apparently rushed past security on the heels of the other three officers who responded to the call about the shoplifter. But John Panopolous, the officer who made that arrest, had already told me that only two other cops were on the scene, both of them on patrol in the neighborhood. They were Doug Holt and Bobby Wu. There was no mention of Varinski.''

"So she used the shoplifter as an excuse to get into the store and sneak her weapon past security."

"Exactly. The other cops never saw her, because as soon as she got in, she snuck right up to the employees' locker room. Dotty bumped into her in the ladies' room. She must have been hiding there until she could make her way to the closet where she concealed herself before surprising Killdaire."

"What luck that there was a shoplifting incident, huh?"

"Not luck. She had planted the kid, Joey Santiago, there in the first place. He was Nacho Ruiz's little brother. The kid idolized Ruiz and would have done anything he asked. Nacho and Katrina paid him off, figuring it wouldn't be a big deal that he got arrested— which was the plan—since he was a juvenile and it was his first offense.''

"That's sick."

"It is," I agreed. "But she's a sick woman."

"So what about Calvino? Why did she kill him?"

"Simple. She, like the rest of the world, had no idea that there was more than one Santa working for Ramsey's this year. When she saw Calvino walking down the hall that night, she assumed he was Killdaire.''

"It was incredibly risky for her to go back to the scene and get Killdaire.''

"Yes, but she was desperate. If he revealed what she was up to, she would have lost custody of her children."

"And now she's lost them anyway."

I nodded soberly. "Their father and his new wife came to get them after Katrina was arrested. I was there. He seemed like a nice man, and his wife appeared to have genuine affection for the kids. He told me that he had married Katrina because she was beautiful and because he felt sorry for her, but that he realized early on that she had emotional problems. He also said that he didn't start seeing another woman until he and Katrina were separated, which disputes her version of the story."

"So you think the kids will be fine with him?"

"They'll be better off. They're moving to California, where they won't have this whole nightmare involving their mother hanging over their heads."

Sybil sighed and shook her head. "It's a good thing she didn't shoot you before the police grabbed her this afternoon, Ed. That was very daring, what you did."

"It had to be done. I knew that once I leaked the news to you that I knew who the killer was, she would panic. She would have no choice but to try to get to me before I got to the police."

"Still, you're very lucky. You put your life at risk."

"I did what I had to do. I'm the mayor of this city. Now things can get back to normal around here. And if you'll excuse me," I said, pushing my chair back, and standing, "I'm late for an appointment."

"At this hour on a Friday night? Where are you going?"

"I promised Barnaby I'd make an appearance at the annual Ramsey's employee Christmas party. I have to go get dressed."

"You're putting on a tux? So it's a formal affair?"

"No," I told her. "It's casual. That's not what I meant by *get dressed.*"

Ten minutes later, when I left City Hall, I found a throng of clamoring reporters and blinding television cameras waiting outside.

"Mr. Mayor . . ."

"Mr. Mayor . . ."

"Mr. Mayor . . ."

They had recognized me despite my full fake white beard and pillow-stuffed red and white velour suit.

"I don't have time for questions," I announced, holding up a hand to silence them.

"Will you make a statement regarding the arrest this afternoon?" somebody called.

"That, I'll do," I said. "Here it is: I am pleased to report that the individual who murdered both Angelo Calvino and Marlon Killdaire is behind bars. The people of New York can get on with celebrating the merry month of December in the most festive city in the world."

"Mr. Mayor . . ."

"Mr. Mayor . . ."

"Mr. Mayor . . ."

"That's all I have to say. Happy holidays to all," I tossed over my shoulder as I walked down the steps toward my waiting car.

And to all a good night.